SECOND CHANCE AT SILVER RIDGE

CLAIRE CAIN

To coffee. (Or Toilet Paper.)
#Quarantine2020

CHAPTER ONE

Jamie

Back in Silverton less than an hour, and as usual, there she was.

She could have been a steel beam and me a high-powered magnet, everyone else around a patch of grass. I left my friend Quinn's side without a word and crossed the street while bracing for Bel's reaction.

"Bel," I called out, a little more gruff than I'd meant, but she was facing away from me, walking in the other direction.

"Jam! I thought you got in later?"

My sister Leo burst into view and hit me with a hug, bodily shifting me back a step as I leaned to kiss her cheek.

But my eyes stayed on Bel, and my stupid chest had tightened even more than when I'd first seen her.

"Hi." I stumbled a bit as Leo let go and my eyes met Bel's green gaze.

She acknowledged me with a nod. "Hi."

"Well, we've only got so long for lunch. I'll see you tonight for dinner at Ma and Da's, right Jamie?"

Leo patted my arm and then physically shifted Bel so she faced away from me before I could respond.

Fortunately, I wasn't fool enough to stick around and watch her walk away. I slipped back across the street to Quinn.

"Got that out of your system?" Her bright blond and pink hair cutting across one eye, she wasn't smirking, wasn't judging. Just asking.

"Probably not."

Quinn and I had always been honest with each other. We'd gone to high school together, played in a band together, and despite rumors and an ill-advised post-concert kiss one night our senior year, had never been anything but very good friends.

She let out a big sigh. "Sorry."

"Don't apologize. It'll be fine."

We started walking again, peering into shop windows I never took the time to admire when back home. The last few times I'd visited had been short at best and mostly spent with my older brother Liam, keeping him from following in our father's footsteps and having a heart attack.

And of course, the visit home after Da's life-altering event had been altogether different, too. It wasn't easy to revisit those months, so usually I didn't. But part of the reason I was here was to change the way I'd been these last few years.

Really, this last almost-decade.

"How long you here for this time?" Quinn asked, hunching against a chilly mountain air gust.

"A few months at least. I have some business here, need

to write, need a break. You know." Shoving my hands in pockets, I glanced at her in time to see the frown. "I mean—"

"Shut it. We've been over this. You don't apologize for your success, and I don't make you feel bad for leaving me in the dust to get knocked up by some jerk at twenty." She gave me a sly smile and nudged me with a shoulder.

"Fair enough."

We walked on quietly then, and my thoughts circled back to where they inevitably wound up whenever I came to town—and anywhere else I found myself.

Bel.

Damn, she looks good.

She always did though. Long, light brown hair sliding over her shoulders, green eyes standing out bold against her smooth olive skin, lips I hadn't stopped thinking about in years.

And even though we'd seen each other more in the last nine months than we had in the last nine years combined, she still looked at me in the same way. Mild loathing, a little fear, fully wary. Like I was about to hurt her again, any minute. Whenever I saw it, that look hollowed me out, leaving me with an aching sadness I couldn't shake for days.

And even though I'd tried to get her out of my head, out of my heart, excise her from my life, my brain still melted a little at the sight of her. My breath still fled when her green eyes met mine—on those sweet, awful times she'd actually look me in the eye.

Hoping it might help shoo away the thoughts of her, I shook my head. I couldn't stay in this addled, mildly lovesick place where I always landed. I wouldn't.

I'd come to back to Utah to accomplish two important goals. First, I had to help Liam with the lodge or, if Jonas

Bauer, our new investor's representative, had his way, the *resort*. It stood on better ground now, but I'd opted out of any responsibility for too long. Things were still on edge, and if I wanted to maintain my relationship with this family, I had to be here. Not just show up at holidays or when disaster struck, but actually *be here*.

Second, I'd get my house and the land I was developing well in hand before I headed back out on tour. It had been too long in coming, and with Da's event a year and a half ago, I'd lost patience. Time to get the construction completed and see that dream—owning my own parcel in these mountains and building a home on it —completed.

I'd done almost everything else I'd ever wanted to— anything else I'd dreamed up as a kid. This was the last thing.

Fine. Almost the last.

But the very last thing wasn't mine to dream about anyway.

"You staying at your folks' house?"

Quinn interrupted my thoughts—probably for the best.

"Yes. They're not back 'til early June, Liam said."

Quinn made a face. "You staying there after they're back?"

"Probably. Nowhere else to go just yet—I'm not about to crowd in with Liam or anyone else for that matter."

Especially now that Liam had Wells, but even if he didn't, his place was nice but not huge. Plus, Ma would never forgive me if I didn't let her spoil me for a few weeks at least.

"You're a braver man than me. I could never live with my mom again."

"Bit different, don't you think?"

We slowed to a stop at the corner where I'd head up to the lodge to find Liam.

She acquiesced with a nod. "Guess so. If the Morrisons were my parents, I'd probably be just fine moving back in with Mommy and Daddy at nearly thirty, too."

My brows raised, and I coughed. "You know I own like three houses in other states, right?"

She rolled her eyes dramatically and bowed. "*Oh, forgive me, your rock-godiness. I forgot who I'm talking to. Please, let me kneel before your greatness and flash you my lady bits in offering—*"

"*Never* say those words to me again, for one. And two, gross. No. That's not what I—"

"Don't try to be humble now, butthead. Unless you're applying for a loan, if you bring up the *number of houses you own—*"

I threw my hands up in surrender. "You're right. I'm a jerk. I admit it. You'll never hear about my real estate port-folio again."

Her arms were crossed, and she slowly shook her head. "You know better, young Jamie. Good thing I know you better, or you'd be in even bigger trouble."

I shoved her just slightly, the same way I would Liam and Leo, and she laughed as she checked her watch.

"Gotta run grab Cara from piano lessons. I'll see you soon?"

"Absolutely. Tell your mini-me hi from me."

"The Great Jamie Morris?" She fluttered her lashes dramatically and sighed. "She'll be positively overcome."

I waved her off as she trotted down the street to collect her daughter. Though I didn't visit often, Quinn had always been a friend to me, and I hoped I'd always been a friend to her. She was someone who should have been doing what I did—in fact, I'd tried to get her to open for a few legs of tours in the past, but she'd had Cara about a year after I left town and that had changed everything for her.

It made sense, but I hated that she wasn't sharing her talent or achieving a dream we'd both shared growing up in the band together. She played local shows and some in the city when she could swing the schedule, but not enough. Not big enough for that voice, that talent. That I'd been the one to *make it* hadn't come between us, but only because Quinn was that awesome. She refused to feel sorry for herself, especially once she got pregnant and her plans changed.

I walked through the rest of downtown and up on the path that wound around past Silverton Inn where Liam's girlfriend worked. As I passed, sure enough, there he was coming out the front, the old screen door cracking closed behind him.

"Hey!" I was sure I had Wells to thank for Liam's notable cheeriness. "Where are you going so urgently?"

"I was on my way back to meet you. We're still meeting?"

Though Liam was the oldest in the family, sometimes he deferred to me in ways I didn't like. It'd been happening for years—one more thing to make me feel like I wasn't just his brother anymore.

"Of course." I reached out to him as he exited the gate that guarded the path to the inn, and we hugged, a tight, back-slapping embrace like always.

"Glad you're back, brother." He rolled out his golden boy smile for me.

"Me too. Happy it's for more than a drive-by this time."

What a relief to mean that, too. So often, I'd felt obligated to come back and had itched to get out on the road. For a long time, I'd tricked myself into believing the fault lay with my troubadour's soul, that desire to be on stage and keep pursuing the music.

And sure, I loved touring. I toured more than most musicians did by double, but coming home had always stirred up too many memories for me, so leaving again brought relief.

Memories of feeling different than my family. Memories of betraying my younger brother. Memories of never feeling like I was where I should be.

Funny enough, though, I never quite got there. I never felt like I'd arrived where I was supposed to be unless I stood on stage, and even there, that wore off when the adrenaline did.

"So what time's this meeting, and who all's going to be there?"

I'd told Liam I wanted in on meetings and information about the lodge *if* he wanted me to be. To my surprise, he'd eagerly accepted.

When I'd offered money last fall, he'd flatly refused. I could have been an investor, could've dug us out of the hole, but Liam's point had been a good one—we couldn't keep bailing the place out. We had to fix the problems so it could flourish and last another sixty years.

"You, me, Leo, Jonas Bauer, Bel..." He trailed off there and glanced at me.

"I just saw her—she was going to lunch with Leo and Wells." I huffed a bit as we hit the steepest part of the walk to the lodge. I worked out regularly which resulted in a high level of fitness, but being this high in the mountains after living in LA was killer—it took me a few days to adjust every time I came back. I always felt I should be exempt from altitude sickness since I'd grown up here, but that, unfortunately, wasn't actually a thing.

He grumped a bit at that. "I know. I wanted to have lunch with Wells but they beat me to it. I'm going to catch you up on everything we've been working on, and they'll meet us in the conference room in about an hour."

"Why were you so happy leaving the inn, then?"

"I left her a note I think she'll like when she gets back."

His ridiculous smile had me shaking my head. "You're a dope for that woman."

"Completely."

I pulled in slow breaths, then pushed them out my nose, focused on calming my heart and breathing as we reached the door to the lodge.

"Always feels like coming home, no matter how long I've been away." I let my hand rest on the cool bronze handle and looked up at the building that used to seem so much bigger.

Liam gave me a perplexed look. "Because it *is* home."

I nodded, though couldn't confirm. It was, but it hadn't always felt like it—certainly, Silverton hadn't.

Just as I pulled the door to open it for us, he pressed a hand against the wood.

"Listen, do we need to talk about you being in a meeting with Bel?"

My answering frown clearly wasn't what he wanted to see.

"I've been with you a few times when you've seen her and it's never even cordial. I don't know what to expect, but I can't have you being... however you are, with her, in front of Bauer. He's now moved into acting on behalf of the investor, and I don't want anything happening in this place that could give him or the investor an inkling that we aren't a solid family board that can make decisions."

His bright blue eyes felt particularly piercing.

"Did you tell Leo that?"

He muttered something under his breath. "Yeah. She knows. Doesn't always listen, as you're aware, but she knows."

My eyes darted around, searching for something to grab onto, when he spoke again.

"I don't know where you stand with Bel, but if you're going to help with the lodge, you've got to know she's involved. And I hope she'll keep being involved. She does good work, even Bauer thought so, and I want her to feel welcomed."

A flare of resentment shot into my gut. "I'm not about to scare her away, if that's what you're saying."

He pressed his lips flat and looked back at me—he'd never looked more like our Da—and watched me a minute.

I couldn't stand that look. I held up my hands and promised, "Nothing to worry about."

CHAPTER TWO

Bel

"Welcome everyone, and thanks for coming."

I pasted a mild smile on my face and did everything in my power not to look at the man sitting across from me. Why was he here?

"We're hoping to create a game plan for the next few months and use the planning we do now to catapult us into summer and into the anniversary in August."

Liam—formerly my friend and colleague and a guy who'd supported my marketing aspirations even while I worked at the coffee shop in town, but who was apparently out to ambush me with his broody brother—kept speaking.

"Bel, could you start? You presented some basic marketing outlines a while back—can you give us a sense of what you've been thinking for the summer?"

Liam smiled pleasantly at me, as though he hadn't led

me to believe I'd be attending this meeting without the biggest elephant ever in the room with us.

I clenched my hands together under the table, then relaxed them. "Of course."

Out of the corner of my eye, Leo was nodding at me in approval. She could undoubtedly tell I was thrown when I walked in to find Jamie seated at the table.

After pulling up mock-ups on my computer, I pointed out the style I had planned for the summer campaign. As he always did, Jonas interrupted, asked questions, forced me to think farther down the line than I had.

He was maddening and a bit pushy, but his input made this place better, and now that he represented the investor, he had a truly vested interest in the lodge succeeding.

I took my seat again, ignoring the way my hands shook while continuing to avoid Jamie, who'd kept his eyes on me the whole time but hadn't said a word.

"I'd like you and Jamie to partner up on this. Bring him up to speed on what you've been doing and then let him help with summer and especially the look of the anniversary stuff. He had a few ideas based on how they market festivals in Europe I thought might be interesting."

Liam's eyebrows were raised expectantly, waiting for me to agree.

As if I had a choice.

I shut my mouth, though I hadn't realized it'd fallen open, and nodded my assent all while dread coiled in my belly.

Why would he do that?

My computer made an excellent focal point for the rest of the meeting, only parts of which I heard. I could feel Jamie looking at me, but I wouldn't return his stare. We'd have to do this, because I wasn't letting him stand in my way on this, but why?

What was Liam doing?

He knew Jamie and I together equaled a mess. He might not know why, or understand, but he knew enough to reckon this was a terrible idea and forcing us to work together was utter nonsense.

"It's idiotic," Leo said under her breath as the meeting ended and everyone gathered their things.

"Agreed." The pasta I'd eaten at lunch sat heavy in my belly, and I wished I could escape to my house—formerly Gran's—and hide out there for the rest of the day. Month. Year.

"I'll talk to him." Leo put a hand on my arm and waited for my acknowledgement.

"Don't. It's fine. It's one meeting, and from there I can e-mail or whatever. No problem."

Her gaze flickered back and forth between my eyes and she must have seen the emotion there, because her frown deepened before she looked to her right and straightened when his words cut in.

"Any chance you want to grab coffee?"

I inhaled slowly, resisting the pull that voice had always had on me. Jamie's voice sounded rich and smooth and felt like an arrow's tip driving right into my sternum.

I turned and smiled brightly, hugging my laptop and notebook to my chest. "Of course."

He didn't speak, just kept looking at me, like he'd done all meeting, those searing Morrison blue eyes eating a hole in my head.

"So... should we walk?" I asked, ready to leave this stifling room and get the coffee over.

"Sure. I don't have a car here yet," he said, shoving his hands into his pockets.

"It's nice enough. I didn't drive either. We'll be fine."

Why my brain thought consoling him about our method of travel fell to me, I had no idea. He was the one invading my space, my territory, *my life*. He'd chosen to leave, and he should have stayed gone.

All this popping in and out over the last few months had become obnoxious, but now, he'd supposedly come back and planned to stay—at least for longer than usual. The only reason I'd agreed to this in the first place? If he'd be wandering around town for longer than a few days, then I couldn't keep doing this. I didn't want people walking on eggshells around me if they saw him in the vicinity. I didn't want to feel stretched thin and become transparent.

I wouldn't give Jamie Morrison the satisfaction of seeing what he'd made of me.

Not shockingly, the walk into town was quiet. Neither of us attempted conversation, which I found to be both annoying and a relief.

I couldn't have him in my house, so we walked to *Rise and Shine*. I waved to Hailey who worked afternoons and found a seat by the window so I'd have somewhere else to look while we talked.

"What can I get you?" Jamie stood by the table, towering over it and me.

"Nothing, thanks. You go ahead."

He didn't even nod, then turned and walked to the counter. I could hear the tones of his voice and Hailey's, but did my best not to concentrate on them. I didn't need him in my head more than he would be by the end of this sham of a meeting.

While he ordered, I focused on pulling up the small ads I'd been making and a few of the larger poster-sized campaign items. Liam had loved them when I'd brought him the idea last summer—vintage ski posters to help promote the mountain and the town.

"That one looks familiar."

Jamie sat and slid his chair in, then leaned closer to my computer screen. I held my breath, intent on not knowing if he still smelled the same. It should've been easy to block out his scent in a coffee house with fresh baked goods only feet away, but my stupid mind hungered for anything it could get from this man.

So I held my breath.

We sat on opposite sides of the small two-person table with the computer between us. Just like it had been years ago when he'd taken me to dinner, the space felt too small. His ridiculously long legs bumped mine under the table, and I tried to ignore the fact that it was the first physical contact we'd had since we'd kissed nearly a decade ago.

"I pulled it from the archives. This is one of the origi-nals from the first few campaigns in the 1960s, I think."

His gaze turned to me and pulled me in. I met his eyes, and the drop and spark in my stomach made me huff.

"That's a great idea. I can see why Liam wanted you for the job."

I opened my mouth, but no sound came out right then. Hearing anything nice from him felt precious and dangerous to me, even something as ordinary as that.

Why is he complimenting me?

A shadow crossed his brutally handsome face. "Listen, before we go any further with this—"

"No. Nothing personal," I rasped, barely capable of speech after meeting his light-socket eyes.

He clenched his jaw. "At some point, we need to have a conversation."

That low voice just loud enough for me to hear had me swallowing hard, working to summon speech. "I guess so. But not now. Let's just get through what Liam asked for and then we can be done."

So we did. I showed him everything I'd worked on and explained what media packages we had in place with different outlets. I told him what Jonas' goals were for the summer season while they pumped in money to build three new lifts and survey land for a hotel property. I explained what a big deal the sixtieth anniversary celebration was and all the places we'd start advertising it online and around the state.

"I know I'm just a musician, but over the years I have gained some experience with events and advertising. I've been in a lot of strategy meetings, watched a lot of albums and tours launch..."

If he'd meant to be self-deprecating, he'd missed. You couldn't look like Jamie Morrison—pardon, Jamie *Morris*—and be anything but arrogant.

"I'm sure. That's great. I'm not saying I don't need help, but it might be a bit different than what you're used to." I waited for him to get that point, but he didn't seem to.

He shook his head, brows furrowing in frustration with my dismissal, no doubt. "Really, Bel, I can help. One thing I was thinking is the way they do festivals in the UK—"

I tsked, impatience rising. "Jamie, not to belabor this point, but that was different."

"Because it's music and not a ski resort?" His frown was deep and his face looked so... disappointed.

With me?

I exhaled my frustration. "No. Well, yes, actually. But with all of that stuff, they're advertising *you*. And *you* are this rare, special thing people wait all their lives to see in person. You're their favorite concert or their dream night out or their most-played album. You're not a floundering ski resort in a remote town with minimal capital and lots of hopes and dreams."

He brought his coffee mug to his lips and squinted toward the door. Was he not going to acknowledge all of that? Was he really *that* stubborn?

But then, he gently set the mug down and revealed his weapon—perhaps second only to his voice.

The smile.

The man didn't smile often, but when he did, *ouch*. Walking on broken glass with bare feet kind of business to my heart.

Had I seen him smile since we'd been friends? No, not even in photos online when he popped up unbidden in a headline somewhere. That smile with his sharp white teeth and perfect lips, his dark stubble dusting his jaw.

Heartache. Heartburn. Heartmelt.

As stupid as it made me, that's what I felt. Not broken, but a real pulse, a pang that shot through me with longing and nostalgia and sadness and hope.

I swallowed that down with a gulp from my water bottle, then tucked it back into my purse. "Why are you smiling?"

"I didn't know you think of me as a *rare, special thing.* But that's good to know."

My cheeks burned, and I clamped my mouth shut as the teasing gleam entered his eye. He wasn't allowed to tease me or make a joke like that. That wasn't what this was.

I shut the computer lid, grabbed my purse, and headed for the door before it all came roaring out. He'd followed right behind me, much faster at stemming my retreat than I would have guessed. Before he could touch me—and it looked like he might have, if I hadn't nearly leapt through the coffee shop's door—I met his eyes one last time.

"Trust me, Jamie. I don't."

CHAPTER THREE

THEN

Bel, age 17

"Isabel Paxton, you better sit and eat with us, or I'm calling your mother."

Alice—Mrs. Morrison—gave me *the look* and I immediately took my seat next to Danny. Her empty threat to call my mother, who most likely assumed I was with the Morrisons anyway but certainly wouldn't be bothered if I wasn't, had nothing on that look.

"Yes, ma'am." No point in arguing with Alice Morrison, my de facto surrogate mother and a woman I greatly admired.

Also a woman who brooked no arguments from her children and their friends.

Danny chuckled under his breath, and I shot him a glare. He bumped me in the side with his elbow. "Told you she wouldn't let you leave."

I rolled my eyes at this. I knew she wouldn't either, but ever since Liam had left for college and Jamie had graduated high school, I felt a little more like an intruder when their whole family gathered for a meal. But William and Alice Morrison insisted I belonged, and even though I knew my cheeks were tinged with pink and I certainly wouldn't look up to meet Jamie's intense gaze or even Liam's friendly smile, I rested assured Danny wanted me there with him, and Leo on my other side always seemed happy to have another teenaged girl around.

"So everyone, tell us how your school years wrapped up. We haven't had a full review yet."

William passed a large bowl heaping with deep green spinach, fresh strawberries, and what looked like crumbled goat cheese. I'd helped myself to some of those berries before Danny and I had been called to come inside for dinner—I'd always loved the bright pops of red against vibrant green leaves planted in two neat rows in the Morrison garden.

"I think Mr. Corbel has unrealistic expectations for his students." Leo piled a spoonful of grilled vegetables on one side of her plate.

Liam rolled his eyes. "Honestly Leo, you think every teacher has a—"

"Don't interrupt me." She shot him a scathing look.

He sat back, conspicuously shaking his head in her direction. "Fine. Please proceed."

Danny, Jamie, and I had all ducked our heads and studiously filled our plates as a matter of self-preservation while William and Alice continued passing dishes, giving Leo their unwavering attention.

Years and years of this dynamic had played out, and we'd all learned that when Leo and Liam went at it, they were best left to themselves. Even their parents seemed to instinctively know they should work it out between them... at least to a point. Despite Liam's being in college, they still wound each other up at a word.

When Leo had finished her diatribe, which stemmed from feeling the teacher had been unfair to three girls who tended to be very quiet in the classroom and not, as Liam might have suggested, from herself being mistreated, the conversation moved on.

"Liam, how much longer do you have until graduation?" I asked, not sure how it worked now that he'd signed up with ROTC and would join the Army when he left school.

"They've decided he's too dumb to graduate."

Jamie said this, completely dead-pan, to his plate, with only a glance up at me, then back.

Danny picked up the torch and ran. "That's right. I heard the president of the university has decided to fire everyone in Admissions since they let him in."

"Ha ha, yes, dumber than a box of rocks, I am," Liam said as they ribbed him.

A few more minutes of insults, and finally, Liam could answer. The evening progressed that way, full of delicious food, some mild antagonism between siblings, but mostly a warm sense of belonging floating around me. I loved family dinner with the Morrisons. It contrasted so starkly with my own family dinners—just my parents and sometimes Gran —less because of the number of people and more because there had never been ease like this between us.

I hugged Alice goodbye and told her I couldn't wait to

see her photos when she returned from her trip to Italy with her sisters. She'd be leaving in a few days and be gone nearly all summer. I hated the thought of the summer without her, but she'd been anticipating this trip for years and I couldn't wait to hear about it when she got back.

Danny hollered to his parents that he'd be back in a while and wandered along the paved pathway that led down to my neighborhood.

"Bel, I have a surprise."

"Tell me."

A gust of excitement blew past me—or maybe that was the June breeze, but either way, I loved having a moment with just me and Danny and thinking of the possibilities this summer held for us. I *loved* that we were so close, I knew he'd walk me home. I just wished he'd grab my hand so we could walk the path together. The sun would shine so much brighter if he did that, like I'd glimpsed in his sunrise smiles for years and years.

I turned to look at my best friend since we met in Mrs. Fletcher's class in third grade when my parents moved us to Silverton. His red-brown hair, pale skin, bright blue eyes were nearly as familiar as my own reflection. As it often did, the urge to reach out and run a hand over his head, touch his cheek, or lean in and hug him gripped me, but as always, I resisted.

Danny and I didn't touch except for a very occasional hug or elbow bump—I'd learned that lesson well after trying to hold his hand in eighth grade, and again when I did it without thinking the summer before ninth and he jumped like I'd burned him at the contact. Anytime in the last few years I reached out to him, or touched him, which felt natural to me, he had clammed up and seemed incredibly uncomfortable. It made me sad, but I'd come to accept that physical interactions outside of friendly hugs or high-fives wouldn't be part of our relationship... At least not until things changed. If he'd admit his feelings for me and let me share mine with him, he'd want to be close, touched, loved.

"My dad's taking me, Liam, and Leo on an Appalachian trail trek!"

He broke into one of his room-lighting smiles and threw his arms wide like the whole town might like to know the news.

"That's... great. When do you go?"

Mr. Morrison had hinted about doing something fun with the kids while Alice traveled with her sisters.

He hopped up on a large rock on the path next to me, his gangly six-feet of seventeen-year-old now thoroughly dwarfing me where I stood. He towered over me anyway with my height being five-foot-four, but he loved to climb—rocks, walls, mountains. He had a constant inertia that seemed to propel him *up*.

"We leave Monday, and he said anywhere from six to eight weeks. I guess he has some stuff he wants to tack on at the end depending on how we're all feeling."

I forced a smile despite the collapsing feeling in my chest, the sun's radiance dimming though it still hung fairly high in the June sky. "Six to eight weeks? In two days? Wow. That's like... almost all summer."

He nodded enthusiastically. "We're hitting so many of the highlights. I can't believe he planned this without us knowing. Jamie's going to be so bummed his doctor didn't clear him to go."

"Yeah? That's too bad." I continued on the path past him, focusing on the horizon and the sun just starting to set, and bit my tongue to keep me from saying what I really wanted, to help push down the disappointment rising in my chest, my throat. "Why didn't he say anything at dinner?"

I could hear him jump down from the rock and jog to catch up, then saw as his sneakers fell into step next to me where I studied my shoes as we walked.

"He didn't want to rub it in since Jam's not going. And I wanted a chance to tell you."

His voice was gentle, like he might know I'd be disappointed, which made me feel both better and worse.

This summer should have been *our* summer. I'd grown restless in the last few years, and as the end of school approached, I'd promised myself this would be the season that changed things between us.

I'd never been kissed except at a handful of spin-the-bottle games in junior high by boys I didn't care about and after one homecoming dance by a guy I definitely didn't care about.

I wanted Danny to tell me what I already knew—to kiss me, to be mine, and move forward. I loved him, and I knew he loved me. We'd been best friends forever.

This summer, the summer before our senior year of high school, would be the time I'd try to show him how I felt and get him to do that for me. Except he wouldn't be here and didn't seem to feel bad about it at all. He had no idea the shadow he'd thrown.

"Jamie'll take care of you though. I already talked to him about it," Danny said.

My eyes jumped to his face as I choked on air. "You *what*? Why would you ask Jamie to take care of me? I'm a grown woman."

Danny slid his eyes my way, and they flickered over me in *that* way. It warmed me, gave that familiar spread of hope in my chest that someday he would make his move.

"I know. But your parents are checked out, working all the time, Gran isn't a reliable source of support because her social calendar is a mile long, and most summers you spend with my family anyway. So Jamie's ready to step in and be your summer buddy, if you want."

I took a deep breath and let it out. Danny was so clueless to interpersonal dynamics beyond what he felt—everybody's friends, and if not, they should be. He epitomized the Golden Retriever of people—always happy, excited, and ready to play. He paired well with my girly adventuresome energy, which I loved, but times like these made me want to slap him.

"You have no idea how awkward that is." My voice shuddered low just thinking about interacting with his older brother—remembering just that one look from him during dinner and how I'd had to ignore the tightening in my belly as I met his dark gaze.

"Why would it be awkward? You've known Jamie as long as you've known me. He's a great guy even if he's a little quiet, and you can keep each other company so you don't get too lonely. It's his last summer in Utah before he heads to LA and becomes a big famous Rockstar—he'll spend it with you!" He pulled me up and into a comfortable hug. "It'll be great."

My cheeks burned at the thought of spending time alone with Jamie Morrison. If Danny was a Golden Retriever, Jamie was a wolf. A dark, broody, gorgeous, and forbidden wolf.

So yeah. Let's talk about that.

The first time I noticed Jamie in *that* way was just before my fourteenth birthday. He was two and a half years older—sixteen. We were all at the swimming hole we routinely spent most of July in, about a quarter mile from the Morrison house.

Jamie was the last to arrive—he'd just finished mowing lawns or something like that. We were all in the water, though the group of the Morrison kids, me, and anyone else bored and hot was smaller than usual.

Jamie sauntered over and said, "Heads up." He never made a big deal of it.

Everyone but me knew what that meant, so they swam to the edge of the deepest part where we'd all been floating. Somehow, I missed that message, but my eyes were glued to Jamie as he stripped off a ratty T-shirt to reveal a tanned, gorgeous torso that made heat jump to my cheeks before he'd hit the water.

But he splashed in right next to me, and he came up almost directly underneath me. His head hit the underside of my thigh, then his hands were grabbing my hips—a place that felt intimate and where no one else had touched me—to shift around me, and when he popped up, his eyes flared as he flicked the water out of his eyes.

"Little Bel, I'm so sorry. You all right?"

His eyes searched my face, dipped down like he could detect an injury under the water, and I swallowed back the flood of humiliation and awareness. He, beautiful sixteen-year old Jamie, was looking at my body in a swimsuit while his warm hands held my hips in the cool water. *Gulp.*

When I didn't respond, he ducked his head to catch my eye. "Bel?"

I nodded while the blush in my cheeks scorched. "Yep."

"Good." He gave me a crooked smile and patted me on the head before swimming over to the older kids.

Despite the way he seemed to think of me as a kid sister, I couldn't think of Jamie any way at all without feeling my nerves light up and my heart beat faster. He was absolutely gorgeous and so sweet, and I hated that he'd called me *Little Bel* and patted my head, but I'd loved when he'd grabbed my hips, even if he didn't know what he was doing, or when his eyes searched over my face.

Or when he stood there laughing, his swim shorts pulling low at his hips, his chest looking far more man than boy compared to the guys my age, certainly. He knocked the wind out of me, just by looking at him. And from that moment on, I'd had to force myself *not* to look.

I never thought of Jamie as just Danny's older brother again. But I instinctively knew he wasn't for me—Jamie's maturity, the age difference, and the simple fact that he held a place in Danny's family meant he couldn't be for me. Danny and I were paired at the hip, and that meant my loyalty and love belonged to him. Jamie was a distraction I didn't let myself notice unless no one was looking. And then I *only* looked—admired what had come together to make a guy like him.

Now Danny was telling me Jamie was going to *watch over me.*

Right. He'd probably pat me on my head while I grew little hearts in my eyes and tried not to drool at him.

What would we say to each other?

What could we possibly talk about?

When Jamie and I did interact, he'd always been kind. Sometimes, I'd look up to find him watching me and he'd nod politely, then look away or disappear, leaving me to Danny's attentions or whatever adventure we were plotting.

We'd shared experiences over the years because I often spent time at the Morrison house or with the family. Danny was my best friend, and the youngest Morrison and only daughter Leo and I got along even though she was two grades younger than me. But usually, Liam and Jamie were off doing their own thing by the time Danny and I were in high school. Liam was in college, and Jamie worked odd jobs, teaching music lessons, sending out demos, playing gigs at venues in the city. The family dinners all together like tonight had become rare, and in many ways, that made things easier.

Jamie had finally gotten a deal to record—a huge triumph, and he'd be leaving at the end of the summer to go to LA and record a full-length album. He'd been itching to get out of Silverton all his life, or at least, that's what it seemed like.

I knew the feeling. Maybe we'd talk about that.

CHAPTER FOUR

Bel

I didn't cry when Danny left, but I kind of felt like it. His leaving meant the summer would stretch out ahead of me and it also meant I'd be lonely. I'd work at the *Elk Street Grill* as hostess on and off, and I'd visit Gran, but no Danny, no Leo, and no Morrison family gatherings, period. Not for the next two months, anyway.

Danny didn't seem bothered, and I couldn't pretend I felt surprised by that. He loved nothing more than being in the mountains, and an Appalachian trail trek had been high on his bucket list since he'd hit double digits. Danny's reassurance that Jamie would keep me company hadn't helped my poor me attitude, even if I could see what a great opportunity this trip was.

He had gone ahead and made a plan for me and Jamie to go to a movie together that night—we'd see whatever was playing on the main screen at the ancient local movie theater. Nice of him to make a plan, and it'd keep me from wallowing, but it did present a problem.

How does one act when going on a non-date with one's best friend's super-hot older brother who one should not be thinking of as super-hot?

I wore shorts and a tank top and brought a sweatshirt in case the theater got cold. My caramel brown hair fell down my back in waves, air-dried, and I had just a little mascara and lip gloss on. See how casual and fancy-free?

"Bel," came Jamie's voice from behind me.

I whipped around to find him leaning against a wall. He pushed off and sauntered to me. He always sauntered—really the only word for it. He might have been slightly bow-legged or something, and with his knee injury, it looked a little off-kilter, but in the end, he always seemed so laid back and self-assured.

"Hey, sorry I'm a minute late." I smiled up at him, then realizing the folly of that as his Morrison-blue eyes stabbed me in the face with their beauty, looked away.

"No problem. You ready? I got tickets." He flared out two paper stubs.

They tore the tickets at the desk—the tiny theater only needed two people working at any time—one person at the booth who then moved to projection, and one at concessions. The Egyptian-style venue featured, as one might guess, Egyptian artwork and pale pastel and gold colors, which had apparently been a popular style for theaters in Utah, though ours wasn't ritzy and revitalized like those in Park City or Ogden. That didn't matter to me—the popcorn was always fresh, and it beat driving an hour to get to a larger, newer theater. Plus there was something homey about the pale pinks and peaches and blues of the building that made me glad to be there.

"Thanks." I tucked my hands into the folds of my sweatshirt and followed behind him into the line for concessions where two guys chatted in front of us. When they turned to look at who stood behind them, they nodded to Jamie and then smiled at me. I returned the look and offered a cheery hello. I recognized them as locals and loved that about Silverton. Though I couldn't wait to get out and explore the world beyond, I found joy in knowing almost everyone around—at least during the off-season.

Once they'd gotten their snacks and disappeared into the theater, I turned to Jamie, bouncing lightly on my toes with excitement and restlessness. "Can I pay you back for the ticket?"

"No." His eyes slid to me, then jumped back to the board.

"So I'll buy the popcorn."

He turned to me, and a dark brow shot up.

"No," he said, though his mouth curved up at the corners.

Just that little bit had me smiling back at him. "That's hardly fair."

"I'm older."

"I'm gainfully employed."

His stern look cracked, and he wiped a hand over his mouth to cover what I assumed would have been a devastating smile and shook his head. "Low blow."

"Just stating facts, Morrison," I said, feeling a little jaunty after winning the verbal spar.

"I'll have a decent job in a few more months." He said this quietly, right before Jenny took our order.

He paid, wouldn't let me, but told me to get napkins and straws for the drinks, and before I knew it, we were seated side by side in a dimly lit theater. I ignored the fizzing sensation in my chest at being so close to him in this setting that suddenly felt intimate and special.

"Are you excited?" I asked, wishing the previews would start so I wouldn't feel compelled to keep looking over at him in the dark. The shadows on his features only made him more alluring—made me want to squint through the dark and admire the lines of his face. Not an option.

He nodded. "I am. I'm hoping I haven't built it up in my head. But if I come back here with my tail tucked between my legs by December, just promise me you won't give me too much hell."

I couldn't believe he'd said that—what so many in town had been whispering, wondering if someone from our small town could really make it big. "I hope it's everything you've dreamed it'll be."

He turned to look at me then, his head snapping to the side and eyes searching my face. Maybe he'd expected sarcasm, but I meant what I said. Jamie had talent in a way most people could only dream. He was born to be on stage— everyone agreed. I hoped whatever waited for him in LA at the end of the summer would let him stay there and see success.

"Thanks," he said quietly, just as the previews started.

We settled in for the movie, and despite my awareness of his nearness, the clean scent of him, our hands occasionally brushing in the large bucket of popcorn, it wasn't awful.

It was nice.

We left that day with friendly waves as he wandered back up toward his house and I split the other way, heading to mine. An odd mix of satisfaction and anticipation swirled in me, and I wondered if maybe Danny's mandate that Jamie and I hang out wasn't so terrible after all.

CHAPTER FIVE

Bel

We saw two more movies before we did anything else.

Danny and I went to movies every week in the summer—the theater was cheap, air-conditioned, and I loved movies. I loved popcorn. I loved Coke. I loved the combination. Danny humored me—or maybe he really liked all of that too, even though it meant he'd be indoors for more than an hour.

Jamie adopted Danny's role, and it turned out to be enjoyable—maybe even easy after that first time—especially once he gave in and let me buy my own ticket and split the concessions. I thought I could enjoy the summer like that, sitting side by side in darkness, only occasional small talk beforehand, and then Danny would come home and we'd all get on with our lives.

I wouldn't have to acknowledge the simmering... *some-*

thing... that lay just under the surface of my thoughts and interactions with Jamie. I wouldn't have to deal with the little thrills that shot through me whenever I caught his eye or inadvertently touched him.

But then, Jamie ruined everything.

No, really, he did. He ruined it all for me.

After the third movie, right when we'd normally say goodnight and wander off under the sparkling summer night sky in different directions, he changed the routine.

"Want to grab dinner next week? I have a gig in the city Wednesday, so maybe Friday?" He glanced up at the sky, then back at me, hands shoved in his pockets.

"Uh, sure. Yeah. Where do you want to go?" I asked, like his suggesting dinner wasn't totally changing the game.

"I heard about a weird little place up the canyon we could check out—I'll find out if it's open. I'll call you next week." He backed up a few steps just looking at me before he turned and walked down the path to his parents' house.

And me? I stood there staring after him like an idiot, my thoughts a tangled mess. He was so casual, I shouldn't have been reading into it, but the whole thing felt so date-like.

Dinner. A Friday night. A new restaurant.

But... this was Jamie—probably just keeping things interesting. Plus, our movie nights had been Wednesdays, and he had a gig next Wednesday. He must feel obligated to make up for that.

It meant nothing. It'd be fine.

Not surprisingly, I spent approximately nine days overthinking how Friday would go. Did *he* think it was a date? Unfathomable.

I wore a summery white dress and slip-on casual sandals and my hair long and wavy like usual. I felt comfortable, but made sure I felt *good* too. Because as much as I wasn't sure what he thought, I knew I wanted to feel good and confident, whatever this turned out to be.

Jamie had mentioned going up the canyon somewhere new, but he'd called early to tell me the place was closed for the summer so we'd just do *Elk Street Grill*. Fine by me—even though I hosted there a few days a week, I still loved the food.

As I rounded the corner of Elk Street and walked toward the far end where the restaurant was located, I thought about Danny.

I should have felt *more* conflicted than I did, shouldn't I? A larger part of me should have felt like I was betraying him or... something. Being excited and weirdly hopeful and jittery about going on a non-date with his older brother should have been a *problem* for me.

But I didn't. It wasn't. I felt nerves, but mostly anticipation. A sliver of conflict in that I didn't want it to seem like a secret—Jamie and I weren't sneaking around, and in fact, Danny had set all of this interaction up. I did feel guilty that I'd fast become interested in and focused on Jamie in a way I never had with Danny, but part of me wondered if that could be because Danny had refused, time and again, to make a move. To be open to that part of me—us.

Plus, I'd never allowed myself to be around Jamie without a buffer in the form of Danny or even Leo, to think about Jamie, to *look* at Jamie. It'd felt disloyal to Danny for too long, but that'd been wearing off as I began to embrace that he didn't see me the way I'd hoped he would. Not after the way he'd left.

But maybe Jamie would.

I stifled a growl of frustration at my messy mental state since, just when I might have given in and let loose, I spotted Jamie leaning against the wall just outside the restaurant.

Each time we'd gotten together, he'd been early. This proved to be the total antithesis to any time we'd ever been together in a group setting. He consistently showed up last and usually left first. He always seemed to be coming from something fun or important and heading out to something much cooler.

Probably my mild years-long crush talking, and the fact that at the age when I became aware of him as a *boy*, he was almost three years older than me, which automatically made him desperately cool and unreachable.

But now, there he stood, waiting for me like he'd been there a while. He wore jeans and a short-sleeved button-up shirt, which I would bet I'd never seen. I hadn't seen him in anything other than a T-shirt aside from shirtless while swimming.

A button-down?

As I walked up, he smiled, his perfect teeth flashing at me. He had great teeth. Something about how his canines were kind of delectably pointy so he almost had a dangerous quality to his mouth. Like he might just consume me if I got too close.

The lips surrounding the teeth—they were nice too. But over time, I'd made a concerted effort not to look at them for fear of sudden dissolution into hormone-addled goo.

"You look great."

He approached, that smile softening as he brought a hand up to my shoulder and softly touched me there before said hand disappeared. I looked to see where, but by the time I found it, it rested at his side, and I'd missed any expression on his face.

"Sorry, didn't mean to startle you."

"By patting my shoulder?" I asked as we walked up the steps.

He chuckled. "Uh, yeah."

"Fear not. I'm not *that* inexperienced." I laughed, then sobered immediately as something I couldn't pin down crossed his face. "I mean... whatever. It's fine."

He nodded and gestured for me to enter the restaurant through the door he now held.

"I never come here for dinner, so this is great."

He paled. "Right. I forgot you work here."

I couldn't help the small smile. "Yeah."

"We can go. It's—I should have taken you somewhere else. I had that place up the canyon in my mind, and when that fell through, I defaulted here." He ran a hand through his longish dark hair.

"It's fine, really. I love their food and I never get to eat their dinner menu." I waved at Jax, the bartender I knew from his occasional dayshifts, and Gena, the evening hostess.

"Hey girl! Back so soon?" Gena asked as she gathered two menus in her arms.

"You know I can't stay away."

"My fault. I had a different place picked out but botched it, so we ended up here—totally my bad." The frown pulling at Jamie's mouth spoke loudly.

"And I told *him*, it's fine. I rarely get to eat off the dinner menu." I gave him a look so he'd know I meant it.

Gena smiled widely, likely unsure what to do with our awkwardness and, no doubt, with Jamie's general existence since he had that effect on women of all ages. But eventually, she gestured for us to follow her.

She seated us at a great table near the back of the *wintergarten* area, an indoor all-glass patio section at the rear of the restaurant. On summer nights when the weather was really perfect outside, you could sit in the garden which housed all the restaurant's fresh herbs and rows and rows of gorgeous flowers, but it was still too hot this late in the day so they weren't seating outside.

Gena left us to the menu and I eagerly scanned it. I'd eaten everything on there even though I wasn't a server—couldn't be until I turned twenty-one, and I wouldn't be around to have the chance at that point—but the owner, Mr. Reiner, was insistent everyone know the menu well, even hostesses.

Quiet had settled over us. I looked up from taking a drink of water and felt myself barreling toward the question I shouldn't ask, but couldn't *not* ask. "So, um... why did you bring me here?"

Jamie jolted back a bit. "I'm sorry the place up the canyon was closed—"

"No, Jamie, that's not what I mean. I don't mean *here*. I mean why are you here, taking me out to dinner, never mind where?"

Here we go—I'd figure him out, figure out this whole date night non-date and what was going on. Then I could stop feeling silly and over-eager and mildly lovesick over my best friend's older brother who was too gorgeous, too talented, too *much* for me.

One brow rose and fell, then one corner of his mouth twitched like he might smile, but of course, he didn't. "Because Danny asked me."

My little blimp of hopes and dreams took the arrow, and down it went, flames and wreckage abounding.

"He asked you to take me to dinner?" My voice raised much higher than normal.

Now a half-smile in earnest. "He asked me to take care of you. He said you guys do stuff all the time and that your folks aren't around much and your Gran is busy a lot, and that you were used to hanging with him or the family, so I should compensate accordingly for the absence of our entire family."

I blinked. I opened my mouth to say... something, but no. Nothing would come.

I should have felt pleased and heartened by the thought of Danny's desire to care for me, even from afar, but only threads of anger and embarrassment stitching in my belly made themselves known.

"Is that surprising?" he asked, naming the painfully obvious.

Yes, but more so, I was surprised by the drop in my stomach at the news that he'd only brought me out tonight because he'd promised Danny he would. I hadn't guessed Danny had been so insistent, and in the last few weeks... well. Some messed-up part of me had thought maybe Jamie had wanted to.

"Uh, no. No. I'm just... I'm surprised you'd do that." Hopefully, I'd covered my real thoughts well enough.

"Why?"

He leaned an elbow on the table to get closer. We were seated at a two-person booth, but at *The Elk*, as locals called it, they were truly tiny. Our knees were threaded even as we tried not to touch, and it felt overwhelmingly intimate tonight in a way it never had with Danny.

Why would I be surprised by this news? I shouldn't.

The Morrisons were as tightknit a family as you could come by, and even though Jamie was the one who wasn't as involved in the lodge and ski area they owned and operated, he was devoted to his family.

I'd seen this demonstrated time and again—him dropping plans to give Danny a ride before he had his driver's license, Jamie running late to something because he'd been helping his mom with a project—he was sweet.

A heartthrob and a supposed lady-killer too, though I wasn't sure where those rumors came from other than the whole gorgeous musician thing. But more than anything, what I'd seen of Jamie proved that he was devastatingly sweet. Hence the reason why I'd promised myself not to think of him at all, because if I factored the external appearance and that internal reality...

Certain doom.

"Uh, I don't know. It's above and beyond your brotherly duty, I'd think," I tried.

He dropped his head between his arms so I could no longer see his face, his longish hair settling back into place with a wisp or two falling into his eyes when he looked back up at me. His hair was longer on top, short at the sides, and often did this fall-into-the-eyes thing which only made him more appealing for some dumb reason.

The half-smile on his face sent a pang of nerves through my belly.

"It's not like it's a hard job, Bel. I'm glad for an excuse to hang with you."

His blue eyes watched me, no doubt seeing my cheeks heat and my lashes flutter, though no way could he know how hard I worked to keep myself from diving head first into the crush I had on him. Encouragement like that would not help.

"Well... thanks." I cleared my throat after my voice came out alarmingly quiet and low.

The waiter took our orders and I was relieved for the interruption, the excuse to focus on the menu and find pleasure in the simplicity of choosing a dish I knew I'd like. We ordered and chatted casually before the basket of bread arrived. Glad to have a distraction from admiring how long and dark Jamie's eyelashes were and how smooth and low his voice sounded, I slathered a piece of bread with butter and shoved it into my mouth.

Once I'd devoured that piece, I reached for another.

"Wow, you're hungry." He chuckled, and I froze with a mouthful.

I chewed and hurriedly swallowed. "Yeah, sorry."

"Don't be sorry. I like that you're not afraid to eat in front of me." He took a bite of his own slice.

"Why would I be afraid of eating in front of you?"

He pressed his lips together to stifle a smile. "See? It doesn't even occur to you—I love that."

"I freely admit not eating has never occurred to me," I said with a smile, feeling warm and fuzzy watching him smiling at me. I was getting moony—not okay, but he was adorable.

Before long, our food arrived. Though I'd feared we'd have little to discuss, our conversation ambled around between my job, his music, his knee... no more awkward pauses.

"So why are you always hanging with the Morrison family?" he asked, eying me before he took the last bite of his roast chicken.

I finished chewing, my heart speeding up as I did. "My parents both commute to the city to work every day, so they leave super early and get back late. I have Gran but she's very social and busy too, so it's just me. When we moved here, Danny adopted me and then so did your parents. They were always welcoming, and my parents were glad for me to have someone to rely on when they're gone..."

Jamie's frown made me bite my lip and take a gulp of water.

"Sounds lonely."

I cleared my throat, set my fork and knife to the side of my empty plate. "It's all right. It's always been this way so I'm used to it."

I kept my eyes on my plate, fiddling with the utensils so they were at a perfect angle and avoiding seeing whatever his reaction was.

"They're missing out," he said quietly.

"They're just... working. It's what they love." Hopefully, he'd miss the suggestion that they loved work and not me.

I mostly avoided feeling that way since Gran, and Danny, and the Morrisons after all gave me so much love, I wasn't lacking. But my parents... they weren't satisfied with life in Silverton. *Understatement.*

The waiter arrived with the check before Jamie could respond. We fought over it. He won by slipping the waiter cash before I could do anything about it and insisting that since he'd invited me, he got to pay.

We wandered home as the sun was setting. By the time we made the fifteen-minute trek to my house, which normally didn't feel too much like a trek but tonight it did thanks to the heat, my hair stuck to my neck.

"We should swim tomorrow if it's this hot again," Jamie said, not looking nearly as uncomfortable and sweaty as I felt.

"Definitely. I only work the brunch seating. I'll be done around two." My voice came out remarkably casual considering the fizzing nerves shooting through my belly at his suggestion.

"Perfect. Let's meet at the hole at two-thirty and by then we'll both be desperate to cool off. I'll bring snacks," he said, a close-mouthed smile on his perfect face.

I nodded, because the thought of seeing Jamie again so soon overwhelmed. We'd only seen each other once a week at most before this—palatable increments I could then tuck away and examine once alone. All this togetherness would leave me off-kilter if I wasn't careful.

CHAPTER SIX

Bel

The *Elk* was insanely busy—in the second week of July, tourists had lingered in town after the 4th to celebrate the lodge's anniversary.

It wasn't a hallmark year the whole Morrison clan would be here for, and the main celebration always happened in August in conjunction with the lodge's anniversary, but July was always the busy month of summer thanks to the fourth and then the uniquely Utahn celebration of the twenty-fourth. Silverton hadn't been settled by the pioneers who'd made their covered-wagon trek from Missouri like Salt Lake City had been, but the town loved any excuse to celebrate and welcome travelers, so they put on a decent show of it.

The brunch and lunch rush flew by. I clocked out at exactly two and had to force myself not to run. Even so, I hurried as I pulled on my practical two-piece swimsuit, some jean shorts and a tank top, sunglasses, a hat, did my hair into twin braids to avoid tangles in the water, and dropped sunscreen, a book, and a water bottle into a small bag before I was out of the house and nearly skipping along the path that led past the Morrison property to the little swimming hole I'd grown up going to.

We called it a swimming hole, but it was really a bend in the Silver River that widened and became especially deep in that little stretch. At the elbow of the curve sat a large tree where Mr. Morrison had hung a rope swing, a perfect launching ground for idiotic feats of bravery and teen invincibility. A line of rocks made a perfect walkway across the water and helped create the pool effect.

Some of my best summer memories had taken place here. The nostalgia for those young, easy years filled me, but also the flutter of anticipation for *now*.

I had one year until I left Silverton behind. One more year and then, like my parents, I'd leave this small town and launch out on my own. Before, I'd always thought Danny would be with me, so not so alone, but I was beginning to realize how misguided that hope had been. The longer we spent apart, the more I began to accept that maybe Danny and I wouldn't always be close—that our lives could and perhaps had already begun to shift and separate. I'd assumed I'd be just shy of miserable without him because I never had been, not since third grade, and yet I'd been having an amazing summer. My job and friends kept me busy, and Jamie provided a sweet bonus. So far, I was just fine without my oldest friend.

I lay a blanket down, then a towel, slipped out of my shirt, and got comfortable with my book after layering on sunscreen. The light breeze pushing through the heat of the day lulled me into shutting my eyes and resting my head on my book.

"Bel," I heard, and felt a cool hand on my shoulder. "Bel, baby, I think you're getting a sunburn."

I blinked my eyes open, and my back ached from the heat. I pushed up to my knees and leaned back as I noticed Jamie, also on his knees, his eyes skating over my body with a kind of focus I hadn't seen before.

"You okay?" I asked, my voice groggy from sleep.

He swallowed. "Yep. Are you? Let's get you in the shade."

He took my arm and helped me stand and walk on strangely shaky legs.

"What time is it?" I glanced back at the blanket where I'd left my book, watch, and small bag.

"It's almost four. Sorry I'm so late—I called *The Elk* but you'd already left." He ran a hand through his hair and turned away from me, glancing at the water.

"Don't worry about it." I shucked my shorts and stepped out of my sandals. "I'm going to cool off. I think I slept for like an hour and a half—I'm fried."

I wandered down the stony dirt path to the edge of the water and dipped a toe. Frigid, but it'd feel good once I got in. I took a breath and dove in head-first where I knew the water pooled deepest, pushing away the thrill that still coursed through me at the memory of Jamie's voice calling me *baby*.

Oh. My.

When I popped out to take a breath, I looked up at the edge to see him standing with hands on hips.

"Wouldn't have guessed you'd be a head-first person and not a toe-dipper," he said with a smile.

"Yeah?"

"Yeah. But anyone who can keep up with Danny would have to be."

He pulled his shirt off in that one-handed grab only guys did. He flicked his sandals off to the side and walked to the rope swing. "Bombs away."

He swung out to the farthest point, and I moved back to the little shelf of stones that helped create the pool while Jamie dropped into the deepest part with an impressive splash. Taller and broader than Danny, he'd always managed to have the biggest splash.

He surfaced and wiped the water from his eyes, then slicked his hair back. The moisture made his locks even darker, his eyes somehow more blue, and the caps of his shoulders bobbing out of the water surprisingly golden.

"How are you so tan?" I asked, knowing the Morrisons tended toward pasty and white—their Irish and German roots made sure of that. At least Danny and Liam sure did. Leo could tan pretty well.

"Probably because I work outside a lot in the spring and summer. I have a little more olive in my skin than Dan and Li—me and Leo tan pretty well. But mostly, it's from repeated exposure." He treaded water until he got up to the rocks and sat next to me.

"I thought you were done working? Someone told me when you got your contract you quit..."

I'd heard he was just biding his time. It was one reason I hadn't wanted him to pay for everything.

"Why would I do that? I got the doc to clear me to go back as soon as I could. Work's good money, and honestly I have nothing better to do."

"So you stayed home from the trip with your family to work?" I couldn't imagine missing an adventure like that—not voluntarily.

He didn't meet my eye. "Wasn't my thing."

That thought settled in my mind, but just didn't ring true. "You've gone on all the other family trips."

He pulled a small stone out and skipped it across the top of the water—a feat considering he sat down in the river itself. After another few moments of listening to the current sliding between rocks, he spoke again. "I have. It's just... different now."

"Different how?"

The look he gave me lay somewhere between irritated and pleased. "You don't let a guy off easy, do you?"

"What do you mean? I'm just trying to figure out why you're here and not with your family. Danny told me the doctor hadn't cleared you."

His lips pressed flat before he took a slow inhale, then let it out. "Yeah. That's what I told them."

This made no sense. I'd always seen him engaged with his family—an active participant. "You didn't want to go?"

He ran a hand through his hair. "I did. I would have. But it's a good time to make the break. I'm leaving anyway, and even though they support me, they don't understand. Don't get how I can leave. Just felt like it might be easier to..."

I waited for him to finished his thought, but he didn't. "To... what?"

"To start getting used to being apart—help everyone move on."

He pushed off and disappeared under the water as my thoughts swirled. I'd never imagined he felt out of place with his family, but he'd said that, hadn't he? That small part of me that had pushed back against liking him, against feeling connected to him, evaporated.

We had far more in common than I thought. And even

though I couldn't understand how he felt out of place in a family where even I felt welcomed, he clearly meant what he'd said. I wanted to know more about why he felt that way, but his disappearing act under the water had effectively closed the subject.

He bobbed up next to me again and wiped the water from his face.

"So now I'm here, working a few jobs. They'll keep me out of trouble 'til I get to LA anyway."

I glanced at him, then quickly away. This close, he was too much.

"Makes sense," I finally said, wondering what kind of trouble he got up to, and wishing he'd take me with him.

Not that Danny and I never did the stupid teen stuff, but mostly, we just hung out, or hiked and skied, or did homework—it all felt fun and easy with Danny. We were good kids, and soon, the time for being stupid would be over. I'd never needed to rebel since my parents were never around, and I had no desire to put Gran through teen drama. My life, despite my parents' general absence, always felt full of joy and fun.

"Back okay?" he asked, craning his neck to see my back.

Turning to him to show him the damage, I held my hair out of the way. "How does it look?"

An intake of breath, then a whisper against my skin as he let it out. A featherlight touch along my spine... "A little red, but not too bad."

I swallowed. "Glad I put sunscreen on where I could. I'm sure there'll be some interesting tan lines tomorrow."

"Sorry I wasn't here to help."

His voice came out quiet, but it might as well have been blasting in my ear since every part of me was tuned to him.

A thrill raced through me. "Really?"

He cleared his throat. "Sure. Danny probably does that all the time, right?"

A laugh escaped before I spoke. "Never. He doesn't touch me."

Only the water made a sound, a happy bubbling and sloshing over rocks behind us.

Then, "What?"

"Danny doesn't touch me. *Ever*. Not unless it's a friendly hug. Not since probably seventh grade."

"How is that possible when you two... *wait*." His look was sharp. He leaned toward me. "I thought you two had been dating for years."

"We have never been on a date."

Heat rose to my cheeks. How could Jamie not know this? Did everyone assume the same? Did I look a fool to him now? I inwardly rolled my eyes but more laughter bubbled up in me at how ridiculous that thought was. How could I control what he thought, or anyone? Even I'd thought Danny and I should be together—no wonder others did too.

He stared at the water in front of him, then snatched at a water skeeter that jumped in front of us.

"What the hell is he thinking?" he asked, as though I couldn't hear him.

There was no point resisting my response. "I have no idea. We don't talk about anything like that. He constantly reminds me what a good friend I am. So I've gotten the message loud and clear. I'd kind of thought at some point we'd...."

I let my eyes wander casually away from him, hoping he couldn't hear the hurt and confusion in my voice. I successfully shoved those feelings down deep and covered them with smiling and jokes when I spent time with Danny, but somehow, it seeped out in this moment. "I guess he just doesn't see me like that."

Jamie made a scoffing sound. "No way that's true."

"Well, it *is*. He's had plenty of chances to change things, including this summer, and he hasn't taken them. At this point, I'm done waiting." I waved my arms through the water in front of me.

Now that I'd said it, I felt the truth of it.

On one hand, I recognized I really was done waiting—I wanted to take the reins and make something happen, and I didn't know how Danny would respond. And on the other hand, I'd been feeling excitement and things I hadn't felt with Danny—maybe ever.

Jamie was quiet, but I could feel his eyes on me. After a few minutes, I nudged him with an elbow. "What?"

His brows pinched together, and his mouth moved like he'd speak, but nothing came out. He frowned, then said, "I have no idea what to say other than he's an idiot."

I chuckled despite the heavy feeling in my chest at the thought of letting go of the years I'd waited for Danny to wake up. "Yeah, well. Most men are."

He humored me, laughed softly, then pushed off the stone bench to swim around.

We waded through the water a few more minutes before I lost feeling in my toes, and we both climbed out.

"I guess I'll see you..." I trailed off as I pulled my shorts over my wet swimsuit.

"Movie night, right?" he asked, toweling off, then running a hand through his hair.

I wondered if he knew how often he did that. It was appealing and maddening and made me want to do it too.

"Sure. Yeah, I'll see you then. Have a good week."

CHAPTER SEVEN

Bel

My parents had asked me to be home by six. I figured they wanted to go to dinner or eat together, something we did every few weeks to catch up since they were gone so often during the week and I tended to work during the day on weekends and hang out with friends in the evenings.

Tonight, they were both buzzing when I walked into the kitchen as I twisted the last bit of moisture out of my hair from my shower and took a seat at the bar.

"Bel, good. We have news." My dad beamed his toothy, wide smile and pulled my mom to his side.

Gran sat at the other end of the bar reading, though at this, she set down her book and removed her glasses.

"Do tell," I urged.

"Well there's no point in delaying," my mom said,

smiling up at my dad who wrapped an arm around her trim waist.

"We're moving to Salt Lake. I got a raise and they need me in-office more, so the drive isn't going to work. We've been looking at houses for months and found something perfect—and we bought up near Little Cottonwood Canyon and everything is going to be great."

My dad spouted this off like it was all of our dream to leave this place, the home of my childhood and the place my favorite person, my Gran, lived.

"I—"

My mom held up her hands to stop me. "You'll stay in school here, of *course*. We don't want to uproot you right before your senior year. Then you go to the U and we could see you weekends more easily. As you know, we'd planned to wait a year but this job and house were too much to pass up, and with your grandmother here, you'll be—"

"I'll be just fine. Of course. Congratulations." I cinched down the tumbling, sinking feeling rising in me, the darkness that rolled in to smother the sunshine.

"We're so happy you're happy." My mom smiled dreamily, not quite looking at me, her focus pulling back to my dad.

I couldn't blame them. They'd always wanted this—back to the city. And I'd kept them from that for years. And now they trusted me enough and had the right opportunity... I couldn't fault them.

I could make it through the dinner my mom had laid out on the table, and I could keep from looking Gran full in the face because if I did, I'd see her compassion and love for me and she'd *know* my words were nothing. They were nothing like my heart.

"Well that's done, so let's eat. We're actually moving

next week, so this'll be our last Saturday night in this house together."

Halfway down the path back to the swimming hole, the tears began to stream from my eyes, and I didn't hold back the sounds coming from the pit of my stomach. I stumbled all the way there and collapsed into the nook of rope swing tree.

My mind couldn't parse out the details well enough yet—I couldn't identify exactly why I felt like the world had been pulled from underneath my feet... except I knew I felt a loneliness I hadn't confronted in a long time—not since I was old enough to fully realize that my parents didn't like anything about where we lived, and I had begun to suspect, even me.

"Bel?"

I sucked in a breath at the intrusion and wiped my face, knowing it looked red and awful—I hadn't heard him approach.

"Hey." My voice came out weak, shaky.

"What's wrong?" Jamie asked, gently setting a guitar on the ground to his right and kneeling in front of me.

"I'm fine."

"You're not fine. What happened?"

His eyebrows were stitched together in concern, his beautiful mouth turned down, and the sight of him made that ache in me grow, nearly to bursting again.

I cleared my throat, hoping I'd find the words without letting my sadness splash all over us. "My parents just let me know they're moving."

"You're moving?"

Pressing my lips together, I slowly shook my head. "*They're* moving."

"What does that mean? How are they moving without..." He trailed off, no doubt realizing what it meant.

"I'll stay here. It's really for the best." I worked at convincing myself too. I pushed some false shine into my voice and continued. "I can finish high school and I'll be here with Gran, so it's really pretty perfect—pretty much like always, really."

He didn't respond right away, but stayed there watching my face. I tried not to let my false smile fade, but it did. I felt nothing but sad, sad, sad.

"Didn't you tell me they'd always planned to leave after you graduated, when you left for college?"

His voice was gentle, but it still cut.

"That has always been the plan." I bent and pulled the bottom of my shirt up over my face to wipe it, no doubt making my eyes and nose ridiculous and red, but I couldn't bring myself to care. At least I hadn't put on mascara before dinner.

"Why now?"

"Perfect job, perfect house, right timing. Lots of factors, I guess."

I didn't look into those blue eyes of his anymore. I wished they'd give me butterflies or make me feel aware of my lips, my neck, wherever they tracked, like his eyes usually did, but even they couldn't break through.

He moved to sit by me and held up the arm nearest to me in question.

Later, I'd look back and think of this moment and wonder at how automatic it had seemed for him to welcome me in his arms and how easy it had been for me to accept, how the sun had peeked out from behind the clouds.

He wrapped his other arm around me and held me. After only a few seconds, I let myself lean into him and rest my head on his shoulder.

He spoke softly into my hair, his chin brushing the crown of my head. "I'm sorry, Bel."

I hadn't seen Jamie since the night he'd comforted me. I'd cried as quietly as I could, mostly because everything around us had been calm and quiet and I'd hated to disturb it. I'd had to assure him I was fine to walk home three times before he let go of me and let me walk back to my house.

He'd offered to go with me, but I'd refused. I was glad he'd been there to comfort me—an unexpected need, and one he'd satisfied perfectly. But I needed the quiet of the night and the time to be alone under the star-flecked sky before I went back inside the house where my parents would only live for a few more nights.

I'd canceled our midweek movie night. It was sweet of him to comfort me, but as the days passed, I felt more upset by my crying. I'd gotten angry.

Why should I care if my parents moved? They weren't making me uproot, and they'd always said they'd move eventually. If it hurt me that they didn't mind living away from me for a year, my last year at home in theory, that was my problem. How could I blame them for taking a promotion and doing something they'd always planned to do—something they'd always told me they'd do?

If it was a bit thoughtless of them not even to offer for me to move with them, it was probably rooted in their knowledge that I wouldn't want to go since my life was in

Silverton. Enough would change in the next year. Of course they knew that.

And if this choice felt a little bit like their final declaration that they were done with me—no longer had to feel tethered to me or like they owed me for having given me life, well... that was also *my* interpretation.

So I was angry Jamie had seen me crying and upset. Not because I hadn't been, but because he probably thought I was a whiney baby, and I hated that his impression of me would be that of weakness. I hated that when I wanted to seem strong and confident with him—when I'd been thinking about what might lay between us, he'd come to my rescue just like an older brother might.

I couldn't have predicted that he'd come to my work on Saturday and demand to see me.

I stood at the hostess desk straightening menus when he walked into the grill just after a big lunch rush.

"Bel."

His voice made my stomach clench, but I resisted looking up at him. Hearing him *and* seeing him would be deadly, especially after my emotional display the other night.

"Hello." I kept my eyes on my work.

I could see his torso in front of me now where he'd stopped. Then he put his hand on top of the menus, and I had no choice but to look up at that startlingly beautiful face.

"You're coming out with me tonight."

"I am?" I swallowed.

He nodded.

"Where are we going?"

"I have a gig in the city. You're coming."

I waited for him to laugh or yell "Psych!" or something,

but no. Dead serious blue Morrison eyes stared back at me, alternately making my toes curl and my mind empty.

"Seriously? I can't even get into the places you play." I nudged the menu on the top off center, then corrected it so the stack was neat again.

"Not a problem. You'll be with the band—they won't care."

He surveyed the room, then his eyes flicked back to me.

"I—I don't know if—"

"Come with me, Bel."

Well, I was done for. There was no going back when Jamie Morrison asked me to do something like that, eyes earnest and face intense. How could I say no?

Plus, it would push my other plans—crying into my pillow and eating every carb in the house—to tomorrow night. I could live with that.

"I have to go get the van loaded. I'll swing by your house at seven." He patted the podium, then turned.

"Seven? Isn't it like an hour and a half to the city? What time do you guys play?"

He stopped before he reached the door. "We go on at ten. See you in a few hours."

CHAPTER EIGHT

Bel

The band was on their last set. I hadn't taken my eyes off Jamie in the last... well, I would have checked my watch, but again, I was unwilling to take my eyes from him.

He was *everything*.

Words didn't exist for the way I felt looking at him. He was damaging my ability to stay calm. I wanted to both cry and laugh as I watched him. Every emotion I'd tried to bury over the last week bubbled up, ready to spill out every time he strummed a chord or nodded in time with a crash of the cymbals.

So... constantly.

He was not just gorgeous, which he'd always been. He took over the venue. Though he kept himself more reserved off stage, he let everything out when he went on—all his charm, his skill, his passion. Alluring. Charismatic. I almost felt bad for the other members of the band, but they were clearly loving performing with him—they must know what they had. They must know what they'd be losing when he went to LA.

His voice was rich and sometimes gritty, sometimes smooth—he could manipulate it to suit the mood of the song. The band was great too, but Jamie... Jamie was astounding. They played music somewhere between Kings of Leon and Mumford and Sons, I'd been told. I wondered if he'd play the same music when he went to LA.

I'd seen him perform before, but it'd always been for a song or two at a festival, or sometimes as a joke where he wasn't fully performing but just humoring his parents or his Grandpa Will. I'd never seen him like this.

"Thanks for coming out, everybody. We're back in two weeks!"

Jamie and the band ended their song with a bang, and before I knew what had happened, there they were, rushing off the side of the stage, disappearing into the tiny green room the club provided.

I smiled at the guy standing guard by the door to the back and who Jamie had introduced me to before they went on, and made my way through the small walkway to the room.

Quinn, the co-lead singer and bass player, guzzled a bottle of water, somehow looking fresh and gorgeous despite her bright blond hair being stuck to her temples and neck.

Jamie tucked his guitar into its case as Darius twirled a drum stick around his fingers saying "Definitely, definitely," and Chase stood with crossed arms, nodding.

"I can take you guys," Quinn said to Jamie while tossing her bottle in the trash.

"You sure?" Jamie asked, still unaware of me in the room.

That wasn't hard to understand—Quinn Darling was just about the most magnetic person I'd ever seen in real life and she was standing straight in front of him.

Well, most magnetic aside from Jamie, obviously.

"Totally. I have to get back. You can let these dorks have their fun."

"I resent that," Darius said with a false-looking frown.

"Hey Bel. You want to go back to Silverton with these two losers, or you want to stay out with the big kids and let us show you the late-night scene?"

Chase flashed a smile that was admittedly charming, but his offer held no allure for me. Not when Jamie stood next to him.

My eyes found Jamie's, which were studying me intently. "Thanks so much for the offer, but no. I'll stick with Jamie tonight."

Jamie nodded and dropped his head as he stood up. It may have been my imagination, but I would have sworn he was hiding a smile at my choosing to stay with him. Or maybe he was just laughing at me for taking Chase seriously at all.

"Your loss," Chase said, then immediately turned to Darius to discuss plans.

Jamie came to me with his guitar case in one hand and a bottle of water in the other. "I just need ten minutes to help break down the kit, and then we'll be ready. Good?"

"Sure. I'll be here."

~

Half an hour later, we were crammed into Quinn's small pickup truck. And small didn't describe it quite right—maybe it could be more accurately classified as a miniature truck, only a small bench seat more likely meant to comfortably seat two people than three. She'd driven separately tonight, and Jamie, Darius, Chase, and I had taken the van, which was basically an old fifteen-passenger with the back seat torn out to leave room for instruments and a few boxes of merchandise. Plenty of room in there. I hadn't thought about the space issue returning in Quinn's ride would pose.

Now I sat sandwiched between Quinn and Jamie, though mostly pressed up against Jamie thanks to the stick shift of the truck taking up all the foot space in front of my seat.

"Sorry it's cramped," Quinn said as she started the ignition.

"No problem," I responded since she must've been mostly talking to me, although maybe she meant it more for Jamie's sake since I was currently plastered to him from ankle to shoulder.

By the time we'd driven about five minutes, I thought I'd light on fire. Being that close to Jamie was torture. Fortunately, he'd changed his shirt, which had been soaked after the concert. I'd missed that, whenever it'd happened, and knew I'd lost out on something spectacular. But beyond that, I was glad he'd done it or I'd be shoved up against him and would *also* be soaking wet.

Sweaty Rockstar—probably only attractive from a distance.

Quinn turned up the radio blaring something I hadn't heard—I wasn't big into rock, so it was unlikely I'd recognize much anyway.

Jamie shifted and pulled his arm out from where it lay

smashed between us and rested it behind me. Not making a move—I knew that—but my heart still dipped and fluttered at how close it was to having his arm around me.

He dipped his head and spoke into my ear. "That okay?"

I nodded quickly, sure I didn't want him to move, both because it was much more comfortable and because being shoved into Jamie's space was absolutely not the worst thing that had ever happened to me.

The next thing I knew, he shook me gently.

"Bel, baby, wake up. We're here," he said, his voice soft and low in my ear.

I breathed deeply, enjoying the warmth surrounding me, the sound of his voice... then my eyes snapped open and I realized I'd fallen asleep.

Jamie's hand rested on my arm. I'd curled into his body, my head resting in the space between his shoulder and neck.

I pulled back quickly, blinking against the strangeness of waking in the cramped truck when I hadn't known I'd fallen asleep.

"Ready?"

I nodded, and he pulled the door handle and slid out.

"Want me to drop you too, Morrison?" Quinn's voice sounded even more sultry than usual.

The clock said it was after two in the morning—no wonder.

"No, go ahead. I'll walk back."

Jamie shut the door behind me as I pulled my purse over a shoulder and turned to the walkway up to my house. Quinn had probably already known where I lived—a product of small-town life. But if not, that meant I'd slept through him giving her directions.

"Sorry I fell asleep," I said, my voice a rasp.

"Don't be sorry."

"You guys were awesome. I'm not sure I gushed enough —you really were." I ran my hands along the strap of my purse as we slowed down to stand by the door.

"I'm glad you came."

"Me too. Thanks for inviting me."

We stopped at the door, and I turned to him, not sure what to expect now. But there he was, right in my space, and before I could freak out or do something awkward, he stepped closer and enveloped me in his arms. I let go of my purse and wrapped my arms around him.

My heart hammered in my chest at this—another unexpectedly sweet moment with Jamie, though why I kept being surprised by him, I didn't know. He'd never shown me anything but this side of him.

And then, because it hadn't been enough of an overload to see him performing in all his glory or to be smashed up against him or to wake up cradled against his body or to be hugged by him, he dropped a light kiss onto my temple, squeezed me tightly, and then let go.

"I'll see you Wednesday?" he asked as he wandered down the path.

A hug. A kiss—to my head, but still. And then, he'd said it again. *Bel, Baby*. A night full of not just light, but heat.

What was this man doing to me?

"Yep. Yeah... see you then."

CHAPTER NINE

Bel

Thanks to Jamie, I arrived home too exhausted to cry about being alone in an empty house.

My parents were officially gone as of Friday. In an effort to be settled before the end of the summer and the busiest season for their work, their company had given them a few days off to make the move—they'd hired movers that week, packed up, and were mostly out. They hadn't taken too much with them since they didn't want to leave me in an empty house, they said, but it might as well have been empty.

I'd needed something to distract me from the fact that their stuff *and* they were gone, and Jamie had done it. He couldn't have known that last night would be my first night fully on my own, but the distraction of the concert and even the late arrival back home had been perfect.

The hug at the doorstep, the kiss to my head... those

things had kept me feeling floaty and anxious as I got ready for bed, but once I lay down, I passed out.

I worked at *The Elk* again, but all day—I preferred going to church on Sundays but had volunteered to work all weekend since I'd known I'd need the distraction and I did *not* need any sympathetic looks or well-meaning friends comforting me and making me sob all over myself in public.

No thanks.

The week went along like that—I took as many shifts as they'd let me, and tried to ignore that my mom's antique writing desk was gone, that the master bedroom stood empty, that the coffee mug my dad left out on the counter all day after his first morning cup didn't leave a ring on the counter anymore.

I'd been looking forward to Wednesday's movie night, but Jamie called to say he had to cancel—something about helping his grandfather, which I couldn't help but find endearing even if it left me hugely disappointed. He suggested swimming again on Saturday afternoon, and I was grateful he'd given me something else to look forward to.

After work Saturday, I changed into my suit, grabbed my bag, book, and water, and walked the very familiar path to the swimming hole.

The walk felt different today though. I didn't know why, but my stomach had twisted in a knot and my mouth had dried out. I felt antsy in a way I hadn't since the first time I'd met Jamie at the movies weeks ago.

I dropped my stuff in the shade by the tree just as he wandered up.

"How are you?"

His face was serious when I turned to greet him.

"I'm fine. How are you?" I asked, surprised to find him looking... almost upset.

Those blue-bird eyes of his seemed particularly vibrant with the backdrop of the sky behind him, even shadowed under his white ball cap. I blinked away from them and searched his face to decipher his mood.

"I'm fine," he said, hands on hips, mouth pressed into a thin line.

"You don't seem fine."

"I'm wondering why you're not telling me how you're really doing."

He stepped closer, and I examined my bag on the ground next to me to avoid his stare. I didn't want to dwell on the ache I'd been carrying around in my chest since my parents had broken their news. I'd been doing a fine job of moving through my days without focusing on it.

"It's fine. They're gone, but they left most of the furniture. I had dinner with Gran every night this week I didn't work, so it didn't feel that different than when they had bigger projects and worked late. It's not the end of the world, and when school starts, I doubt I'll even notice the difference."

Jamie dropped into a squat right next to me and forced my attention to his face. "It's okay to be upset."

"I know." I snapped the words, knowing I sounded petulant even though he was just trying to be a good friend.

"Do you?"

His face was so full of concern, I swallowed hard against the rush of longing to ask him to hold me and let me cry in his T-shirt again. I didn't want that from him or anyone. I didn't want to cry anymore.

Instead, I nodded. "Yep. Thanks."

I busied myself with shimmying out of my shorts,

pulling off my tank, and jumped into the water before he could say anything more. By the time I climbed out and back to my towel, he was watching me with an entirely different expression.

"What now?" I asked, restlessness inching up my spine.

Typical Jamie, he just stared, the barest start of a smile at the curve of his lips.

"Seriously? First you tell me it's okay to be a wreck about my parents, which I appreciate. And now you're looking at me like... *that*. Whatever that is."

He ducked his head and chuckled, then set down the book he held but hadn't opened and turned to me as I settled onto my towel next to him.

"I was looking at you like I can't believe Danny hasn't made a move for you."

My eyes shot to his. "What?"

The breeze disappeared and the air turned thick, almost humid, around us. Small drops of water slid down my chest, beaded off my thighs, my wet hair warm in the sun, and yet somehow, at the same time, I couldn't feel anything.

His face darkened, clouds passing over a calm sea and gathering a storm, and he pushed out a breath from his nose. He shook his head like he was having a conversation with himself, then shifted his attention back to me.

"I'm saying Danny's an idiot." He pulled his hat off, ran his hand through his hair, then smashed the hat back down on his head.

My heart hadn't let up its tripping, tumbling pace. I could take what he said at face value, but I wanted him to say more.

"Why?"

He slumped down on his towel and rolled to his side. I

lay back down and turned on my side to face him just in time to see his eyes wandering over me from toe to chin.

"You've always been beautiful, Bel. But you're also strong, sweet, funny.... If I was him..." He stopped—just trailed off like he wasn't holding my heart in his hand.

I waited a few seconds, a minute, for him to speak.

"What? If you were him, *what?*" My voice was nothing above a whisper, but he heard me.

He was close—only a foot from me, facing me, all his attention on me.

"I—" He pressed his lips together to stop.

He was killing me. What was he going to say? The quiet weighed heavy on my chest as I waited.

"What, Jamie?"

Something about my voice must have snapped him out of whatever hesitancy he had, because as soon as I said his name, he reached out at the same time he leaned over, and his mouth met mine.

Jamie Morrison's soft, warm lips were on mine.

Me. Bel Paxton.

I reached up to steady myself with a hand on his shoulder, but he moved closer, and soon, I lay on my back, and he bent over me, one elbow planted by my head, one hand smoothing a path from my ear, down my neck, over my collar bone.

Every part of me lit on fire, and the heat from Jamie's body didn't help. His kisses were a confusing mix of sweet and passionate, pulling back from the heavier sensation just when it seemed like we'd dive head first into something else.

Then he did pull back completely, his lips a fraction of an inch from mine, his eyes boring into mine, his hat lost somewhere in the last few minutes.

"I'd make you mine. In every possible way, Bel. I'd want

you every way, and if you wanted me too, I'd make you mine." His breath skated over my lips, now parted in disbelief and overwhelm.

We stayed right there, body to body, eyes locked on each other, for another minute before he closed his eyes and pushed back, rolled over, and sat up to locate his hat.

I just lay there, surprised to find I was still a corporeal being and had not, in fact, combusted under the heat and flooding desire that had rushed at me since the beginning of our conversation, let alone the actual physical contact of the last few minutes.

Seconds?

I had no idea how long we'd kissed, but I wished it wouldn't stop.

I cleared my throat, willing my voice to come out confident and solid so he wouldn't think I was as befuddled—even if in a good way—as I was.

"Jamie—"

His head jerked to the side, but he wouldn't look at me. "Bel, I don't think—"

"There you guys are!"

My head snapped to the new voice coming from the pathway leading to where we sat.

Danny's voice.

"I'm so ready for a swim—this is perfect! Being cooped up on a plane for the last five hours... not awesome."

My body seemed to know what to do before my mind did. I stood and moved to Danny as he trotted to me, his face a huge sunrise smile, his sweet blue eyes so familiar to me. I wrapped my arms around him and he did the same, lifting me and spinning me a bit.

"There's my girl. I missed you!"

I should have been happy—elated—at his return. But

my heart felt like it was collapsing in on itself as I caught Jamie rolling up his towel out of the corner of my eye.

"I'll let you guys catch up, then. I'm sure I'll see you at dinner tonight if everyone's back?" Jamie said, his voice nothing like the warm, delectable sound I'd heard only moments ago.

He didn't stop to look at me or talk to Danny as he stepped onto the trail.

"Ma comes Tuesday. We ended up heading back a bit early and decided to surprise you guys. We'll be ready for dinner tonight for sure," Danny said as he slung an arm around my shoulders and turned us to watch Jamie go.

"Great. See you later." Jamie raised a hand in farewell as he walked.

I still couldn't find words, couldn't speak, couldn't even figure out how I was feeling. My mind still reeled from Jamie's kiss and still wished it hadn't ended.

My first real kiss. My first real... anything.

I was still waiting for my chance to say *I do want you* and see what happened.

But here, now? Danny, my best friend, who'd been gone for over six weeks and now looked like all he needed to make him happy was the sight of me.

"You're back," I croaked.

He pulled me in for another hug, then set me back and looked me over. Normally, him checking me out in my swimsuit would spark some kind of hope that maybe, someday, he'd figure out he was in love with me.

Today, it did nothing but make me turn and slip back into my shorts and shirt. "I should probably get out of the sun."

"Really? I mean it, I could use a swim—I can run back

to the house and get my suit in less than ten minutes, and then you can catch me up on your summer."

I grabbed my bag, water, book, sunglasses, all of which had spilled out and required my attention in a way that let me avoid Danny's inspection.

"Yeah, sorry. I've been here a while and I don't want to fry. But I'll see you at dinner? Or is that a family thing—"

"Of course you're coming. We're doing *The Elk* at seven. I haven't had non-campfire food in forever. Leo told me to tell you to wear a dress because she wants to dress up after being part of the unsanitary hiking crowd the last while."

I nodded, smiling brightly, and took the path to my house, hoping I'd feel like myself once I got space from the scene of one of the more intense moments of my life.

CHAPTER TEN

Bel

Why didn't I call Jamie? Why didn't he call me? Who kisses a girl and then just leaves? Who kisses a girl *like that* and doesn't want to...? I don't know... discuss what happened?

Yes, I knew it was unrealistic to expect him to want to talk the same way I did, but that had been more than just a peck, more than just a simple kiss. It might have been my first real kiss, sure, but I could tell. I *knew*.

The kiss and the words and the... just... wow.

He'd shut all the way down when Danny had arrived, but what was he going to say? *"Bel, I don't think..."* and that was it. I didn't get the rest. *I don't think we should do that again?* Or something more like *I don't think I can wait until we do that again?*

And now, as I walked to the singular restaurant of my life lately, *The Elk Street Grill*, decked in a coral-colored sundress and curls in my hair, a little makeup on my face, and sandals on my feet, how could I sit across from Jamie and *not* talk to him about this, not look at him and study every breath he took in an effort to figure out what was going on?

Maybe he'd been worried about Danny. He'd clearly thought Danny and I were together and had been for years, which made the whole situation a bit more complex, to say the least.

But I could say with freedom and a lot more surety than I'd had six weeks ago, I owed Danny nothing more than a clarification. He so frequently called me *buddy*. Clearly, he didn't think I was his girlfriend, but dating his older brother —that merited discussing.

A few minutes after seven, I stepped inside the doors of *The Elk* determined to make the best of dinner with the Morrisons and then have a heart to heart with Danny. Then if, or ideally when, I talked to Jamie, I could make sure he knew that wasn't an issue in any way.

"Bel! So glad to see another female. It was like ninety-nine percent dudes in my life for the last six weeks and I need some estrogen exposure." Leo grabbed me and hugged me, then smiled as she took in my dress and did a small curtsy when I smiled at hers.

Leo and I were two years apart at school, so we didn't spend as much time together as we might have if we'd been closer in age. But the older we got, the more fun we had and the less those years between us mattered, and I was glad I got along with the whole Morrison family so I could see her often.

"You look great, and very tan," I said, eyeing her shoulders about five shades darker than Danny had ever been.

"Showers work wonders."

"*You* look great Bel. Man, I've missed you." Danny stepped close and pulled me into another hug. "Your hair's longer."

I shrugged. "I don't know."

"It is. I'm sure." Danny was extremely laid back, but also intensely observant in a way that often proved startling. The one thing he'd never seemed to notice was *me* in that certain way I'd always wanted to be noticed by him.

But standing there in the circle of his family, smiling at his dad and older brother Liam, feeling the heavy stare of Jamie who looked particularly broody tonight with his hair falling in his eyes and his hands tucked into his pockets, I couldn't help but notice that the way I felt about Jamie looking at me and noticing me was nothing like what I'd felt with Danny.

I'd been barreling toward it all summer.

I loved Danny, and I always would. I'd grown up loving him. But maybe I'd wanted to be with him in that way because he was familiar and my dearest friend. He was cute and maddening and clueless and smart all at once. I did love him.

But I could tell after weeks apart that I wasn't, nor had I ever been, *in love* with him.

We sat at a circular booth in the corner of the restaurant and Mr. Morrison, who I refused to call William even after all this time, regaled us with stories of his children. He just beamed when he talked about them.

Once or twice, I felt Jamie's eyes on me, but when I'd look at him, he'd snap his head in the opposite direction. Maddening.

A few times, I gave in to the desire to watch him as Danny or Liam told stories about Leo's unending bravery and stupidity in a particularly harrowing portion of the trek, and found his head downcast, his shoulders sloping instead of steady, his eyes staring at his plate in a distant way.

It made sense. He'd opted out of the adventure and had missed all of the moments they were sharing.

"And how was your summer, Fancy Pants?" Leo asked Jamie.

He chuckled then shook his head. "Pretty uneventful. Just biding my time 'til I head out."

If my heart had been a hopeful little paper airplane about to take flight, he would've just crumpled it into a useless ball. *Ouch.*

He didn't look at me—hadn't really even acknowledged me.

"Did he keep you company, Bel?" Danny asked, his voice hushed so only I could hear.

I nodded, unable to use words just yet.

Fortunately, the meal was nearly over at that point, so I could stay quiet without drawing attention. Plus, at a table with Mr. Morrison, Leo, and Danny, it was rare to find a quiet moment in which to insert myself. They were used to me enjoying the show.

Danny took my hand in his and pulled me down the street toward my house. We waved to the others as they meandered and chatted, though Jamie was already fifty feet down the path and staring up at the mountains as he walked.

"So what's up?" Danny squeezed my hand as we wandered down the street.

The sun was setting and lighting the mountains on fire with pinks and golds. One of my favorite times of day.

I let out a breath, gathering courage and praying I'd be able to be clear, and that this conversation wouldn't be as awkward as I thought it might be. We stepped onto the path that led to my neighborhood, and I was glad to be off the street where people were still milling, shouting at Danny every now and then that they were glad he was back.

"Jamie kissed me."

Well. Now it's out there.

Danny stayed silent as we walked on, and I couldn't read his face when I looked at him. He still held my hand, so apparently the news hadn't repulsed him too much.

"Just today. I don't really know what happened, but I like him…"

"That's great." His voice was the same—friendly, sweet, normal Danny tone.

"I—I think so. I mean, what he said at dinner… it's probably nothing. But I felt like I should tell you since you're my best friend, you know?" I stopped to look at him.

He dropped my hand and gave me a close-lipped smile. Not his usual glaring, full-bodied grin.

"I'm glad you told me. It's cool. Jamie's the best, and I can—well it makes me—it's cool." He nodded emphatically.

Despite his words, I knew I'd hurt him. Maybe it was the surprise, or maybe he just didn't like the idea and couldn't find a reason to say so, but I could tell he didn't like this. That strain in his voice, that thin smile. No.

We'd never had a conversation like this before—I'd always been with him, his option, his person, his friend, his *girl*, but not in the way I'd thought I wanted.

Now I was saying I wanted to be someone else's. Of course he wouldn't understand that, even if he didn't really want me as something more.

"Well, I doubt it's anything, but I didn't want it to be weird. I wanted to talk with him about it, and I thought I should probably let you know."

"Sure. Yeah." He kicked at a rock and shifted restlessly.

"Well hey, I have to go work on laundry and some stuff before bed—my dad wants the house and the garden and everything ready for my mom this week so we're starting tonight..."

"Of course. I'll see you..." I stepped forward to hug him, and he pulled me in for a quick pat on the back, then was halfway back to the road before I ever turned toward home.

"Bye, Danny."

CHAPTER ELEVEN

Bel

I 'd been waiting for a chance to find Jamie alone. I had to talk to him, and he was not easy to pin down. After two days of hoping he'd magically appear, I sent him a text. I didn't like using my phone—we really hadn't used phones in the course of our relationship except to work out logistics, and he didn't strike me as a guy who'd want to talk on the phone any more than I did, so finally I broke down and asked him to meet.

"Thanks for meeting me."

"Sure. What's up?" He picked up a stick and tossed it into the little stream that ran along the path I walked to his house.

He'd agreed to meet me at a little bridge in the path. Technically almost exactly halfway between our houses, it was *not* the site of our first kiss, which I thought I should avoid. Especially if anyone else ended up being there.

The fact that he was going to pretend nothing happened wouldn't derail me.

"Uh, can't you guess?"

He leaned against the bridge's railing. "I guess I can."

"So…" I tried, hoping he'd say something else.

"So?"

"You kissed me."

He sucked in a slow breath and let it out. If he wasn't him and always understated, I would have called it dramatic.

"Yeah. I did. I shouldn't have." His eyes jumped to mine, then back to the water.

"Why not?" Fair question, and I'd managed it without letting the hurt swirling around my heart show in my voice.

He shook his head, but didn't speak.

"If you're worried about Danny, I told him. He said he thought it's great."

Finally, he turned to me with wide eyes. "You told him? Why would you do that?"

"I—I thought he should know. I'd typically tell my best friend about my first real kiss." I cleared my throat, regretting saying that last part, especially when he flinched, then continued. "He could tell I had something on my mind, and I thought he should know. I'd do the same if it'd been Leo or anyone else, but especially someone related to you…"

His expression hadn't changed, but his eyes were darting around like he was trying to make sense of what I said.

A hand ran through that hair. "There's no way he's okay with it. You get that, right? He's just trying not to be a jerk because it goes against his nature to be anything but easygoing and happy. But this…"

I stepped close to him and put a hand on his wrist. He

looked down and frowned, but I inched closer. "I think we should try it. Date."

He stepped back and pressed his hands to his eyes, then let them drop. "No way, Bel."

In all of my imagined scenarios of this moment, *no way, Bel* was never one of the phrases that came from his lips. I'd known he might resist, since whatever he'd started to say after he kissed me hadn't exactly been enthusiastic, but he'd been interested enough to kiss me. He *was* interested. I knew he was. And I was too. There was no reason we shouldn't just... see what happened.

He interrupted my internal madness. "You get that, don't you?"

"No. I don't see why—"

"Bel, you're seventeen. You're in high school. I never should have kissed you, if not only for that reason, then for the fact that my younger brother is in love with you. I am a jackass of the worst kind. Add to that the fact that I'm leaving in less than a month and I have no idea when I'll be back, and it makes no sense."

"If things went well, we could be long-distance. I don't mind that—"

I stepped closer just as he stepped back.

"You're not hearing me, Bel. You're great. You really are. But you belong with Danny."

"I'm Danny's friend. I don't want him that way..." The truth of that resounded in me for the nth time that summer.

Jamie shook his head, ran a hand through that maddening hair of his, and looked up at the sky for a minute.

"Listen, Bel. I'm not—" He cleared his throat. "I'm not the kind of guy to do long-distance. I'm about to start a new career and the last thing I need is some girl back home pining away for me when I have nothing to give her."

Some girl.

I opened my mouth, but I'd been handily silenced by his words, like instead of cavalier words he'd dealt me a sucker punch to the gut. I'd been foolish enough to think he cared about me—wanted more from me than something physical. Those words he'd said by the pond had a different ring to them. *I'd make you mine.* But now, it was clear. He had no intention of being faithful, of being a partner. He had no intention of being with me.

"I've got to head out. I'll see you around."

I nodded, sure that if I spoke, my voice would betray me.

I stayed in place, refusing to move until he'd rounded the corner of the path. When he disappeared around the bend, I turned and trudged back to my house with leaden feet, gutted in a way I hadn't expected.

How could I have been so wrong? How could I have thought we had something when he apparently couldn't care less about me? *Some girl.* The darkness returned fully to block out the sun now.

How could I have thought I liked him, let alone that I might be falling for him?

And how many times had I thought he was sweet? *Sweet?*

He was wrong about me being too young, wrong about Danny being in love with me, and wrong about him having nothing to give me. But I couldn't refute him on that, because if there was nothing he wanted to give me, then that was that.

Bullet dodged.

And even though I talked myself through that—the idea

that I'd been saved from humiliation, frustration, possibly the embarrassment of him being unfaithful to me since he sounded a lot like he planned to go for broke and live the musician life when he left here... even with all of that, I couldn't help but think I'd lost something I'd only just begun to grasp.

Good thing I'd cried all the tears in my storehouse over my parents and had determined not to bawl about stupid, meaningless stuff anymore. If I hadn't, I might have curled up in a ball and let myself sob at the loss of something my heart wanted so desperately.

CHAPTER TWELVE

Bel

If anyone noticed something different about me in the following weeks, they likely blamed it on my parents.

That wasn't all wrong. I still hurt from their leaving. But I was angry enough and also resigned at the same time, so it didn't really influence my day-to-day.

Jamie's departure from town, his obligatory smile and hug and pat on my back paired with a refusal to fully meet my eye at his going away party, were more to blame.

But what happened a few weeks after that, a few weeks after we'd returned to school and everyone was tittering excitedly about the homecoming dance—that's what really locked in the feeling I'd known all my life.

"Can we talk?" Danny asked one day after school as we walked home.

The school was west of the small downtown, which meant Danny had to walk past my house to get home anyway, and ever since I'd known him, he'd come by my house on the way to school and dropped me off on his way home.

"Of course."

"You seem... different." He crossed his arms, and when I glanced to the side where he walked, his face was drawn and his eyes were studying me.

"Sorry. It's been weird with my parents gone. I guess I'm still trying to get used to it." I crossed my arms too, not sure what else to do with myself.

"Is that really it?"

"What else would it be?" I asked before I could stop myself.

"Jamie."

We stopped at the little gate to my backyard.

"It's not—"

"I know it's Jamie, Bel. I'm not an idiot. I don't know what happened between the two of you, but you told me he kissed you, and that you liked him, and then you never said anything else about it. What's going on?"

This conversation was nails on a chalkboard. I didn't want to talk about Jamie, and I especially didn't want to talk about him with Danny.

"Uh, he wasn't interested." I turned the handle of the gate and walked inside, ready to close it behind me, but he caught it and held it.

"I don't buy it. What'd he say?"

Danny didn't usually act like this. I couldn't tell what he had on his mind other than clearly, I'd upset him.

"Just that he was leaving and it didn't make sense for us to date, which, you know, makes sense. So we're just friends." I avoided his eyes, inspecting the faded bird house hanging from an oak tree in the corner of the yard.

"And you're good with that?" he pressed.

"Of course," I said, hoping my voice sounded as nonchalant as I meant for it to be—*nothing to see here, folks! Same old carefree Bel.*

"Okay."

I turned to look at him, unsure of where this was going. Usually, Danny wanted to talk about a new trail he'd planned to cut on the mountain or when he would start his winter training program to strengthen his legs so he could ski longer every day... He didn't talk about this stuff often and when he did, he didn't do it like this.

"Okay?"

"So, if I asked you out. Would you want to go with me?" His eyes were locked on mine now.

I swallowed. "What? We hang out all the time."

"Yeah, but if I wanted to take you out on a date, would you go?"

"I—I don't know what you mean."

He forced a laugh. "It's not all that complex, Bel. I'm asking you to go out with me. I've been in love with you basically since I met you, which I guess you were totally oblivious to, but I'm telling you I'd like to take you on a date."

I wasn't sure whether I felt the blood drain from my face or if I just knew it was gone. My heart was suddenly beating out of my ribcage, my hands clenched together against my chest like I was shielding myself from him.

I opened my mouth, but couldn't force a sound. He'd nearly spat those words at me, angry with me for not knowing how he felt despite the fact that he'd kept that secret from me so well.

More than a minute ticked by as my mind filtered for

words. The look on his face passed from frustrated to resigned, and finally something infinitely worse.

Hurt.

"Danny, you know I love you."

He pressed his lips together and nodded, a reluctant breath escaping from his nose. "Yeah."

"I just don't—"

"Please, Bel. I'll just go. And we'll pretend like this never happened." He looked me in the eye again, his mouth hard and his jaw locked down. "All right?"

"Yeah, sure."

He nodded once, a final closure on the conversation, and then let the gate slide shut as he turned and left.

I made my way to a chair on the patio and slumped into it. I couldn't parse out what I was thinking or feeling except the terrible irony of the last three months that I couldn't escape.

What Danny had just said to me was exactly what I'd dreamed of him saying to me for years. But when he'd left for his trip and given me space—more space than I'd ever had from him, actually—I'd realized that what I felt for him was love in a familial, friendly, lovely way, but not romantic love.

I'd fallen, at least to some degree, for his brother, who had no interest in me besides a stolen kiss.

And now, Danny wanted to date me, and I couldn't date him. *I couldn't.* Because as much as I hated to admit it to myself, I did like Jamie—maybe even sort of loved him—and I couldn't think of dating Danny now.

What I couldn't have known then was how irrevocably my friendship with Danny had broken. In the months that followed, we never spoke of what he'd said, we didn't talk about Jamie, and worst of all, we started simply not talking.

Before long, just after Christmas, we weren't spending much time together at all. I went to senior prom with Tyler Jasperson and Danny took Chalice Wallace. By graduation, we were barely cordial, and his parents were more than a little confused when I begged off of their throwing a joint graduation party for me and Danny.

Just shy of a year after my first time hanging out with Jamie, I'd lost my parents, Jamie—who I'd never really had to begin with—and Danny.

With Danny went my support system in the Morrisons, my friendship with Leo though she never treated me differently. I just didn't get to see her. Even Liam, who'd always been like an older brother, was lost to me.

It was time to leave Silverton and not look back. Two days after graduation, I left the town having said goodbye to the only person remaining in my life.

"I love you so much, Gran. I'm sorry I'm leaving."

Gran pulled back, her eyes sparkling with tears. "Nonsense. It's time for you to go out and conquer the world."

"Well, I'm only going down the mountain. I'll be an hour away." I summoned a slight smile.

Gran reached a weathered hand to my face and smoothed away a tear. "I'll be here if you need me."

The tears filled my eyes again. "I know."

"You'll be great, Bel. And I'll always be here for you."

We hugged again, and I left her there in her kitchen at the small table where I'd eaten so many meals in my life. I left her place, a tiny little house she kept immaculate, feeling more desolate and lonely than I ever had.

I got in the beater car I'd saved all year for, took a deep breath, and drove out of Silverton, promising myself I'd never look back.

CHAPTER THIRTEEN

NOW

Jamie

That went well.

She made it out the door before I could stop her. At that point, she wouldn't have stopped anyway, but it made me feel worse to know I'd lost the chance to sit with her a little longer without that persistent hostility simmering between us.

Swirling the now-cold coffee in the bright blue mug in front of me, I remembered how much more quickly coffee, and everything, cools down up here in the mountains. Da would microwave his coffee ten times over the course of the morning because he couldn't stand it cold, but half the time, he'd forget the mug altogether until it was time for another warm-up.

I slugged back the last of the bitter drink and nodded to the girl behind the counter as I left, unable to fully push away the feeling that I'd done something very wrong with Bel.

Aren't you astute?

Of course I knew I had. I'd done the wrong thing with her over and over again years ago, and here I sat, at it again.

Back then, I never should have agreed to *keep her company*, as Danny had called it, nor should I have taken her to dinner, or comforted her when she'd been crying, or kissed her and told her how I wanted to make her mine when I knew I couldn't.

When I knew I never would.

The problem was, I thought I'd had it all on lock-down. I'd thought I could talk myself into thinking of her as a sweet kid, my little brother's girl, but the minute I spent more than, well, a minute with her, there it was. The chemistry, the interest, the sense that she knew me better, saw me better, than anyone. Once she made clear she and Danny weren't together, and never had been, that part of me that'd pushed away my interest in her broke down.

After years of feeling like the odd man out, it was a heady experience to sit next to someone who didn't judge me for not being more engaged in the family business, who wasn't faulting me for not going to college, who didn't doubt I could make it in the music industry. She had innocent, blind faith that felt too good to avoid.

And Danny was gone. So it became ridiculously easy to ignore the fact that the girl I was getting to know, was hanging out with, wasn't mine at all. Wasn't available. Even after she'd made it clear Danny, like an idiot, had never made a move on her and had made it seem like he never would, I knew she was wrong. She had no idea what she was talking about, but I did. And I'd kissed her anyway.

And as he should have, he'd miraculously appeared, and we'd split apart before I could try to make up some lazy excuse about how we shouldn't have kissed and couldn't be together—or worse and far more likely, gone back for more.

But by the time I did talk to her, it was too late. She'd already gotten excited about the prospect of us, Danny had already been hurt, and I had already descended into accepting my role as screwed up brother for wanting the girl my brother loved.

I'd hurt her when I fled, but it'd been a last resort. Because I had wanted her too. Almost desperately by the time I left, so that in order not to grab her and kiss her and tell her I'd wait for her as long as she wanted me to, I'd avoided her, frozen her out, kept myself from her in an effort to retain one shred of dignity and familial loyalty intact as I ran away to LA.

She deserved better. They all did.

The blast of fresh mountain air as I wandered along Main Street had me smiling, even as I confronted those dismal thoughts.

I could accept that I'd run away. Yes, I'd been taking an opportunity that ultimately changed my life, but the timing of it, the *way* I'd done it, both with Bel and with Danny, and really the whole family—running.

"How'd it go?"

Liam's voice interrupted my thoughts, and I turned to see him and Jonas Bauer a half block behind me.

I shrugged. "About like you'd expect, I guess. Maybe slightly better."

Or worse. Especially since she was still so wary of me.

I'd have to rectify that somehow. Maybe we'd never be together, never even be friends, but I couldn't stay here and have her constantly expecting me to harm her in some way.

Liam nodded, but as he did, I remembered I was mad with him.

I stalked back toward him. "You know, you could have given me a heads up you'd planned for us to work together."

"I did."

"No, you didn't. You said she'd be in the meeting, but not that you were having us work together. Very different things." My eyes bounced to Bauer, whose neutral face looked unreadable—something evidently typical of him.

Liam let out a dramatic sigh. "Fine. I should have. But now it's done, so you can go ahead and thank me."

"What are you thanking our big brother for?"

Danny's voice set my heart racing just a tick faster when it came over my shoulder.

Liam smiled immediately. "He's thanking me for getting him involved in company board meetings, that's what. No longer the wayward son, he's getting his hands dirty with the lodge."

Danny's brows raised, impressed, and he smiled at me. "Good for you, bro. I'm working on putting on my big boy socks and joining the fun a bit more too."

He never did carry any hint of anger or upset about what I'd done, and we'd never discussed it. Wondering if he'd ever forgive me had occupied a large portion of my mental energy during my first year away. By the second year, it'd faded some. By the fourth, I came back just before Christmas, and Liam told me Danny and Bel were dating. It'd felt like a strange dagger to my gut, and yet it'd felt like appropriate punishment, too.

If I couldn't have her, and the reason I couldn't was Dan, then Danny *should* have her.

Confusingly, it didn't last long. Liam found a way to drop in that they'd broken up just after the New Year. The shroud of guilt I carried around after the flood of relief had hit me at that news was heavy, ugly, thick.

I cleared my throat, shoving the thoughts away. "Well good on us. I'm sure Liam and Leo are more than ready to see us take more interest. And you, Mr. Bauer?"

"I'm glad to have you on the team, Mr. Morris. The more help we can get, the better. Happy to hear you're investing in the local economy."

He straightened, somehow taller than he'd just been, which was maybe an inch taller than me, but stiff and direct in a not-unpleasant way.

I met his eye, wondering what he knew about my investments. Liam couldn't have told him because so far, no one but my lawyer and realtor knew. "Please call me Jamie."

He nodded, just once. "Of course."

"Well, I've got another meeting in a bit. I'll see you guys for dinner."

I held up a hand, my new awkward way of parting with people right in front of me, apparently, and turned to go. The chorus of goodbyes followed me a half a block before I turned the corner and walked the rest of the way to realty and developer's office on Elk Street.

Before I could step in, I felt a hand on my shoulder.

Dread jolted through me, the familiar fight or flight response gathering between my shoulder blades, until I whipped around to see Danny.

He backed off, hands up. "Whoa, sorry. Guess I shouldn't be surprised you don't like people touching you without permission."

I blew out a breath and shook my head. "Hard to remember I'm here and not somewhere people who don't know me might be trying to get my attention."

I never stayed in Silverton long enough to acclimate to being in a relatively safe place. Of course, there were tourists and people who had moved to the town in the last few years, but overall, I'd never had issues here. A few requests for autographs, a few stolen photos on the sly, but really, nothing invasive.

But everywhere else, people knew me. Even with sunglasses, even in nondescript cars, even grabbing coffee in sweatpants on a Saturday morning at a time most musicians were still sleeping. Somehow, they knew me.

No benefit to complaining, and I accepted that. But I'd had some weird run-ins with fans in the last few years, and it had been often enough to keep me on my guard, particularly when I was without a security team.

But this was Danny. Danny with a look on his face like he'd work all day to figure out what was going on in my head.

"Let me make you breakfast tomorrow."

"Can you cook?" The question kept me from asking the larger question—*why?*

"You've missed a lot these last few years. One of the key developments is my breakfast prowess. It's high time you were educated."

He grinned, his whole face cheery and sweet, and suddenly, I was looking at this man and not the gangly fifteen-year-old I always thought of him as. That made no sense, especially since we were only three years apart, but memories were funny things.

"All right. Tell me when and where, and I'm there."

CHAPTER FOURTEEN

Bel

Gran folded me into her arms the minute she pulled open her door.

I closed my eyes and let myself breathe in the familiar scent of her, and must have held on a bit too tight.

"All right now, honey, release. *Release.*"

I backed away and chuckled. "Sorry. Weird day."

One penciled eyebrow arched in question, but I could tell by the set of her lips she knew. Gran didn't smirk, but this expression didn't have a name, so it might as well have been a smirk.

"Did Jamie Morrison have anything to do with that?"

I didn't hold back the frustrated grunt that came so naturally now, at the end of the day, after I'd mentally rehashed the conversation with Jamie no less than twenty times.

"How'd you even know he was here?"

Who knew why I bothered asking? She always knew everything—the Silverton Springs retirement community teemed with gossip and the latest news about the town and its inhabitants.

She clucked at me and waved me inside her room as she shut the door behind me. "You know Will Morrison lives here. He's always crowing about his grandkids, who's doing what. Jamie is always making the news so we have to hear about all his fancy awards and Oscars and platinum records and lawsuit settlements." She rolled her eyes like any of that was normal news.

"Lawsuit settlements?" I'd instituted a rule about halfway through my freshman year of college: *No searching the Internet for Jamie.*

I'd failed to follow it a few times over the years, and each time I did, the failure had brought only a brutal sense of separation and sadness with it. He'd changed—he'd grown up, and his music had matured, like his voice, but he'd kept that same soulful style he'd always had. He'd only become more attractive. It all made me ache. Having learned that lesson a few too many times, it'd now been years since I'd looked him up.

Gran arranged plates at her small table so I sat the pasta bake and bag of sides in her tiny kitchen. The tight quarters were small but very nice—granite countertop, stainless steel fridge, and the kitchen itself less than five feet squared.

"Yes. *Oh.* Did you not know? A fanatic broke into his house even after he'd taken a restraining order against the person. No one ever said what happened, but I guess there was a big debacle with Jamie's security company giving out his information or some such nonsense that clearly endangered him and several of the company's other clients. Bad move in that business."

I dished servings of pasta onto our plates while suppressing the chill of horror running down my spine at the thought of someone breaking into Jamie's house. I'd not given his level of fame much thought, particularly because I'd made an effort to avoid knowing just how famous he was, but in truth, it wasn't really something anyone could ignore.

He showed up on gossip magazines, on headlines, on radios... he was everywhere.

Gran rifled through the bag with salad, bread, and cookies inside.

"Ah, yes. I assume this is Sadie's?" she asked, holding a baguette in a paper sleeve to her nose and inhaling deeply.

"Of course."

"Then you've proved your love yet again, my dear."

She pulled out a serrated bread knife and began slicing while I served salad and ignored the mild fear that ran through me any time I saw her gnarled hands holding a large knife. Not a fair thought—she'd never given me any reason to worry, but something about her lately had me jumpy.

Maybe it's you.

Yes, my anxiety had been higher in the last few months. About everything. But that wasn't it. This was... concern for my favorite person.

"I make you dinner, but the way I prove my love is by buying a baguette?" My mock-hurt rang clear.

"You know as well as I do that the most thoughtful gift a person can give someone else in this town is something Sadie made. Don't give me the sob story. I know you feel the same." She narrowed her eyes at me until we both broke.

"It's true. I'll skip the bouquets and bonbons and take bread any day of the week."

We sat at the table and Gran blessed the food before we dug in. Then the inevitable, despite my hope to avoid it, arrived.

"And so? Will young Jamie be dropping round to deliver you ciabatta rolls? Perhaps a nice honey whole wheat?" She fluttered her lashes, then took a large bite.

I laughed. "You are ridiculous, and no, definitely not. In fact, I kind of yelled at him today, so I doubt he'll be *dropping round* at all."

Of course then I had to tell her all about the meeting, the coffee, my storming out in righteous indignation only to get all the way home and realize said indignation was possibly not so righteous and maybe Jamie had been attempting to lighten the rather leaden weight of our meeting.

Ughhghg.

No simplicity existed in my interactions with him. The few times I'd seen him this past year had been fraught with high emotion, stupid words, and hurt feelings in the aftermath, even when the interaction had been nothing more than coming face to face with each other.

Good grief, it was exhausting.

"My guess is he tracks you down in the next seventy-two hours if he's any kind of man."

Gran liked to make statements like this. She'd done it with Jamie years ago, once she'd found out what'd happened between us.

If he's any kind of man, he'll call to apologize.

If he's any kind of man, he'll recognize what a jewel you are and he'll be begging on your doorstep before sunset.

When that failed,

If he's something short of an idiot, he'll visit you the first time he comes home.

Then, inevitably,

When he hears you're with Danny, if he's worth his salt and the nine long months Alice Morrison had to carry him before he was delivered a week late, he'll congratulate you both.

Then of Danny after we'd "dated" for three weeks over Christmas break my senior year of college,

If he's any kind of friend, he'll keep being your friend, even if he's in love with you and you aren't with him.

If only she'd been right about that one, at least. But Danny and me... we broke that summer before senior year of high school, and even the key years of college, of being away, couldn't push me back into seeing him as anything but a formerly faithful friend.

Gran expected men to make sense—to do the right thing. Maybe it resulted from being raised just outside the Greatest Generation and being friends with so many still of that era, but she expected men to do what they *should*.

Little did she know, as far as I knew anyway, no one did what they should anymore.

"I don't think so, Gran. I think he'll probably go back to avoiding me like he has the last nine-or-so years, and then before we know it, he'll be gone again, back to tour and hook up with famous women and get his house broken into by weirdo fans."

Gran pegged me with green eyes, a shade or two darker than mine unless she wore yellow. "Bitterness is bad for your laugh lines, Bel. Scrap it."

I frowned more exaggeratedly, and she shook her head.

"Just wait. He'll be knocking on your door before Saturday."

CHAPTER FIFTEEN

Jamie

I knocked on Danny's door at seven in the morning, astounded he planned to be awake that early for me in the off-season. Granted, some people were still eking out a few runs in the spring snow, but he didn't have many patrolling shifts this late in the year, or so I'd gathered. Fewer people equaled less need for patrollers except for blasting to keep avalanches at bay.

"Thanks for coming!" Danny's broad smile greeted me as he held open the screen door.

I'd never been to this place, but so far it suited him—the collection of skis and boots inside the door marking the path.

Something smelled great as we stepped through a tidy living room and into a small, vintage-looking kitchen, complete with old-timey blue fridge.

"This place is ridiculous. Did you outfit it?" I ran a hand over one sparkling countertop and eyed the oven, which must've contained whatever smelled so good.

Danny pulled coffee mugs from a white painted cabinet and raised a brow at me. I nodded.

As he filled the mugs, he shared details. "The lady who lived here loved retro style. The fridge is one of those that's actually new and insanely expensive, but looks old. She had a bunch of retro Coca-Cola stuff all around here too, but took that with her. I kind of dug the look, so never bothered changing it."

I smiled into the mug he handed me. That was so Danny. If it wasn't broken, why fix it?

"Food should be done in a few. Want to sit?"

He pulled out a seat at the small four-person table and I did the same.

"How long have you been in this place?" I ignored the flare of shame at not knowing. A man should know this information about his brother.

"I rented it right out of college—actually rented the basement place until the landlady said she planned to put it up for sale. Rent was stupid cheap, so I asked her if I could submit a bid to buy first. It worked out perfect."

The shock of his statement made me take a too-large swallow of coffee. "You *own* this house?"

Danny's smile was small, satisfied. "Yeah."

"I shouldn't be so shocked. It's just... I didn't ever—"

"No one thinks of me as a responsible homeowner, I know. That's never been me, but this place was a good first step toward actual adulthood. I have a few more lined up too."

Who was this kid—I should say man, really... What had

happened to make him change so much from the bum I'd always known?

The oven beeped and he jumped up. I watched him pull out a large cast-iron skillet full of food and plunk it down on the stovetop.

"Oh yeah? Do tell." Maybe I could dig for answers.

As he dished the food onto plates, he did. "Like you, I'm trying to be more involved. I know you saw Liam struggling off and on when you visited last year, but you didn't see the worst of it. It was *bad*. That, and a few other things, woke me up to the fact that it's time for me to make a move. Maybe get a real job. Get a real life. Get out of limbo."

A few other things... Like a girl, maybe? Bel? No, it hadn't worked between them.

I covered the disbelief flooding at his words by looking through the doorway back toward the living room—I didn't want to hurt him. We'd all been waiting for Danny to *grow up*. Even if he and I weren't close, Liam had kept me up on his life—or the part Liam knew about, anyway. He'd had the same job since he'd graduated college years ago and didn't seem to want anything else. He'd just... coasted along. Or, at least, that's what Liam thought—what I'd thought.

"That's great."

He set the plates down on the table and leveled me with a look that was very... un-Danny, if I had to name it.

"One of the things I have to do is talk to you."

We watched one another, then each grabbed forks and took bites. He'd made some kind of awesome skillet meal with sausages and potatoes and roasted vegetables and eggs. *Mind-blowing*.

"I didn't know you could cook."

Danny chuckled and shook his head as he swallowed.

"There's a lot you don't know, bro. That happens when you systematically avoid your place of birth for long enough."

That one hit.

I blew out a breath. I'd been awake particularly early this morning with thoughts of how to broach this subject, let alone actually apologize almost a decade late. "Yeah. I know. That's why I'm here for more than a long weekend, and one of many reasons I need to apologize to you."

Danny set down his fork and leaned his elbows on the small table so we were practically face to face.

"Yeah, that's why you're here."

Well, that was unusually direct. "To apologize to you?"

He reared back. "No, doofus, for *me* to apologize to *you*."

No doubt my eyes were wide. "What?"

Danny shoveled a few more bites in like he was fueling up. "I've done a bad job reaching out and checking on you, making sure you're okay. I've never come to see you on tour... I've just..."

I shook my head, my chest constricting with a flood of affection for this idiot kid beside me. "Are you kidding? How is that something you should apologize for? I left like a toddler having a tantrum. I left after I'd—after everything with Bel, and I knew—"

"That. *That*." He pointed his fork at me. "That is what I have to apologize to you for. You shouldn't have felt bad about that, and even though she thought I was fine with it, you knew I wasn't. But I never said anything to make it better. I never did anything except sulk around you, and that was wrong."

"No, Danny. *I* was wrong. I never should have kissed her, and I knew that. I knew it immediately. I knew it *before*. She was yours, she always had been, and I—"

"See? That's exactly the problem. She wasn't mine. She was her own, and I messed up not telling her how I felt for years and years. By that summer, I should have known she'd spend that time with you and fall for you." He frowned down at his plate.

"She wasn't yours, but she wasn't mine, either." My voice was low, and even to my ears, even after all this time, it sounded regretful.

We ate in silence for a few minutes, only the clinking of cutlery against plates accompanying us, until Danny set his fork onto his empty plate and leaned back. His eyes were on me, steady and patient. I didn't know what else to say now, but I hadn't said enough.

"Listen, I know you think she wasn't yours, but she was. I did a stupid thing and broke your trust, and hurt her, and I regret it. You have no idea how much." That was simplifying, big time.

"You regret it?" He narrowed his eyes and inspected me.

"Of course. I messed up, and it only served to drive us apart, and you and Bel…"

His head dropped to his chest, then he sat up and hit me with a big, sweet Danny smile. "You know, you did mess us up. And when we tried to date in college, she couldn't see me as anything other than a friend."

I'd wondered. How could I not have? But I'd never asked Liam what happened between them. I'd assumed the short stint together just meant the timing wasn't right.

"I'm sorry. I'm sure that was hard."

Danny chuckled. "You have no idea. Getting shot down *twice* for my older brother could easily make a guy paranoid, and one of those was before you were a world-famous Rockstar."

No bitterness in his voice showed, no real malice. He was too good.

"Not *twice*. And she was confused the first time."

His face darkened then. "No. That's the other part of this, Jam. As far as I know, Bel hasn't dated *anyone*. She and I dated for just shy of three weeks, and that was, what, more than four years ago? Not to sound like a creeper, but I'm fairly certain she hasn't dated anyone, at least not seriously, since then."

My body's reaction shouldn't have been a surprise, but sitting there in his retro kitchen, the pace of my pulse came to a sprint.

"That can't be true."

"It is. And I know why." Danny was all focus now, his blue eyes blaring sincerity and some meaning I couldn't read.

"Why?"

"*You*. She's hung up on you. She'd never admit it, and she might not even realize it, but she's never gotten over you."

My stomach dropped, the food I'd just eaten weighing leaden in my gut. "I messed her up that bad?"

Could that be possible? Could feisty, charming, independent Isabel Paxton still feel *that* wronged by me? A nightmare, but it explained her being so upset, so wary, every time I'd seen her. It explained her clipped speech and her quick exit yesterday when I'd tried to lighten the mood.

I rubbed at my eyes, now feeling tired and just... bad.

Danny stood and patted my shoulder, then stopped until I pulled my hands away from my eyes.

"What I'm saying is not that you messed up. I'm saying if you've ever wondered what would have happened if you took away the guilt and the running away and *me* from the equation, then maybe you should see."

"See what?" I asked, wondering when Danny had become the poignant voice of reason in the family.

"See what could happen between you and Bel."

Bel

People packed the coffee shop—the veteran's group took up the large table on the left side, and each of the smaller tables held small gatherings and couples sipping lattes and delving into the last vestiges of Sadie's baked goods. We'd sold out of everything at just past eight a.m.

Fortunately, she held her ground back there in the kitchen, headphones blocking out everyone, producing world-class bread and baked items that would soon refill the display case and bread baskets. And thank goodness, because I hated telling people we'd sold out of everything.

Jonas Bauer occupied the table nearest the front windows on the left side of the shop. He'd taken a room at the Silverton Inn but ended up here at least three mornings a week. He sat tall in his chair, in perfectly pressed dress shirt and slacks no matter the hour, and sipped espresso.

Once he finished his coffee, he'd only linger a few minutes. Just until...

"Are you taking a morning break?" Garrett asked as he handed me an iced mocha for the customer in front of me.

"If I can—does that work? I just need to run home for a minute—I can be there and back in twenty." I smiled at the customer, bid them farewell, then slumped a little as I turned back to Garrett.

"It's no problem, Bel. It's slowing down, and Sadie will have some new stuff for us any minute. Go ahead before the niner rush comes through."

Garrett's orangey-red hair, bright blue eyes, and pale skin made him seem almost comically young in that moment. He was eighteen, had graduated high school early, and worked at the coffee shop while saving up money for college.

"Sounds good. Be back in twenty." I untied my apron and walked into the kitchen where I hung it on the hook by the door.

I noted Sadie, bent at the waist, hunched a little to see into the oven. She wasn't likely to speak to me, even if we made eye contact, even if she'd forgotten her headphones, which she never did. It'd been so strange the first few months I worked there, but after years, I'd adjusted to her dynamic and knew any attempt to talk with her would just throw her off course.

Coat and purse in hand, I headed to my house. Only five minutes by foot from the shop if I walked just shy of a jog. I didn't usually run home during one of the busiest times of day, but my cat Squish had been sick and he needed medicine.

Could I be a bit more single twenty-something female

who lives alone? Maybe—sure. Maybe I could be pining for some super famous Rockstar.

I rolled my eyes as I hustled down the street. Squish slept on the couch and barely lifted his head to greet me. He'd curled into himself, a little piping hot cinnamon roll of cat right there on the cushion. His fur was creamy with accents of reddish brown. He'd stayed unusually small for a fully-grown cat, mostly fur and a little potbelly.

"Let's get it over with."

Once I administered the medicine, I switched the laundry I'd started before I left hours ago—just this morning? This week had been long, and it was only Wednesday.

"See you in a bit, Squish."

Back out into the chilly spring morning, only thirteen minutes down, I'd make it back to the shop with two minutes to spare if I hurried. I pulled out my phone, wondering if Wells and Leo wanted to meet up sometime soon—time for a catch up, and I wanted to see if I could wheedle Leo into talking about Jonas Bauer.

Because that's who he seemed to wait for. Not always. And he didn't say much to her other than a curt acknowledgement. But I people-watched as part of my job, and I'd swear he waited to see her.

Back out on the path toward Main Street, I flipped through notifications, wondering if we'd stay this busy once the spring breaks were over, knowing we wouldn't but it was always—

Ooof.

A hand grasped my wrist as I stumbled back from running into what might as well have been a coat-covered brick wall.

"Bel—I—I'm so sorry. I wasn't looking."

Jamie's voice had my gaze snapping up to meet his frowning face and of course, piercing blue eyes.

"Me neither, obviously. I'm sorry too."

My lungs must have been stunned by the impact, by the unexpected close contact, and not because I was breathless in front of him, not because of the faint scent of coffee and detergent I'd caught when my face had virtually been shoved into his jacket. Definitely not because seeing him just after eight in the morning on the streets of my home-town looking downright human and touchable and a little flustered gave me a thrill.

"Are you okay? Did I hurt you?" He looked me over, leaning a bit this way and that as if to see all of me.

I swallowed back a wild giggle at the question. Had he hurt me?

Only irreparably, I often feared. But just now?

"No, really, I'm fine. You all right?" Taking him in now, all six-foot-three of him, wasn't any easier than it had been moments ago, but I noticed he'd dropped a portfolio full of papers. "Your stuff..."

We both leaned down, hands reaching together to pick up the leather-bound folder. I should have seen it coming, but I reached for just the same place he did and set my hand on top of his. I pulled back immediately, ignoring the jolt of... whatever that horrid gushing, racing feeling I felt when he came near was, and studiously checked the time, then tucked my phone into my pocket to avoid his attention.

"Thanks."

"No problem. Is that stuff for the lodge?"

"Uh, no. It's some other business I have today."

He squinted just a bit, just enough to let me know something about that statement made him uncomfortable—or at least telling me about it had.

"Cool. Well... I've got three minutes until I'm supposed to be back at the shop..." I leaned forward in the direction I needed to go, then took a few steps, but he followed.

"I could use a coffee. I'll walk you." He tucked the portfolio under his arm and caught up to me.

Searching my mind for something to talk about other than ask the million things I'd wanted to ask for so long, I landed on, "What brings you out so early?"

He chuckled. "I'm always up early—not a good sleeper. But this morning, Danny made me breakfast at his place."

At that, I turned to look at him. I didn't know what kind of relationship he and Danny had, but from what I could tell, it wasn't nearly what he had with Liam and Leo. I'd wondered, in my more vain and small moments, if they'd fought over me. I inwardly cringed at that thought, but couldn't deny I'd had it more than once when desperate for any evidence that Jamie had really cared about me.

"How was that?" I could see *Rise and Shine* now. Half a block and we'd be there.

"Good. We hadn't really talked in years. We cleared the air, which was long overdue."

His voice dropped low, and I felt his hand on my arm as he slowed and we both stopped.

"I need to—"

"We need to clear the air too, Bel. Can we find a time to do that?"

Those blue eyes bore into mine as his hand dropped away.

My stomach bottomed out at the sound of his voice, at the thought of that conversation. What would he say? After all this time, what could he possibly say to clear the air?

But the conviction hid there, in his drawn brow and

serious, lovely mouth. It lay there in the way he waited, as if frozen, for me to respond.

I nodded, not sure I could summon my voice at that point.

"Good. Soon, okay?"

I nodded again, because I wasn't about to squeak out a reply and let him see how much the idea of talking to him about what had happened nine years ago affected me.

A small group burst out of *Rise and Shine*, and he held the door for me. I scuttled past him and through the swinging half-door, straight into the kitchen and away from him. My cheeks had flooded with heat, my heart beat wildly, and I needed just a minute in the warm kitchen, without an audience, while I recovered from that much back and forth with him.

As for clearing the air, I couldn't think about that. I wouldn't.

CHAPTER SEVENTEEN

Jamie

The house was coming along.

It'd been months since they'd broken ground, laid the foundation, and gotten the outer façade up. They'd done the work in the fall, so I'd been happy with the progress when I checked in on my brief trip at Christmas. Things naturally slowed down in the snowiest months, even with the outside complete.

The contractor had gotten the kitchen built except for appliances. The staircase, fireplace, and flooring were in. The carpet upstairs had been laid. The heated floors in the bathrooms had been installed. All bathroom fixtures were done except one shower because a slab of marble for one wall had been cracked upon arrival and they were waiting for more to come in that matched.

It was a damn fine house, and I couldn't wait to see it truly completed. I inhaled the raw scent of wood that hung around still—exposed beams above, wood floors... all different phases of the process still present for a while longer.

The stirring to have a place of my own here had started before I'd ever left, and it'd only grown stronger. Seeing this dream come to fruition, and being here as they finished it out these next few months... that would be true satisfaction.

My phone buzzed in my pocket, interrupting my little reverie. "Great timing."

"Is it? How so?" Julian Grenier, my partner in this development and a man who'd become my friend over the years since we'd met, sounded typically unenthusiastic and distracted.

"I'm in the house now. It's coming along."

"Happy?"

"Very. They're pouring roads in June." This neighborhood would be an exclusive one, and we'd built it out of nowhere. We'd be paving for miles.

"And the airport?"

He'd required putting in an airport as part of the development in order to agree to partnering with me on this project. It'd be small and cater to private jets—precisely the kind of transportation people who would own houses in this community might use. If this took off, and it would, this little settlement could draw all kinds of people and crowds up to Silverton and the lodge. The fact that it'd mean I'd have neighbors appealed to a lesser degree, but my fifteen-acre lot would give me plenty of privacy.

Julian's unimpressed grumble came through loud and clear. "Permits still pending. I might need you to go in person and light a fire under the county's seat."

"Nope. We agreed we're not using my name on this. I'm sure some of the people up there know I'm Jamie Morrison, but most of them probably think it's just another Morrison kid starting a project. And no one out here knows the name Julian Grenier." That last part just to needle him.

He harrumphed. "Of course they don't. They shouldn't. But if we don't get this done this summer, it sets us back. We can't—"

"They'll approve it. Winter slows everything down—things will wake back up and move faster in the next few months."

"They better."

"Well Pollyanna, if that's all..."

Julian coughed out a laugh. "I know, I'm a delight. That's all for now, Morris. Talk soon."

Never an exchange of goodbyes—or greetings, for that matter—with Julian Grenier. The man regimented his schedule down to the minute. No doubt he'd left four minutes for that conversation and we were edging up to three and a half. He'd put the extra thirty seconds to good use.

I didn't even remember how Julian and I met. Probably through my financial advisor. I'd decided I wanted to invest in small tech companies who were doing interesting work. I met with his people, and he convinced me to invest in a project he was funding for increased robotics tech for prosthetic limbs.

Not long after, I started having trouble with security at my house in LA. He approached me with a connection he had to the security company he used, and from there, we'd become... well, not friends. Friends would be overestimating it for me because we didn't have much in common except wealth, even if mine was a sliver of his, but I suspected he considered me to be a *colleague* and that, for Grenier, proved to be a prime place in his roster of relationships.

With one last lingering look through the house, I headed back to town. The development sat a quick ten minutes outside of Silverton city limits in the unincorporated part of town. That gave us a bit of anonymity—at least for now. The small community dynamic meant people had to be aware *someone* had submitted plans to build on the land, but like almost anything I did lately, all of the business holdings, contracts, and permits were filed through various entities that would take more time than anyone around here was willing to give to figure out they were linked to me.

If it made me odd I hadn't told my family about the project, then so be it. At first, the land had been a way to connect to my roots without feeling tethered by obligation to be there all the time, to develop it into something important. I didn't need any more pressure to succeed than I already had.

And now, years after I'd purchased that first parcel, now that we were developing six luxury homes not including mine and Julian's with almost thirty more lots lined up, now that there were roads being routed to the space and an airport going in within the next six months, I hoped, I found myself thinking maybe this would be one of the difference-making things Liam, and everyone, had been hoping for.

I shook off that thought. Liam had the hero complex, not me.

I parked outside my older brother's just in time to see Bel wave to Liam, who turned back inside the lodge, and watch her stroll down the sidewalk with Jonas Bauer. Just the sight of her proved enough to throw my pulse into a riot.

Danny's words had been playing in my head since breakfast days ago. *If you've ever wondered what would have happened if you took away the guilt and the running away and me from the equation...*

And so had the look on Bel's face when I told her we needed to clear the air. I couldn't think of any other way to put it, but I needed an excuse to meet with her, and I needed it to be something she'd be ready for. I couldn't spring that conversation on her when we were supposed to be talking about the lodge's marketing campaign or when I swung by the coffee shop and happened to see her—she had too many good excuses to escape.

No. I needed her captive.

That thought sent a thrill of wanting through me. Interesting thought. Bel, captive to me, and no one else. Just Jamie, not *Jamie Morris*. Just her and me, no Danny or the ghost of her relationship with him between us anymore. No need to push her away, to run away. No need to hide.

I didn't have to guess at what she felt for me. Danny thought she'd been waiting for me—that just showed his positivity, his tendency to look for the good side of things. But Bel had made it clear in every interaction we'd had in the last nine years—she loathed me.

And God help me, but I wanted to dismantle that look she got on her face—the one that said she felt both angry and scared, anticipating my next move and wishing I'd jump off a cliff. I wanted to cut through it and see what *really* grew there at the heart of her. What had set us so at odds after a simple kiss almost a decade ago?

Was there anything left, and after apologizing, could I pull it out of her?

CHAPTER EIGHTEEN

Bel

Jonas Bauer escorted me into town like he was doing *me* a favor.

I had my theories.

We'd had a good meeting with Liam, who'd asked me to say hi to Leo and Wells when I met them. Wells must have told him we were getting together for an early dinner. Jonas immediately declared he had business in town and would be happy to walk with me.

Never mind the fact that I'd lived in this town all my life, that the clearly-marked path to Main Street had always been safe and a pleasant ten-minute walk, and that the late March sun had just begun to set since the days were getting longer. No reason I needed him to walk me.

"I'm glad to hear pairing up with Mr. Morris has worked out."

Jonas' first words to me since we'd left the lodge.

The one unpleasant part of the afternoon—Liam had grilled me on how our meeting had gone. Certainly, Jamie would have told him it hadn't gone particularly well. But if I took a step back and removed myself, I could see that the business aspect had gone just fine. We didn't see eye to eye, but Jamie'd had some ideas, and that was frankly more than I'd expected.

Truth be told, other than making me feel panicky, unco-ordinated, and a confusing cocktail of heartsick and angry, I didn't expect much at all from Jamie. That's probably why I couldn't stop thinking about what he'd say whenever he decided to move on his threat—yeah, I'd wrapped myself around it enough to decide it felt a little like a threat—to clear the air.

Initiating that little gem of a conversation fell under his purview, and until then, I'd keep on living my life, ignoring the fact that I couldn't simply ignore him and actually live said life.

"It did." No need to give Jonas any of the nasty history —I took a drink from my water bottle to give myself an excuse to keep my response short.

"And are you... quite close with Mr. Morris?"

I choked on the water.

"No. I wouldn't say that." I wondered how to summa-rize our history and leave him with an appropriate picture without seeming unprofessional. "I suppose we used to be, but that was a long time ago."

Silence. Jonas didn't talk unless he had something to say —he didn't fill the air. I admired it, because I rarely felt comfortable in silences like this.

To exemplify that perfectly, I spoke again. "I hope we'll become friends again. Maybe working together will help."

Jonas nodded, which I saw from the corner of my eye as we passed the inn.

"This town needs more development. More business, more housing, more rooms, more everything."

I looked over at him to see him carefully eyeing the inn, and a little roar of defensiveness popped up. "Wells has doubled the number of rooms in the inn since she arrived, and it's thriving."

"Exactly. We need more."

"We do."

He gestured for me to proceed in front of him, so I did, keeping up my pace since his legs were probably a foot longer than mine. We hit the sidewalk on Main Street one after the other and I wondered if he'd walk me all the way to *Basta*, where I'd meet the girls.

"Your Mr. Morris may have some ideas about developments. He has vast real estate holdings."

I resisted the urge to give Jonas a *why are you telling me this?* glare, and instead said, "You should ask Liam to talk to him. Or ask him yourself. He seems to like you."

"Mr. Morrison has expressed he'd prefer not to."

It took a moment to let that settle in, but I deciphered that he meant Liam, Mr. Morrison, did not want to ask Jamie about his real estate.

"Ah. Well... he must have his reasons." What else could I say? How did this pertain to me, the underexperienced marketing freelancer?

"Perhaps you could ask him." He stopped walking a few doors down from *Basta*. "I would consider it a personal favor. I do not want to operate against Mr. Morrison's wishes, but I believe he is under-utilizing an asset merely because it is his family member. If you were to bring up a discussion, perhaps Mr. Morris would decide to offer his extant knowledge and convince his brother of its value."

His cool gray eyes locked on mine a moment more, then he turned, and we both continued down the street.

Nothing but his stride slowing changed about him upon arriving at the door to *Basta*. He addressed Wells first. "Good to see you, Ms. Bryant."

"Good to see you, Jonas."

Then he turned to Leo, who looked stunning in a blue off-the-shoulder top that made her eyes look like mini Caribbean Oceans.

He cleared his throat. "Ms. Morrison." A slight nod. Then a turn to me. "Talk to you soon, Ms. Paxton."

And then he departed, long, sure strides with a clipped gait, somehow efficient even in his walk.

Leo watched him walk away before I interrupted whatever thoughts burned through her mind. Based on her expression, they were... notable.

"Everything okay?" I asked.

Leo pursed her lips as Wells and I looked on. "Yep. That's about the extent of our interactions lately. Come on, let's go eat."

"So why are we eating at five o'clock instead of later in the evening like normal people over the age of eight and under the after of eighty?" Leo clearly felt inconvenienced by our early gathering, even though she looked completely relaxed.

Wells smiled down at her plate. "Liam's taking me out for dessert."

"Really? On the same night we're doing dinner? He

can't let us have you for one full night?" Leo's face exemplified disgust.

Wells chuckled. "Of course he can. He does all the time. But I'm working something like the next ten days straight with arrivals for the weekend, so this will be the only evening we have without me trying to work and get people settled."

"I think it's great." I flared my eyes at Leo. "Plus I have to be up early so this isn't far from when I normally eat."

"*Fine.* But I'm going on record and saying finishing dinner before six p.m. is silly, even if it is a Thursday."

"I'll make a note of it, and convey your sentiments to your brother."

Wells was all grins now that she and Liam had worked through their misunderstanding and professed their undying love for each other. They were too sweet to be annoyed by—or so *I* thought. Obviously, Leo felt otherwise.

A throat cleared at the side of the table. "Bel? Could I have just a minute?"

Leo threw down her napkin and glared up at Jamie, who'd materialized at our tableside and looked... *ugh.*

"Really? How are you here right now? Can't my brothers leave me in peace with my friends for *one night*?"

"Just grabbing takeout, saw you guys, thought I'd see if Bel—"

"Sure. Let's just... pop out front," I offered, sliding my chair back and leading the way to the exit.

Anticipation, nerves, little flutters of that hopeless feeling I got when I looked at him flooded my chest. He stayed close behind me, and even though he had no reason to, I wished he'd put his hand on my back as we walked.

Stop that nonsense.

He followed me outside and came to stand next to the

door under the awning, then fixed me with his attention, which must have been a little like standing in a tractor beam.

His jaw flexed and the moment hung between us as he just... *looked.*

What was he waiting for? He'd asked me—interrupted my dinner (never mind we hadn't even ordered yet), like there was urgency. And now, he stood there, mostly unreadable.

A hand shot through his hair, just like he used to do. My memory recognized the movement, and a jolt of fondness and longing had me rocking back on my heels as my pulse raced.

His gaze switched back and forth between my eyes. "Can I take you to breakfast on Saturday?"

My lashes fluttered, and I released a breath.

"Um..." What else could I say? Nowhere to hide. "Sure."

His shoulders dropped in relief, I assumed. My gaze slid over his face, and my heart sped as I took in his eyes, lips, jaw... nearly painful to look at this close up.

What would he say in this conversation he'd requested? How antagonistic would I be without even meaning to? It'd be a messy sideshow for anyone within view, and no matter where we went, everyone would be watching.

No, that wouldn't work. We needed privacy, even if the thought sent alarm racing through me. "But... maybe not *out* to breakfast?"

Jamie swallowed, nodded slightly. "Of course. I'm at my parents' house for now..."

"Just come to me. If you want."

I didn't want to be at the Morrison family home. I loved the place, but if we were rehashing history, all my messy cuts and bruises, I didn't want to be in a place that held so many memories. I wanted my own territory.

My eyes found his. "I mean, you should come to my house, if that works."

"Absolutely. But I'm still bringing the food."

"Good." I nodded once—strong, decisive. "I'm at 10 Meier Street."

"See you then."

CHAPTER NINETEEN

Jamie

It stung that she didn't want to be seen with me. Was I that bad?

Clearly, she wasn't so upset with me she feared being alone with me. I would hope not—she had to know I'd never hurt her physically. Of course she knew that.

The look on her face when I'd mentioned taking her out... *ouch*. Whether she didn't want the attention, or she didn't want people to know she was spending time with me at all—either way, brutal.

But since I'd talked to her Thursday night, I'd realized I couldn't keep letting my own excuses stand in the way of apologizing, and hopefully moving past this awkwardness. Everyone in town knew about the tense dynamic between us, and that did nothing to help us work through the issues. Whenever we came near each other, it seemed like anyone in the vicinity held their breath in anticipation of what would happen.

Enough of that. Time to clear the air and take the next step.

How we found this next step largely rested with her. Just seeing her across the damn room made me want to get to know her again, figure out what her life had been like, and hope she'd want to get to know me like she had that one ridiculously short summer we'd shared.

I took a deep breath and let it out slowly as I walked through the neighborhood. Everything was quiet except the light chirps of a few early spring birds and the gentle trickle from the Elk River. Spring run-off wouldn't start for another month, so there was hardly anything to call a river.

When I came to the door of 10 Meier, the realization that I knew this house hit. It was her grandmother's house. Did she live with her gran these days? Had she planned to have a chaperone for this breakfast all along?

The thought soured my stomach as I knocked with my free hand, the other clutching a bright canvas bag from *Rise and Shine.*

My pulse sped up as I heard the locks clicking, the knob turning, the door opening.

"Hey, come in," she said, a tentative smile on her face as she held open the screen door.

"Thanks."

I moved past her, reminding myself it was inappropriate to greet her with a hug or kiss on the cheek. It wouldn't be acceptable for me to run a hand along her smooth jaw and look into her grass-green eyes and allow my own eyes to take a closer look at the perfect lips I'd kissed only once and thought about a thousand times.

We were barely past antagonism; affectionate greetings,

even if friendly, weren't welcome, let alone me touching her —*really* touching her on purpose. Not allowed.

Not *yet*.

I followed her through a small, tidy living room that looked nothing like I would have expected an older woman's home to look, and into a gleaming, modern kitchen.

"Isn't this your gran's place?" I set the bag of pastries on the table and admired the mottled granite countertops, stainless steel appliances, and light, painted cabinets.

"It used to be, yeah. I bought it from her a few years ago after I moved back and she decided to go to the retirement community." An unrecognizable expression flashed across her face—pain, sadness, something—then fled.

"So it's just you here?"

I held in the rushing relief that brought me. She *hadn't* felt the need for our conversation to be supervised. I may not have been her favorite person, but she didn't feel she needed a chaperone. That counted for something.

She pulled water glasses from a cabinet as she spoke. "Just me and Squish."

"Squish?"

"My mutt of a cat, yes. You'll meet him. He's shy for about ten minutes and then you'll be begging me to get him off you. Are you allergic?"

Her face was soft and sweet as she spoke of the cat, and the strangest pull of jealousy at the thought that her cat had so much more of her affection and attention than I did tugged at my insides.

All right. That's enough of that pathetic line of thinking.

"No. No allergies that I know of." I resisted the urge to roll my eyes—if we were discussing my medical history, things were not going well.

"Coffee? Cappuccino?" She held up a mug where she stood by a regular drip coffee maker and a very nice espresso machine.

"Coffee's fine. I'm sure you get sick of pulling espresso at the shop..."

Her lips flattened a touch. "I don't mind it."

She turned to the machines, and I wanted to bang my head against the wall. Things had been so easy between us when we were kids. Maybe because we were kids and there wasn't a pile of awkwardness and mistrust stacked between us.

"Do you have plates? I grabbed a bunch of pastries and some fruit from *Rise and Shine.* I hope you don't mind eating from there. It's the place everyone I asked recommended."

She whipped around. "You brought me pastries?"

Something about her expression told me that despite her tone—mildly suspicious and disbelieving—my bringing pastries was exactly the right thing.

"Yeah. I hope it's not a problem—"

"It's perfect." She handed me a bright yellow mug full of dark coffee. "Thank you. Just a minute while I make mine."

She fiddled with the espresso maker, which I couldn't see when she stood at the counter where her body blocked it. I couldn't just sit there and stare at the denim-clad backside of her, though that would be no hardship because, well, the years had been generous to Bel in so many ways, based on what I could see.

Had to shake that off.

I wandered back to the living room and admired the bright colors and cozy feel—certainly nothing like what my taste tended toward, but my artificial taste developed because I paid for someone to create it. I made a note to get more color in the house up here—that made sense considering I wanted this Silver Ridge house to be a kind of hideaway for recharging. My house in LA contained all modern lines, sleek glass and steel, and grays, blacks, and whites. Not all that comforting, but I'd grown used to it.

Two paws startled me just above the knee. I looked down to see what must be Squish, a furry little ball with front legs stretched up on my knees, face looking both sleepy and expectant.

"Hey, Squish."

Squish looked back at me, at full attention now and head bobbing just slightly as he sniffed my jeans, still leaning up, front legs and paws stretching, reaching up my leg.

I bent down slowly, let him smell my hand, then pet his head. He leaned into the touch, rolling his head side to side to capture more sensation. Chuckling, I set my coffee on the nearby table and scooped him up. Normally, I wouldn't chance picking up a cat, but it was like he was sitting there, waiting for me to grab him. I cradled him and stroked down his nose, admiring his full surrender into ecstasy at the contact.

"Jamie? Oh... Squish found you." She stood in the doorway to the kitchen, one hand on her chest.

"Hope you don't mind I picked him up. He seemed like he wanted me to."

She bit her lip to stifle a smile, and oh, how I wished she wouldn't. Hunger for those smiles filled me.

"He probably did. He loves being held. He loves being touched. He particularly loves men, for some reason." She swallowed and cut herself off from saying more.

What men? Who else does he like? Are you dating someone?

These questions, I did not ask. I simply set Squish down and washed my hands before taking a seat next to her at her small table. She'd set plates and utensils, so I pulled out the pastry box and container of fruit.

She took not one but two pastries and filled a small bowl with the fruit. She passed the box to me and must have caught the grin I'd been trying to hide.

"What?"

"I'd forgotten how much I like that you eat."

Was that an idiot thing to say? Probably.

"I'm sure the women you spend time with now don't usually eat pastries." She ducked her head to take a studied sip of her cappuccino from the bowl-sized mug.

There was no good response to that, nor should I have said anything in the first place.

We both bit into pastries, chewed, swallowed, painful silence nearly humming around us. Or, maybe that was Squish's purr, which sounded like a distant roar coming from where he sat on the chair next to me.

All right, this had gone on long enough. I wiped my mouth, sipped water, ignored the nerves slicing through my gut, and dove in. "I am sorry for how I left."

Bel gulped down the sip of coffee she'd taken, a small cough punctuating her surprise. Her green gaze found my eyes, but she didn't speak.

"I was scared of what I'd done." I forced a laugh—that was putting it mildly. "I was scared of a lot of things, but one of the big ones was that I'd betrayed Danny the moment I kissed you."

Bel's lips parted, but she still made no sound.

My pulse hammered in my throat, my head, my wrists.

"I didn't know how to handle it, so I ran away. I'm sorry I hurt you. I should have talked to you, treated you better, and I'm sorry."

She focused on her mug then, slowly bringing it to her lips, sipping, moving so purposefully I knew she was buying time. When she set her cup down, I braced.

"You should have. I wish you had."

"I do too."

Sitting this close to her should have felt warm and intimate, but she felt far away. There was more to repair.

"I'm also sorry for ignoring you for so long after. Avoiding. Everything. I couldn't really handle seeing you. I built up a lot of shame and guilt over what I thought was betraying Danny. It's not that I didn't care for you, but I was terrified of what kind of man it made me if I'd betray my own brother like that."

Bel huffed a small breath and shook her head. "It drives me insane that you two insist on playing martyrs. I know you didn't mean to betray Danny. He knows it too. And you kissing me was independent of Danny. It had nothing to do with him. And I kissed you back, and wanted to do it again, because *I wanted to*. Danny wasn't a factor because I'd made peace with the fact that I loved him, but wasn't *in love* with him. I wish you could have seen that as clearly as I did."

"Me too."

"And for what it's worth, Danny and I did date. A few years into college. It was awkward and we never should have started. It... it never would have worked, whether you'd come along or not. So... just... stop making it this big wrong you've done him." She sat back in her chair and crossed her arms, watching for my response.

"I told you Danny and I cleared the air. That was also

long overdue. This is part of what we talked about, and he said the same thing in different words." I ran a hand through my hair, tugged at the knot at the back. Probably time for a change from the style I'd had the last few years, but I couldn't bring myself to care enough to do anything to it.

"What did he say?"

"He said we were both wrong to think of you as anyone's but your own. He'd thought of you as his, and I'd done the same. We were both wrong."

She sat up straight. "Exactly. Yes. *I am my own*. Always was."

She collected our dirty dishes, clanking plates together as she stacked them on the counter by the sink.

"But I wanted you to be mine," I mumbled.

"What?" she asked from the sink.

I looked her straight in those gorgeous, green eyes. "I wanted you to be mine."

She swallowed, paused, seemed to be turning that thought over. "I wanted to be yours too."

She turned back to the sink, rinsing dishes and then loading them into the dishwasher. She'd stunned me in place so all I did was watch, until mercifully, my body unlocked and I moved to stand next to her.

"Would you... want to try that? With me?"

I'd closed in on her, standing closer than we'd been in years and years. I'd forgotten how petite she was—not that I wasn't around petite women all the time, but she'd always seemed strong, and in the last few weeks, she'd seemed like a little font of ragey looks and emotions. Add to that being friends with Leo, who occupied the majority of any room she stood in by virtue of her demanding presence, it was easy to forget Bel was petite.

Fine-boned, thin and muscular from distance running

regularly, or so I'd heard... no artificial voluptuousness or manicured beauty. Just free, glaring loveliness.

"I—try what with you?" She hadn't broken eye contact, but was searching my eyes for clarity.

"Would you want to try again with me? Maybe see what would have happened if I hadn't run away?"

Her brow furrowed, and the corners of her mouth pulled down. "I'm sorry, but what are you talking about?"

I'd been prepared for a bit of confusion. Maybe even some disbelief. I'd considered outright rejection an option too. In each case, I'd had a plan.

"Danny told me you haven't dated. He thinks you've been..." *Waiting for me.* "Waiting for the right person. And I'm wondering if you'd like to go out sometime, spend more time together, see if I might be that person."

Her jaw dropped open, and her hands froze in front of her where she dried them on a kitchen towel. "Jamie, I—"

"Don't answer now. I'm going to go and let you think about it. I've been an idiot for nearly a decade, and I don't expect you to forget that. But if you can forgive it, to start, then maybe we can move forward. I'll check in with you later this weekend, and you can tell me what you think then."

CHAPTER TWENTY

Bel

"Is he insane?"

I stalked around the space in front of Gran's couch as she watched with an amused smile.

"I'm genuinely asking. Do you think he's lost it? Has all that stardom and fame gone to his head?"

Gran stayed quiet and watched me continue to pace. Odd, I realized after a moment, because normally, she'd be cackling at my dramatics.

"Are you feeling all right?" I approached and surveyed her.

Hair normal, but makeup not quite as on point as usual. No earrings or watch today. Energy seemed low, but nothing obvious, or I would have spotted it the minute I walked in.

"I'm tired today—didn't sleep well last night. Nothing to

worry about." She waved me off and straightened the blanket resting on her lap.

"Are you sure? Should we ask the doctor to swing by and check you out?"

She sat up taller and leveled me with her most imperious look. "Absolutely not."

We eyed each other another minute before I continued my route around her living room to burn the energy that bubbled inside me. Had been since Jamie'd said what he'd said and didn't let me speak and then left.

Like that wasn't his area of expertise. Like that wasn't at the very heart of this issue.

Like that wasn't at the heart of my *issues.*

"Fine."

She chuckled a little then, maybe summoning the sound for my benefit. "So go on. Tell me."

"He comes to my door looking like... *himself.*" It'd been hard not to see that as its own form of an attack.

He'd worn jeans, sneakers, and a zip-down sweatshirt-style layer. He'd looked comfortable and at ease and completely, terribly beautiful. His hair was up in that *I-should-hate-this-but-it-works-too-well* man bun style, his jaw dusted with a day or two of stubble. His blue eyes were typically, irritatingly gorgeous and unavoidably blue. His lips...

I let out a frustrated sound falling somewhere between groan and growl and refused to look at Gran. I could imagine the look on her face, and it wouldn't help things.

"So he apologizes for being a jerk, for running away, for ignoring and avoiding me for years, and then drops a bomb on me right there in my kitchen. Do I want to see if he's my person? *Is he serious?*" My voice rose and pitched at the end, and I turned on a heel and marched back across the living room.

Really, this was the worst possible place to pace and decipher my feelings. But this was Gran's place and I needed her, so here I was.

"I may have been off on my timing, but I told you. If he was any kind of man, he'd be knocking at your door, groveling at your feet, and.. voilà."

She looked perfectly pleased with herself, a sly little grin and fluttery eyes telling me she had more than one *I told you so* lined up for me this morning.

"That's nonsense. I mean, I get the apology. I'm glad for it. I'm not sure I forgive him, because please, that's too easy after all of this time... though it did seem genuine. And I'd be glad to have that tension and drama out of the way every time we see each other, especially while he's home. But I'm just supposed to.... to... what? Want to date him again after all this time?" I crossed my arms and stood at the window that looked out on walkways and gardens at the center of the complex.

"Yes. You are. Because you do."

I whipped around. "How can you say that?"

She raised a brow. "Bel honey, be honest."

I swallowed, the jumble of nerves and *feelings* I liked to avoid at all costs building a bird's nest in my belly. "I can be honest. But Gran..."

She knew. To some degree, she knew how hurt I'd been, and how hard I'd found it to be with anyone. That wasn't all Jamie's fault—I didn't blame him for my failed dating attempt with Danny or the other small handful of guys I'd tried going out with over the years. That wasn't his fault.

"You've got a decision to make. You can avoid him and go back to this ridiculous stand-off you two have played at for years. Or you can accept his apology and tell him *yes,* which is what I bet you'd like to tell him if you'll be honest with yourself. And then you go slow, and you take your time, and you feel no obligation to anyone but yourself and figuring out what's right for you each step of the way."

Her voice was gentle and wise, as usual. She had a way of softening the most direct advice so it felt more palatable, but truthfully, she could tell me just about anything and I'd hear her. She was the only person I trusted completely. Since I'd moved back and Leo and I had gotten closer, I'd learned to trust Leo too, but no one compared to Gran.

No one was a guarantee like Gran. Everyone else might leave.

I cleared my throat. "I guess I know what I'll tell him when he finds me."

After that, Gran mercifully changed the subject and we talked about marketing for the lodge, my thoughts on Leo and Jonas and their weird dynamic, how she'd heard Danny had been volunteering at the library, her friends, the usual. We ate in the cafeteria for lunch since I'd had plans that morning and had told her I was too nervous to do much other than obsess about Jamie's arrival so she'd insisted I not worry. I always enjoyed sitting in the big room and catching up with so many of the people who'd been a part of Silverton, and my life, growing up.

As I left, I felt... not quite relieved, but better. I had a plan, and though it made me want to lose my lunch if I thought about what it meant that I'd see Jamie again and he'd have a very specific question for me and I knew what answer I planned to give him and that *terrified* me, it was still better than feeling so tangled up.

My phone rang as I stepped onto the path leading back home, and a thrill raced through me before I saw who it was. I let out a long breath and released the disappointment

—Jamie didn't have my number, anyway. And it had been a little over a month, so we might as well get this over with.

"Hey Mom. Dad. How's it going?"

"We're great! How are you? How's your gran?"

I kicked a rock off the path in front of me as I took my time wandering home. The spring air warmed in the sun and it'd be enough to go without a layer this time of day soon. I loved spring.

"I'm just leaving her place after lunch. You guys should call her."

"Oh, she doesn't want to hear from us any more than you do! But you're our baby, so we have to check in every once in a while."

I gritted my teeth against that sentiment. "Well, here you are, checking in. Any news?"

Best to keep the conversation moving.

"Your mom is up for a big promotion—she'll be president of her division. Otherwise, same old same old here. What about you?"

Dad, chipper as always, upbeat and oblivious to any nuance or change in my voice, only reported on their status at work.

It made sense. Work and life were the same to them and had always been that way.

"No news here. You know Silverton."

They both laughed a little too loud. "We sure do. Well okay kiddo. We'll talk to you again soon!"

Yep. They'd call in exactly four Saturdays. They'd call around this time of day. They were faithful that way— thanks to the reminders they set in their calendars, surely.

They knew nothing about me. They'd probably never really known me, but since they'd moved away from town, they'd had no opportunity. I'd gone to school at Miller State, not quite as close as they'd expected me to. And when I graduated, instead of moving to the city to find a job, which might have given us some common ground, I moved back here to Silverton.

It hadn't been my plan. But Dad let slip, one day just before graduation and fortunately, just before I'd accepted a job that would have started right after I finished school, that Gran wasn't in good health and was thinking of moving into the retirement home. It wasn't an *old folks home*, he'd emphasized. Wasn't a *nursing home*. It was a retirement community, but they had care available should the need arise.

And then it hit me.

I'd left her. She'd been the only constant, the only person I could count on, and I'd left her. And I was going to keep leaving her if I took this job. Her own son had left her, evidently feeling no obligation to his mother or daughter. I couldn't do it.

I moved home with the thought that I'd be there for her to help her get well and back on her feet, and then I could always move to Salt Lake City. It wasn't like it was another country—just a long drive and a few boxes in my car.

In fact, the only way Gran had let me move into the guest bedroom of her small house was on the promise that I'd leave when she was well—that, and my parents had sold my childhood home as soon as I'd left for college, so I'd had nowhere else to go. It'd taken a few months because her cough had developed into pneumonia. I'd gotten a job at the new coffee shop in town—*Rise and Shine*.

And I just... never left. At first, making plans scared me because I couldn't stand the thought of losing Gran, of not being there for her if she got sick again.

Then, she'd announced she wanted to move into the

retirement community, so we decided to work on getting her house cleaned up and ready to show in the spring since houses just didn't sell in winter in Silverton.

And then, she'd said, "Of course you know you can have the house if you want it, Bel. Anything that's mine is going to be yours anyway. If you'd rather have the house than the money, it's yours. I have plenty set aside for the move and paying the retirement home."

At that moment, the thought of having her home, of being close to her and keeping that little house where she'd lived all my life and much of hers, sounded perfect. It'd been right. I'd said yes, but insisted I pay her something. She'd sold it to me for a dollar and the promise to visit her regularly at her new place, and I'd had no problems keeping that promise.

I'd often wondered what would have happened if I'd said no. Over the years, Gran had even told me I should move to the city and get out there—that the house would always be mine, and I could rent it for income to support me wherever I wanted to go.

She was right. But where would I have gone? After working as a manager at a coffee shop for the first few years after college, after having a small handful of freelance marketing projects and no other real-world experience, what would I even do?

That my heart ached with the sense of missed opportunity, of missing... *something*, never left me, but I'd learned to banish that self-pity. Just liked I'd learned not to keep track of Jamie's tour schedules and awards and news articles... All of that hurt a little too much, and definitely wasted time and energy.

CHAPTER TWENTY-ONE

Jamie

Thinking about something other than Bel had been impossible.

In some ways, that could have applied to many times in my life. Any time I'd planned a trip home. Any time I'd talked with one of my family members on the phone. Any time I'd attempted spending time with a woman and ultimately felt hollow and sad in the aftermath.

But now, thoughts of her were inescapable. No ignoring the reality that I was mentally and emotionally consumed by her, and the worst part of it was I had no idea what her answer would be.

I would have sworn there was excitement, maybe even a kind of alertness, in her as I said goodbye yesterday.

Yesterday.

Had it really only been a little over twenty-four hours since I'd made my play and then wandered back home along this well-beaten path, restless and hopeful? Impossible.

It felt like days had elapsed since I'd stood there, looking at her flushed cheeks and genuinely shocked eyes. It'd taken everything I had to walk out of there and not to kiss her—to make her see we could try again and it wasn't too late.

I'd become convinced of that—it *wasn't* too late. We were different people, yes. We'd lived entire lives since that summer, but there was a reason I'd never been able to get her out of my head. There was a reason she'd never found anyone to be with.

Attempting to enjoy the scenery on my walk from the house failed. I simply couldn't focus on anything but getting back to 10 Meier and hearing her answer. Or, first, confirming she was home. Why hadn't I gotten her number? Why hadn't I set a time to meet?

I forced myself to slow the pace. I'd purposefully spent the morning dragging my feet so I wouldn't show up at her house too early. If I hadn't, I would've ended up there before eight a.m. And while I was eager, and I didn't mind her knowing that to a degree, I didn't want to freak her out.

I knocked on her door just shy of three in the afternoon. Miraculously, I'd made it that long.

Bel opened the door, and the sight of her turned my insides liquid. My heart pounded in my chest to a base beat I couldn't hear, and my feet tingled like they used to when I got nervous to perform.

"Is it a good time to talk?"

She nodded and stepped back. "Let's go out on the porch in the back. It's too nice outside to be cooped up."

I followed her through the living room and kitchen, then out on the back porch and into a nice little garden that looked surprisingly manicured considering trees and plants hadn't quite started budding yet.

"Coffee? Water?"

"Water would be great."

She nodded again, a sure sign she was nervous. I'd noticed, even in the short, awkward, at times antagonistic encounters we'd shared in the last few years that she tended to reserve her words. She hadn't been like that as a teen, but she'd never been as loquacious as Leo, for sure.

The screen door snicked shut behind her. I admired the little deck with a wooden table and chairs that looked surprisingly clean and not sun-bleached or weather-damaged like most outdoor furniture that got left out. I wondered how she managed that.

Everything about the house spoke of Bel's meticulous approach. She'd organized and thought carefully about her home, and she took care of her things—no waste, no big piles, and nothing that seemed excessive. After being exposed to some insane levels of wealth and privilege, Bel's home, her way of doing things, struck me as perfect.

The screen door jiggled and shut slowly behind her as she came to sit across from me at the small, two-person table and placed two glasses of water on the surface, one in front of me.

"Thank you."

"You're welcome."

I took a moment to inhale a long draft of the warm spring mountain air. The crystal-clear day bloomed around us, and the view from her backyard looked back at Silver Ridge, mighty and snow-covered and seemingly touchable, even from there.

"Have you thought about what I said yesterday?"

Her chest rose and fell, like she'd taken a deep breath to

steady herself for the response. My stomach tightened, bracing, sure this couldn't go the way I'd hoped and genuinely dreamed it might.

"I have."

Waiting had never been an issue for me, but it was torture in this moment. I searched her face, her eyes, for any clue. Her shoulders were tense, her hands clasped in her lap, her gaze on me.

I wouldn't speak until she did. I'd left it up to her. Her chance to have her say rested in this moment—I'd had mine yesterday.

Evidently, she wanted it to be as slow and miserable a process as possible.

My pulse continued to race through me. My hands gripped the sides of the chair where I sat. *Please just say whatever you have to say!* I wanted to yell.

"I think it would be okay."

I mentally rewound to what I'd said. How I'd phrased it. I'd asked something like, did she want to see if I could be the person for her. So... this was good, right?

I swallowed the confusion. "So, yes? You want to..."

She nodded. "Yes."

Her lashes fluttered, and she looked out into the yard. Her cheeks and neck were red, and her chest rose and fell more quickly now.

"Bel, are you saying you'll go out with me?"

She bit her lip, tentative. "Yes."

The smile broke out on my face before I could stop it, and I chuckled with relief as I dropped back into my chair, not even realizing I'd been sitting straight-backed at the edge of it. "Oh, thank God."

She raised a brow at me.

"I wasn't sure what you'd say. Obviously, I'd hoped it'd be this, but... I know I have a lot to atone for."

She frowned at that. "You've apologized, Jamie. I accept that apology. You can take me out, and treat me well, and that'll put legs on it."

"Works for me."

We both sipped from our water glasses and enjoyed the view. It would have been a calm, lovely moment, except for the riot in my body and mind. *What now? When do we get this party started?*

"So, uh... when are you free?"

Glad her attention on the mountain kept her from seeing, I scraped a hand down my face and couldn't suppress rolling my eyes. One would think being a world-famous rock star would give me some kind of advantage with this scenario. I should have been charming and appealing, but here we sat in awkward quiet, me fumbling through asking a girl out who'd just told me I could ask her out.

I guess all those years I hadn't dated were finally paying off in a cruel way.

"I work weekdays six to two or three depending on who's taking afternoons from me." She still wasn't looking at me.

"So, evenings are best?"

"Yes. Though I get up pretty early, so I go to bed early too. Consider me a senior citizen in terms of the hours I keep." Her eyes flickered to me, and a half-grin creased one cheek.

"I've always wanted to eat off the early bird menus around here."

She laughed lightly. "Well then, you're in luck."

I checked my watch—time to go. I stood and followed her back through the house to her front door.

Yes, time to go. But first, "How about tomorrow?"

Her brows shot up. "Oh, tomorrow? Um... sure. What are you thinking?"

"Let's keep it simple. How about we go to *The Elk* for old time's sake. Then this weekend, when we have more time, I'll find something that'll be more involved."

Just the thought of time alone with her where I could get closer to her sent anticipation flooding through me.

She flashed a broad smile at me, then reined it in, tucking it away like a cruel trick. "Sounds good."

We stood there a moment, and I turned to the door, about to push through the screen and leave her.

But I couldn't do that. Not yet.

"Sorry, can I just..."

I turned back and slipped my hands behind her and pulled her to me gently, but insistently. I hugged her close and closed my eyes at the feeling of her hands pressing against my shoulder blades where she hugged me back.

I released her, wary of letting it go on too long, fully cognizant of how much more I'd like to share with her and how far we were from that.

"Okay. See you tomorrow."

CHAPTER TWENTY-TWO

Bel

Jamie trotted down the walk to the path that would take him out of the neighborhood. I stayed staring through the screen door for longer than I could tell, until finally my jackhammering thoughts broke through the calm his hug had gifted me.

Jamie just hugged you. Jamie is taking you out tomorrow.

Days ago, I'd barely been able to stand still in his presence. I'd felt overwhelmed and sad and angry and angsty and *everything* near him.

I chuckled at the thought—not altogether different from what I felt now. Though not angry anymore. But overwhelmed, a little angsty, and a bit sad? Yes.

As much as I wanted this to go well, so far we'd been less than comfortable in each other's presence. It'd been stilted, and while that wasn't a shock considering the years of avoiding and dramatic silence that lay behind us, it didn't exactly set us up for riveting conversation and a successful date.

Plus, what on Earth would we talk about?

He wasn't the Jamie I'd known. The summer we'd spent together had come after years of spending time together—or at least adjacent to each other. I'd known every member of his family and seen him regularly, even after he was out of high school since he'd stuck around and worked and played local gigs while he wrote his demo, or whatever it was he'd been doing all that time.

Now? Jamie Morris and I had exactly nothing in common. Far less than we might have if I'd ended up in Salt Lake and didn't still live a small-town life, but that was me now, no chance of changing it.

He'd spent the better part of the last decade traveling the world. He toured more than he stayed home—he'd probably been to hundreds of countries. I'd been to exactly one.

And all of that avoided the subject much more concerning to me—the actual dating part of things. I dropped my head into my hands.

I hadn't dated more than a small handful of people, and it'd all been surface level, easy, a few stolen kisses and hand-holding sweetness. No sizzle. No burn.

Just standing next to Jamie lit me on fire, set my insides to fizz and whirl to a dizzying effect. In the same way that I lived a small-town life, and he lived a Hollywood, rock star, travel-the-world glamorous one—we had to be incompatible in that regard too.

I shut my eyes against the swirling panic. *What am I doing?*

My phone buzzed in my pocket, and my heart nearly jumped out of my chest.

"You need to chill out, woman," I said aloud to myself,

because that's what happened when you lived alone with only your cat for company.

"Hello?"

"I just saw Jamie. *You're going out with him tomorrow!?*"

Leo's voice projected out of the phone well enough that Squish's ears twitched at the sound, even from across the room.

"This town is too small."

"It's nothing to do with the town. I ran into him, and he looked like he was living his life to the soundtrack of 'Walking on Sunshine,' so I pried it out of him. Tell me. Everything. *Now.*"

I sighed. "He apologized. Asked if he could take me out. I said yes. Now I'm panicking, second-guessing, and trying to remember how to breathe."

"Do you *want* to go out with him?"

She could sound so reasonable sometimes. It was times like this I wondered why she couldn't exercise that gentle, calming voice more often. But the earlier moments of our conversation were just as typical of her. She was demanding, whether in her requirement for honesty or her insistence on dealing with me with gentleness.

I blew out another breath. "I think so. Yes... no. I don't know."

I rubbed my eyes as I toed off my sneakers and let my feet rest on the couch.

Leo's chuckle was mercifully subdued. "Well, which one's winning out?"

"Obviously, the wanting to won out, or I would have said no. But... am I a total idiot?"

That was the thought I'd kept coming back to since he'd

asked yesterday, and yet, I couldn't stop myself from ignoring it and saying *yes* despite myself.

"No. You're not an idiot." She was quiet for a moment— long enough I thought she might have been done with the thought, but then she spoke again. "But I do think you need to think about what you want. I think you need to consider not just what you want with Jamie, but what you want in *life*. It's a good time to evaluate, and you'll be happier with yourself if you know what you're expecting to get out of this situation before you go in."

~

I thought about Leo's words the rest of the day.

Well. Not true.

I thought about her words, and the feeling of Jamie's arms around me, pulling me to him. And how solid and warm he was. And how good he'd smelled.

But I tried to keep my mind focused on Leo's words. *What* do *I want?*

The reality was this: I'd forgiven Jamie, but I hadn't forgotten.

What I wanted was to feel good walking around and not dread running into him. I wanted to feel satisfied with my life and at peace with the choices I'd made. I wanted to stop worrying that I'd be left by someone else who mattered to me.

My answer rang clear: I didn't want to be left. Dating Jamie had a big Las Vegas-sized sign blaring at me and telling me that no matter how much fun we had, or how much he apologized, he would leave. He wouldn't be staying in Silverton because that didn't even make sense for his life.

Jamie Morris had records to make and tours to go on, and probably a whole slew of women lined up waiting to be his escort to whatever awards show he'd be attending next.

But I couldn't ignore that I wanted him—I wanted a sliver of what I'd glimpsed years ago, and if I let myself be honest, I wanted the version of him *now* too. I wanted both Jamie Morrison *and* Jamie Morris. But I damn well wasn't about to get left by either one of them.

This time, I'd do the leaving. I'd enjoy the here and now without having a total emotional breakdown over the past *or* the future, and I'd do it by making sure I ended things, whatever things developed between us, well before he had a chance to leave me.

Perfect plan.

Exhaling some of the tension that'd worked its way into my back and neck as I tossed and turned last night, I unlocked the door to *Rise and Shine*. After hanging my jacket and purse, I walked straight into Sadie's field of vision so she wouldn't be terrified—she wore her usual head-phones to block out sound and maneuvered all manner of pans and pots at the oven and stove, her hands moving at hyper speed.

She acknowledged me with the subtlest nod possible and kept at it—she'd be out of there within an hour, and the smell of everything she'd baked thus far was enough to make me glad I'd run a few extra miles this morning so I could fully justify indulging.

I moved through the motions of opening the shop's front, though as usual Sadie had already loaded up the big baskets of bread that hung on the wall behind the counter, piled pastries into the glass case, and filled the fruit basket and cups and parfaits. She'd done all that, likely starting around four this morning. At quarter to six now, the woman had baked enough to feed a small town.

I wondered what time she went to bed—if we ever had a conversation, I would have asked, but so far, all communication other than the silent greetings and farewells we'd shared, or me speaking to her if we needed something while she was in shop, had happened via e-mail.

The first fifteen minutes of the shop's day were slow, but by six-fifteen, even in the off-season, people were up and about in Silverton. Several regulars came through before they opened their own stores, but the first hour typically belonged to the same few people. The daily slice of bread sold well, as it always did—today a sunflower honey whole wheat, and I knew why since I'd treated myself to a thick slice with a healthy slathering of local salted butter... glorious.

Truly. Between the sun cresting over the mountains in the east and shining into the front windows of the shop, to the breakfast, bread, and coffee happily fueling me, and the lull between customers, the knot in my shoulders had eased.

Or, maybe the plan I'd made had done the job. Leo's prediction held true—I already felt better knowing what I wanted.

At seven, like most days, Jonas Bauer came in, purchased his usual espresso and pastry, and set up his computer at a table by the window. Leo, as she did nearly every day, popped in around fifteen after seven, and looked comfortable and unaccountably gorgeous.

She'd braided her hair into a halo around her head, and for some reason, she had on a German Dirndl, the traditional Bavarian dress she wore for our Sommerfest and Oktoberfest celebrations.

"Uh, hi there."

She sniffed and slapped her phone down. "Is this too

tight? I am overhauling my closet today and I was thinking I might need to order a new dirndl before the celebration this summer. We're doing the fest as a part of the sixtieth anniversary, and I don't want to look like I'm spilling out of this thing."

I thanked God no customers sat close enough to hear her and let loose a cackle. "You're asking me if you look stuffed into it? No. Isn't it supposed to be really tight around the ribs and, uh... accentuate your assets?" I glanced around, glad neither of the high school boys who worked a few hours here and there at the shop weren't here.

Leo wrinkled her nose. "Sure, to a point, but I don't want to look trashy. I want to look... authentic. I got this like six years ago when I visited and I was a little less... endowed than I am now."

Leo's confidence seemingly knew no bounds but, perhaps because she'd grown up with older brothers, she never liked talking about her body. Who did, really, but this was such a rare and anomalous thing for her, it stood out.

"I'm not really sure, but you know who might know? Our resident German expert." I raised my chin and pointed to Jonas Bauer, studiously typing on the computer. "Jonas, can you advise Leo?"

On his feet and walking to us before anyone said another word, he stopped, hands in pockets, next to Leo, but looked only at me.

"How can I be of service?"

"Leo here is wondering whether this dirndl looks authentic or if it's a bit too... revealing." I pressed my lips together in an oblivious smile and ignored Leo's skyrocketing rage.

Her cheeks and chest were growing red, her neck stiff,

and the look in her eye said I'd regret this moment for years to come.

"Ah—" He cleared his throat. His gaze swept over Leo from head to toe, slowly back up her torso, and then, fairly reluctantly I might add, met her eyes. "It is acceptable."

He turned on a heel and marched back to his chair, never looking back or showing a hint he might participate in the conversation any further.

My smile died when I looked at Leo. She was bright red, a furious blush enveloping her whole face, neck, and the rather ample amount of décolletage showing. I expected a verbal lashing, but instead, she seared me with a livid look, her eyes practically glowing that cerulean blue that typified the Morrison family's youngest, and stormed out of the store.

I'd pay for that. She might've simply been embarrassed or maybe more—she'd been embarrassed because *Jonas Bauer* had seen her dressed that way. Time would tell. I'd regret it whenever she exacted her revenge... But for now, I hummed to myself and reveled in the beautiful morning.

CHAPTER TWENTY-THREE

Jamie

I ducked against the rain splattering my jacket and hustled into the restaurant.

Bel had agreed to meet me at *The Elk*. No idea why she didn't want me to pick her up, but I didn't press it. A few minutes after I arrived, she scuttled in with a rain hood leaving only a small space for her eyes and the jacket covering everything down to her knees. She had on rainboots, which for some dumb reason made me smile.

"Hey," I said, stepping to her, because I had apparently come with my most sparkling conversational skills on deck.

"Hi. I thought I might beat you, but ended up getting caught. I'm sorry." She pulled the grommet of the cinched strings that kept the hood tight around her head and released it, then unzipped her jacket and hung it on the rack next to the door.

I fought for breath. She'd shucked the outer covering so

quickly, leaving me no time to prepare for her in a light green dress that fit her every curve without looking tight, her hair cascading over shoulders in gleaming waves. *Stunning.*

"No—no problem. Glad you had a jacket."

"Me too. Could have been rough. I thought it was just going to sprinkle."

We chatted about the unexpected rain as we followed the hostess to our seat—a little spot tucked back into the *wintergarten,* a glass-enclosed space that had a surprisingly intimate feel thanks to the fireplace roaring and the rain pummeling the transparent ceiling and walls.

Just as Bel sat, I reached out and took her hand. "Wait, come back."

She frowned at me, understandably, but stood. I leaned in and kissed her soft cheek, grateful to be near her.

"Oh, thanks."

Her voice was shy but she had a small, pleased smile on her face when I looked as we both sat down.

We studied our menus, not speaking, for a few minutes.

This had to stop.

I set my menu down and spread my hands on top of it. "We haven't spent time together willingly, or without... strain... in a long time. But this silent, awkwardness thing is killing me. So I'm just going to dive in, okay?"

One eyebrow raised at me. "Seems reasonable."

"Good. So... tell me about the last eight and a half or nine years of your life." I folded my arms on the menu and leaned forward.

She chuckled, shaking her head. "No, no. That's not how this works. You go first."

"What? I'm not supposed to sit here and talk about myself. That's boring."

She didn't answer, just shook her head. Clearly, my tactic to get her talking wouldn't work as easily as I'd hoped.

"Fine. I've been making music, touring, avoiding Silverton..." I watched her face, her brows dipping with a look of concern that asked the question for her. "Not all because of you, or Danny. I don't know how much you remember in terms of how I felt with my family... that contributed to my staying away. Mostly, my schedule was insane and I didn't have seniority or clout or room in contracts to work in time off for visits. And after a while, the longer I stayed away, the easier it became to stay away."

I'd never been less happy with myself than when I'd looked up and realized I'd gone eighteen months without stepping foot in my parents' house. I'd seen Liam, who'd come to visit me before he deployed, and I'd seen Leo, because she insisted on visiting at least once a year, and my parents tracked me down, but I hadn't been *home* in over a year and a half. And I hadn't seen Danny.

Or Bel. But back then, I'd talked myself into that being a happy side effect of not visiting, and not a primary motivation not to.

"You've been back a lot the last year or so, or at least it seems that way. What changed?" She folded her arms and rested them on the table, matching my pose.

"Well, Da's heart-attack, honestly. I don't know how much longer I would have gone acting like an idiot if it hadn't happened. I'm just glad it wasn't too late for me to repair things with him."

What a selfish child I'd been the years leading up to Da's attack. He and Ma didn't even seem hurt—they'd been so supportive of the music career, and they would have been even if I'd never found success. I knew that, but I still felt so far away from them for wanting something other than a life in Silverton. Seeing Da in that hospital bed had brought it home for me: I could live my life, and love them too. They could love me for living my life. I could have both, but it'd take dedication.

Since then, much of what I'd been working on had been with an eye toward having both—music and family. Touring and performing, and *home*.

"I'm so glad he's doing well. Seems like he and your mom are loving their retiree status."

Her sweet, genuine smile caused a pang to race through my chest.

She knows me.

She still knew me better than anyone I'd tried to date or connect with over the years. She knew what my family meant to me and knew what this place meant to me—she could see past my being gone so long. Or, I hoped she could. I'd help her see that.

"They are. Their quick trip back at Christmas only confirmed it, apparently. Ma has declared that she'll be happy to never wear a winter coat again."

Bel's laugh was all delight. "I'm sure. She never did love the cold."

"No. She loved the mountains, but the cold's hard on her. Even though I wish it could have happened without the medical emergency, I'm glad they had an excuse to make a change."

"Me too. I'm glad for them."

The waiter came then, so we ordered. Just as he left, someone dropped off a basket of fresh bread, steaming hot, with a side of butter. Bel reached for a slice just as I did, fingers brushing in the process.

A ridiculous thrill shot through me at that small contact. I remembered feeling that way anytime we touched before, but I'd been a kid. How could it all be so charged, even still?

"So, your turn. Tell me about college, and how you ended up back in Silverton."

"Went to school at Miller State for marketing and design. Had a job lined up in Salt Lake, but the month I graduated, Gran got terribly sick, so I came back thinking I'd help her through it. By the end of the summer, she'd decided to move to Silverton Springs Living, and I figured I'd wait a few more months and get her settled and make sure her house sold. But then she offered me the house for a dollar—literally, and the firm where I'd been hired had filled the position, so I stayed here. And then I just... stayed."

She took a bite of bread, not looking at me. So many questions filtered through my mind. I'd been wondering what'd happened for years. She'd always planned to leave, so the fact that she'd landed back here had been more than a little surprise when Liam had mentioned it years back. That she'd stayed, even more so.

"And your folks?" I kept my voice quiet—gentle, I hoped.

She pressed her lips together, a look of regret or maybe disappointment. "They sold their house as soon as I moved for college the summer after high school. They're still in Salt Lake, doing fine."

I nodded, accepting that for now. They still caused her pain—I could see it. I'd never forget her sobbing in my arms at the base of the tree the night she found out they were leaving before she'd even graduated. I'd never actually felt someone's pain like I had that night.

"Good. I guess. And Gran?"

At that, her face brightened completely. "Sharp and sassy as ever. She's good friends with your Grandpa Will, and everyone else over at Silverton Springs, so she probably knows more about your life than I do."

"If she's friends with Grandpa Will, she probably knows more about my life than *I* do."

We laughed together at that—Grandpa Will was a gossip if there ever was one, and he loved nothing more than to share the details of his grandchildren's lives. Apparently, his children were too boring, and so me and my siblings made the perfect fodder.

The waiter delivered salads, and we both dug in. Bel and I chatted a bit about Silverton Springs and what a lively, fun place it seemed to be—nothing like a dreaded nursing home or "old folks' home" you might imagine. Once they'd cleared those plates, I went in for it.

"Is what Danny said true? Have you really not dated?"

Her eyes went wide. "Uh... I have. A few people in college, including Danny. But since living up here..." She sighed. "You know how it is—or, maybe you can remember. It's too small. I wouldn't know where to start, and I'm sure everyone feels they've known me too long to be interested. It's fine though."

I shook my head, but kept the *that's insane* or *what are these idiots thinking* internal. I didn't want it to sound like a line.

Before I could take a bite of the steak that had arrived, she asked, "And you? Have you dated much?"

CHAPTER TWENTY-FOUR

Jamie's eyes bore into mine.

He squinted. "A bit."

I let out a chuckle. *Sure.*

"Really, not much. You may not remember, but I'm not outgoing. Between touring and the weird stuff that happens when you're famous, there have only been a few people I've even attempted to spend time with." He looked down, pushed the food on his plate around.

"I'm sure you sowed your wild, Rockstar oats, or however you want to put it..." My cheeks heated. I shouldn't have said anything—why bring up the idea that he'd likely slept his way across the world while I'd lived, nun-like, in our small hometown.

He leaned forward, very stern-looking. "Absolutely not. That kind of life has never appealed to me."

I raised a brow because... sure.

"I'll admit, in the beginning, it was exciting to have so many people want my attention. But very quickly, you figure out none of them want it for anything other than their own gain. I tried to date a few girls over the years, ones who seemed normal, but it never got far. They never really knew me."

"Sounds... tough." I probably should have summoned more sympathy than that, but forgive me if I couldn't quite feel sorry he'd never hit it off with anyone. "But you've dated celebrities, right? Isn't there a kind of common bond that helps?"

He nodded as he took a drink. "Yes. There's a different level of understanding, but then there's even less anonymity. I dated Whit Grantham for a few months, and she's great—she's probably one of my best friends. And that's really where we've ended up, and probably should have been all along except I think we both wanted the other person to help solve our problems and thought another equally famous person might do the trick."

I pushed back against the jealousy welling in me, building like lava in my chest. I had no right to jealousy, but hearing about Grammy award-winning country star Whit Grantham being one of his best friends, dating him, solving his problems, made me want to turn the table to ash.

"What's that face for?" Jamie ducked his head to catch my eye.

I gulped down water, attempting to quell the unwelcomed burn in my throat. "Nothing."

His lips quirked, and he watched me as I dabbed my lips with a napkin and carefully avoided his ridiculous eyes.

"Are you jealous?"

My gaze found his. "Of course I'm jealous. You got to date Whit Grantham."

His head reared back as he laughed loudly.

"Well, I can't blame you there." He leaned forward again, no reprieve from his soulful blues in sight. "But you should know, we kissed a handful of times, that's it. And Whit is happily committed to a good man named Ben, who is also a friend."

The heat in my ribcage began to cool at that thought—that he wasn't hung up on Whit. As much as I'd successfully avoided tracking his career in any detail, it'd been impossible to miss the Oscar win for Best Original Song right before he reappeared in Silverton. And I may have tortured myself by watching the clip of them singing together, that beautiful, heart-wrenching song.

"So you're telling me you're not here in Utah, pining for a Nashville girl?"

A smile flashed. "Absolutely not."

I nodded, too overcome by relief, by a strange sense of victory, to speak.

"And you? Are you pining for anyone these days?"

His words were light, flirty even, but his energy carried an inescapable intensity. It created the sense we were alone in a room, huddled in a dark corner, and he was offering me something I couldn't name.

"No pining for me," I managed.

"Glad to hear it."

Dinner ended too soon. After the relationship recap, we moved to talk about a hundred other things. Before we realized it, our food was gone, the table cleared, and only dessert menus sitting in front of us.

"Anything catch your eye?" the waiter asked, waiting patiently, especially since he'd had to come back three times before he found a chance to insert himself and ask.

Jamie looked at me, brows raised in question. "What do you think?"

The pang of regret that hit felt all too real. "I wish I had room for anything else, but I'm so full."

"Same for me. We'll take the check, please."

With that, the waiter disappeared, and we were alone. The night was sliding by too quickly—I'd gone from mild dread and anticipation to a sense of sadness our time together was nearly over. In the course of a little more than an hour, I'd remembered how much I liked this man.

"Thank you for dinner, and for asking in the first place."

He smiled, one of those bright, lady-killer smiles that launched a thousand screams and made my insides flip, likely because they'd always been fairly rare.

"Thanks for saying yes."

Minutes later, we walked side by side under an umbrella he must have packed, the rain less aggressive now, but still coming down heavy. He'd insisted on walking me home, and I'd had no desire to refuse him.

After a block or two of bumping shoulders, he snaked an arm around my back and pulled me close to his side, our bodies huddled together under the shield against the rain.

"Better," I thought I heard him say, and then felt the press of his lips at my temple.

His arm around me, his nearness, his thoughtful steering of the umbrella to block the most rain from me, even if it meant he got wet, reminded me so much of the person he used to be. I'd had the realization then as I did now—Jamie Morris was still sweet. For all the miles he'd traveled, the millions he'd played to, the fame he'd earned... part of him was still that sweet boy holding me as I cried over my parents leaving.

I pushed that thought away. We'd had a nice time, sure, but Jamie had clearly placed my brain, my logic, under his spell. He was sweet—*maybe*. Or he simply knew how to manipulate people into getting what he wanted.

That thought made my shoulders stiffen, which I hoped he didn't notice as we turned onto my street. What *did* he want? Why was he doing all of this?

We stopped at my door and I unlocked it, then pushed it open. "Come in. Get out of the rain for a minute."

He followed me in, the storm door hissing shut behind us. I closed the main door and stood on the hardwood, watching the raindrops dribble down to the floor as he dropped the umbrella into the rubber tray I used for boots and muddy shoes this time of year.

I pulled off my jacket and hung it on a hook. "Jacket off. Let's warm up and dry before you have to go back out in it."

He didn't acknowledge me verbally but removed his jacket and hung it, then pulled off his shoes and set them neatly by the umbrella while I moved to the fireplace that centered the living room and started a fire.

I padded into the kitchen to start some milk heating in a pan for a warm drink. When he didn't follow, I peeked back into the living room to find him sitting on the couch in front of Squish, his whole body twisted so he could talk to the cat. He murmured low, so I couldn't make out his words.

"Are you trying to date me just to get to my cat?" I leaned against the door frame and crossed my arms.

He shot me a dark look and flashed his eyebrows as he petted the wrinkled fur on my traitorous cat's head. "Maybe."

The milk in the pan was close to scalded, so I added the chocolate shavings I kept for special occasions. Normally, I'd have tea, but since we'd skipped dessert, and the rain had made everything feel cold outside and cozy in here, it fit.

Plus, it was a little decadent to have hot chocolate on a Monday night with a man you'd been half in love with all your life. Jamie's presence demanded that decadence from my subconscious, and at this point in the night, how could I refuse?

I set mugs of rich, dark chocolate melted into milk and a bowl full of marshmallows in the middle of a small tray, a few small cookies I'd smuggled home from day-olds no one had bought at the shop earlier on a plate too.

At this point, there was no surprise in finding Jamie with his head resting on the couch next to Squish, staring at the cat while Squish's ears twitched from being watched.

"Don't steal him, please. He's the only thing between me and despairing loneliness." My tone came out light, but the words rang with ugly truth.

I swallowed against that realization—why had I said that aloud... and to *Jamie?*

His head popped up. "I know what you mean. I had a cat for a few years. He was a good companion... I miss him."

He eyed the tray, but didn't seem to see it.

"What happened to your cat?" I asked, keeping my voice soft as I handed him a mug.

His eyes focused on me as he took the hot chocolate and made a reluctant frown. "Someone let him out of the tour bus... it was awful."

"Oh no. I'm so sorry... that's terrible." I put my hand on his arm and found genuine sadness and regret on his face. I'd never thought of Jamie as an animal lover, but more and more, he proved he was.

"Never had the heart to get another little bud. That's probably why I'm obsessed with your cat now." He flashed that smile again, trying to lighten things.

"Well, you can see he's miserable from your attention."

We smiled at each other, sipped our hot chocolate, and a calm, quiet mood fell over the room. The fire crackled in the hearth and the flames sent shadows flickering on the walls. With only the fireplace and a sliver of light from the kitchen, the dimly lit room was just bright enough to see each other.

"That's delicious," he said, breaking through the quiet as he set down the mug.

"Dessert." I smiled, holding the warmth between my hands.

Something in his eyes changed and he shifted, coming closer to me on the couch. He reached for me, took the mug from my hands, and set it down.

"Bel." His voice was low, a little rough.

At that sound, my heart sped up. The heat from the chocolate must have seeped into me faster than I'd though, because suddenly I was too warm, as if his voice saying my name had flipped an internal switch.

"Jamie."

His fingers brushed over my knuckles where he held my hand—when had he taken my hand?

"I've thought about kissing you again since the first time."

I huffed a little breath, unable to force a laugh. "That's been a while."

He'd put me under a spell. That's what this was. There could be no other explanation for the electric currents running through me—it had to be some Jamie Morris Rock-star voodoo.

"It has. It doesn't make much sense, but it's true."

Those eyes never wavered, never looked way, never released me from their mesmerizing gaze.

I swallowed, my breath coming quickly as I watched him for a beat before he was *right there*, right in my face, so close he became almost a whisper on my lips.

He searched my eyes, one to the other, asking permission without voicing the words. I couldn't have said who moved first, but after an excruciating moment there just waiting, waiting, our lips touched.

The contact began unbearably softly, barely more than a shadow of a touch—not tentative, not unsure, just... slow. Purposeful.

My heart hammered in my chest as the hand already holding one of mine slipped up my arm, over my shoulder, and settled just under my ear, his warm skin and calloused fingers their own delicious thrill.

The kiss, at first tentative and sweet, deepened, all dark chocolate and smooth lips. All Jamie, sweet and terrifying.

My hands found their way to his face, the rough scruff of his beard making me smile as I experienced one of those strange out-of-body moments where I realized *I'm kissing Jamie Morris* and also a brilliant flashback to the smooth skin of his jaw when he'd kissed me all those years ago.

Some things had changed.

Some things, like my response to him, that feeling that *this* was right, had not.

It was that thought that had me pulling back a bit, just

an inch at first, enough to catch his eyes lit like blue flame and feel the burn in my cheeks more clearly.

"You okay?"

A smile broke out, and I laughed. Right there in his serious, unrelentingly gorgeous face. "Definitely."

He ran his thumb across my lips and leaned in for one more peck. "Thank God."

CHAPTER TWENTY-FIVE

Jamie

I left Bel's house sometime after eight that night. After the long-awaited kiss, we'd managed to talk a while longer before I knew I needed to leave or the leaving part would be far too difficult.

Not that I assumed that was something I could control. But I didn't want to rush things, and if the kiss had proven anything, it had shown me I wanted Bel even more than I thought possible.

It'd been three days since I'd seen her. I'd called her the next day and asked if I could take her out Saturday. Even though the date had gone well, I'd had a momentary drop where the world got a little fuzzy as I waited for her to answer the phone and after that, as I waited for her to say yes again.

"When are you thinking?"

She sounded so small on the other end of the line.

"Saturday. I'd pick you up late afternoon so we can take our time and still get you home for a good night's sleep."

I firmly ignored the mental images that threatened to flash through my mind of all the ways we'd take our time, of how I'd get her home, of how she might get that good night's sleep.

Chill, man.

The pause as I waited had my heart racing faster than all those scenarios teasing at the edges of my mind did. Had I gotten ahead of myself? I'd become determined immediately after hearing Danny give me the go-ahead. I'd like to say I played it cool mentally, but no. I'd wanted Bel for too long to not be enthusiastically in favor of taking whatever she'd give me, but of course that didn't mean anything in terms of what she wanted to give.

"Sure."

Not as enthusiastic as I would've liked, but I'd take it.

"Sure?" I had to ask. I didn't want her to feel anything but happy about it.

"Yeah, sure. *Yes.* Let's do it."

I held the phone away from my face and let out a long exhale. I could hear the smile in her voice as she spoke. *That* was what I'd been hoping for.

"Excellent. I'll see you Saturday, then."

And I'd planned on seeing her Saturday, not sooner.

But because I'd become a dependent idiot incapable of going even a handful of days without seeing the woman I'd recently admitted to myself that I'd been mildly obsessed with for nine years and who I finally let myself want without feeling like the worst kind of man, I found myself walking to the coffee shop where she'd be working.

Really, it was miraculous I'd managed the three days since the call. I hadn't wanted to talk to *anyone* on the phone, probably ever, and yet hearing her voice, just the thought of it, had my heart racing and my palms tingling.

So I walked to *Rise and Shine*—never mind that my clock showed just after seven in the morning and I didn't have meetings in town for another hour, or that I should probably leave her alone and not smother her. I'd left her alone for too long.

The bell jingled overhead as I stepped inside, but I found an empty shop save for Jonas Bauer, who sat at a table in the corner by the window. When I walked through, his head jerked up and looked at me. I could have sworn he seemed disappointed, but maybe I'd become too accustomed to people going into mild shock at seeing me and his was simply a neutral face.

"Mr. Morris." Bauer stood and extended a hand, which I shook.

I'd told him to call me Jamie, but we could stay formal if he insisted. "Bauer, good to see you. How're things?"

I'd been at the board meeting this week, but had been called out thanks to an issue with my manager, who I couldn't ignore. Ultimately, he gave me the room I needed to breathe. He'd gotten me going, and I'd stuck with him through the grueling pace he'd set—it'd worked for me and it certainly worked for his bottom line. But now that I'd demanded some time and space, we still had the occasional run-in where he panicked that I wanted to *run away to the mountains and become a pottery-slinging hermit*, as he put it.

"Going well. I heard a rumor you might be working on a project aside from the lodge while here."

His even tone, calm face, unchanged body language said nothing. But I could read the subtext.

I heard about this project and I want information.

It wasn't the kind of aggression I usually encountered—often people wanted to "meet me" but really, they wanted to sell me on their product, their service, becoming their poster boy for whatever it was they were hoping my fame or bank account could do for them.

No, Jonas Bauer was a shark in a gray suit, and he wore it well. He technically played for the Morrison family team —or at least we thought. And my development project with Julian would absolutely be a good thing. But we didn't want it leaked to the town just yet—we wanted to come in with more houses bought out, and I didn't want Liam to know I'd kept this from him yet.

I certainly didn't want Bauer finding out first.

"Writing the next album, mostly. It never ends," I said, tacking on a pleasant *whatcha gonna do* smile.

"Jamie. You're out and about early," Leo said as the bell chimed again and she entered the space.

Bauer stood straight. "Ms. Morrison."

"Bauer."

Leo's reception of Jonas Bauer struck me as strange, but nothing about Leo could be called predictable other than she would inevitably have her own opinion about whatever took place.

I hadn't seen her since the date with Bel. Suddenly, I realized that before me stood an untapped resource. She might have talked with Bel—might have a sense of how Bel thought it had gone. Might know how Bel felt about me.

As though she read my mind, she held up a hand. "Nope. I will not divulge anything about anything. That is all."

She turned and marched to the counter and drummed on it to get attention as I flared my eyes at Bauer and shook my head. He gave me a curt nod and returned to his seat while I moved to stand in line behind Leo.

"Sorry! Sorry, sorry. I'm coming. Had a small issue with —" Bel stopped as our eyes connected over Leo's shoulder just as she rounded the corner from the kitchen. "Oh, hi."

"Hi." The breadth of the English language at my disposal, and... *Brilliant.*

"Can I get you something?"

Her smile was too lovely. Seeing her this early in the day had apparently short-circuited my brain. I'd had a perfectly normal conversation with Jonas Bauer moments ago.

"Uh, yeah. Me. You can get *me* coffee and stop staring at each other."

Ah, the record-scratching sounds of Leo.

Bel's face broke into an embarrassed laugh. "Of course, Your Majesty."

One thing I'd always liked about Bel, even before she and Leo were close friends, which hadn't happened until long after I'd left town, was how well she handled my sister. Leo could be prickly and pushy, but with that came incredible loyalty and a fierce kind of love.

Bel's temperament complemented Danny's very well— Danny embodied the laid-back, easygoing guy, and Bel fit perfectly with that. She had a backbone, but she didn't assert herself unless she needed to. She was vibrant and fun and smart, but she didn't like being the center of attention. Or, at least, that's how she had been for all our growing up years.

I'd wondered once or twice when we were kids if she and Leo didn't get along—she spent so much time with our family, I'd always been surprised she and Leo weren't better friends. But Leo was two grades below Bel and

Danny, and that was a large enough difference when kids are young, so I figured it all came down to circumstances back then.

Seeing them together a few times lately, I could tell Bel had earned Leo's friendship and couldn't ever lose it. Lucky for her, and lucky Leo had Bel—someone she couldn't walk all over, and someone who'd known her most of her life.

I envied that. Anytime I came back here, I felt the fish-out-of-water sensation so strongly because I'd been gone, but there were these flashes of belonging, like this odd little moment at the coffee shop, where I forgot how long I'd been away.

"Jamie?"

Bel stood in front of me, eyebrows raised, waiting for me to respond like she'd been talking to me for more than a minute.

"Sorry, must have spaced out. Still waking up, I guess." I gave her a half-smile, surprised how inside my head I'd been. I'd missed her helping Leo, Leo paying... all of it.

"Can I get you something?"

The temptation to say *you* flared, but I resisted. Too much, too soon.

"Black coffee and slice of the day, please."

She nodded, a grin sprouting lines at her eyes—a delightful detail I reveled in when she smiled considering most women I encountered in LA had no evidence of aging past adolescence thanks to Botox and whatever else.

"I'll bring it out in just a sec."

I took a seat after saying goodbye to Leo, who'd gotten her order to go, and scrolled my phone until the bell above the door rang again and I looked up to see women walk through the door. The first one in stopped, causing the person behind her to run into her back. I quickly ducked my head back to my phone, dreading what I could already feel would happen.

"No way."

"What? Move aside, weirdo."

They must have come inside because I heard the door close. Bel walked over just then, setting a bright blue mug full of coffee on the table and a plate with a thick slice of something wheaty and wholesome, slathered with butter, next to it.

"Can I get you anything else?" she asked, already moving back to the counter.

"No, thank you. This is great," I said, my head still ducked, voice low.

The women were waiting at the counter when Bel got back, their backs to me, though I could feel their eyes on me every so often. The first one ordered, then the next, and Bel served them their coffees to go. Then they appeared at my table, bodies smashed together at the hip like they held each other up next to the empty chair at my table.

"Uh, are you Jamie Morris?"

I raised my chin, forcing a pleasant grin on my face. "Yes." I'd learned long ago that usually it was futile to pretend otherwise.

The woman standing closest to me gripped the back of the empty chair while the other one laughed wildly, loudly, and flushed red.

"Cool. Cool. Well... nice to meet you!"

They scuttled out the door, no autograph request or any further propositioning, and relief flooded me. My eyes immediately found Bel watching, biting her lip to hide what I could have sworn was a smile.

Unexpected.

"Saw that, huh?" I asked, sweeping a few crumbs from

the table into my hand, then sprinkling them back on the plate.

"Hard to miss."

The smile escaped, and my stupid chest expanded at the sight.

I'd expected her to be annoyed, or... something other than amused, at least. She didn't seem at all impressed with my fame or money or even my music—we hadn't talked about it at all, really. I'd figured women giving me attention would be a drawback.

"Sorry about that." I took the last swig of my coffee and stacked the mug on the now-empty plate.

"You can't possibly control people recognizing you. Plus those two were sweet, don't you think?"

Warmth spread through me. *Yes. Yes, exactly.*

The few women I'd dated before Whit Grantham had become unmanageable after a few run-ins with fans. I hadn't expected it—had naively assumed they'd know that was part of dating me. Their reactions at the first run-ins were never so... easy. They weren't overtly upset or unkind after the first or second time, but there always hung a clear sense of displeasure and annoyance.

Bel's apparent... delight, for lack of a better word, felt awesome, and unsettling.

"They were. It's hard to tell what's going to happen, but especially around here, it's usually pretty low-key—the only reason I don't have to have security with me here." Fortunately. Because I wasn't ready for Bel to see how some people approached me.

"I'm sure that gets tiresome, but you handled it well."

Smiling—she still smiled, like all of this was adorable to her.

"It does sometimes, but again here in Silverton, it's

never bad. Plus I can't really do what I do without fans, so that's part of the deal."

I believed that, which helped when people got overwhelming, asked for too much, *took* too much. I'd had some tough encounters with fans, not to mention a few break-ins at my house in LA, and those events threatened that sense of gratefulness. But there were always parts of the world where I wasn't so conspicuous, and Silverton provided a fair amount of anonymity—one more reason to get the house finished and be here more often.

"Makes sense." Bel leaned on the counter with an elbow and reached a hand out to take the plate and mug.

"Thank you." I held the edge of the plate even after she'd taken it, keeping her there with me for just a minute. I needed a few more seconds to take in those green eyes. "I'll see you Saturday afternoon, right?"

CHAPTER TWENTY-SIX

Bel

The day started off well enough, and seeing Jamie had left me fluttery and smiling long after he'd gone, his tall, broad frame darkening the doorway as he left with one backward glance and a smile I'd think about later. But I could easily say Jamie qualified as the highlight.

Not a surprise—lately, it felt like any glimpse of him became the best part of my day, and I still had mixed feelings to an irritating degree. Still, I looked forward to catching sight of that distinctive bun at the back of his head, or those eyes...

I'd fallen behind on a project for the library. I typically worked on marketing stuff nights and weekends, and for some reason, likely rhyming with *mamie jorris*, I'd had a terrible time concentrating once I got off work at the shop.

But the new librarian, who'd moved to town about a

year earlier and was trying so hard to revitalize some of the programs, had put up a flyer asking for help a few months ago. I'd responded and had been genuinely elated to use my ability to help her and the library—*libraries are one of the last pure, good things on Earth*, Gran says, and I agree.

The librarian, Mia Parker, came in around ten that morning.

"Bel? I'm so sorry to ask this of you, but do you think you could get that logo made for me by the end of *this* week instead of next?" Her dark eyes were wide and pleading as she spoke.

"Uh…" I ticked through the things I had left to do—not a ton for just that, but it'd mean a long night ahead.

"I understand if you can't." She shook her head anxiously, clearly unhappy at imposing on me.

I'd gotten the sense Mia didn't like being a burden—and really, who did? But she often canceled requests after voicing them, and some part of me knew it came from her feeling like she asked too much. The nature of me being a volunteer did make it tricky—as a client, she relied on my goodwill rather than a paid contract, but I'd had her sign a contract for my time anyway. It helped me budget my time, and it helped her feel good about what she could expect.

Even so, I could tell this killed her to ask. Her petite frame stood rigid at the desk, one hand clutching a canvas bag at a shoulder, the other tucked to her chest like she was calming her heart. Her long, black hair was pulled into a tight, orderly bun at the back of her head. She touched the section just above her ear and smoothed it back while I fumbled around, cursing my slow response.

"Of course. I can do it, yes. I'm off at three today and I have the evening to finish it. I'll have it to you before nine tomorrow morning. Does that work?"

I offered my most encouraging smile, wishing I knew her just a bit better so I could chat more comfortably with her. I'd only interacted with her at the library itself or on occasions like this and through e-mail. Someday, I should invite her to dinner with Wells and Leo—she had to be about our age and must be lonely living in a town this small.

The bell rang as Danny walked through, and I smiled at him as he approached the counter and stood a few feet behind Mia to wait his turn.

"Thank you so much. You're a life saver. I messed up the date for—well, never mind. I don't want to take more of your time. Thank you so much and—" she turned to go and ran smack into Danny. "Oh, I'm so sorry... *oh.*"

"You okay?" Danny ducked his head to look at her face with a steadying hand on her shoulder, then loosed a gigantic smile. As if his whole world had lit up when Mia had looked up into his face. *Hmm...* Something brewing there?

She spoke, an answering grin on her lips. "Didn't mean to attack you. How—"

"—How are you?" Danny's face brightened even further as he accidentally interrupted her. "Sorry. How are you? It's been a while since—"

"More than a month, right?" Mia added, then dipped her head, a little tinge of red at her cheeks.

"Yes. Too long," Danny said, rocking back on his heels.

"I owe you breakfast." Mia tucked her purse under her arm and stepped back.

Danny chuckled. "I wouldn't say you *owe* me..." He dropped his hand and moved to the side so she could pass. "See you soon, Mia."

And there he was, smiling like a doofus all while she waved as she exited the shop, Danny's attention not leaving her until she'd walked far enough down the sidewalk that she couldn't be seen anymore.

Interesting.

"How do you know her?" He set a hand on the counter and turned one more time to look after her before giving me his full attention.

Curiouser and curiouser...

"I do some marketing for the library, but don't know her well. She's really nice and seems to be doing a lot for the library from what I can tell. Do you know her?"

Obviously, he did, and wanted to better. Danny had never been the kind to give second glances—he was too busy racing forward to the next thing, ignoring anything that might slow him down or saddle him with responsibility.

I'd thought about that a lot lately, actually. With Jamie around, I'd found myself remembering our childhood, all the interactions Jamie and I'd had, but with that naturally came my childhood friendship with Danny. I'd been so surprised when he said he'd been in love with me for years and hadn't said anything, but looking back, I wondered if maybe it didn't make perfect sense.

If he'd said something, it would have stopped us—at least our friendship as we knew it. It might have enriched it, but it might have set us off course, and Danny was never one to rock the boat or choose change.

To be fair, though, it seemed like maybe change was afoot.

His face certainly indicated it might be, if that crimson tide of a blush covering his cheeks and neck said anything.

"Uh, yeah. I know her."

Nothing more—just that, and he scratched the back of his neck.

I hid a smile. The same tell he'd always had when he

didn't want to admit something—some things hadn't changed. I could show him some mercy though—after all, he'd made the huge step of confronting Jamie on their years of strain, so making fun of his interest in Mia wasn't fair.

"What can I get for you?"

The day continued with my steaming my own wrist—I know, it really took quite a bit of skill and if it hadn't given me a scalded strip of skin that ached the rest of the day whether I iced it or not, I might have been impressed. I dropped someone's coffee, and by the end of the day, I had to work incredibly hard not to snap Garrett's head off. He was in goofy high school boy mode when he arrived, and after only half an hour together, he'd turned sullen and disturbingly obedient.

Who am I?

None of this made sense. I didn't get moody like this— that was Leo's territory.

Which really wasn't fair to say about her. I'd been shrouded in the mood since Mia had come in, and even if I didn't want to admit it, I had to.

As giddy as seeing Jamie had made me, I had legitimate concerns. I had real hurt that, yes, I'd forgiven him for, but ultimately still lived in me. It didn't just go away because the guy who'd crushed me emotionally years ago had said sorry and wanted to go out.

If only it were that easy.

I believed him when he apologized. I knew he wasn't solely at fault for the damage that had been done, and that I had my own weakness and inability to move on from being hurt by him and my parents to blame too. But I also knew that my promise to myself to be the first one to leave, at least based on how every part of me lit up at just the mention of his name or the sight of him, would be incredibly hard to keep.

My phone buzzed next to me on the bedside table—I'd been lying in bed for hours, wishing I could sleep. I'd finished the project for the library and sent it in around seven that evening, and had hoped I could get to bed soon after since I felt so weirdly run-over by the day. It hadn't been a bad day, but it had been emotionally draining.

I looked over to find a message from Jamie. I dropped my head back into my pillow and covered my eyes with the hand not holding the phone.

Taking stock of the feelings chasing through me did nothing to make me feel better about how all this would go. My heart rate had increased. I'd definitely smiled when I saw the message came from him, and opening it proved to be the only thing on my mind besides a mental image of him holding Squish, which would likely never be erased from my brain as it'd no doubt been burned into my memory.

I exhaled dramatically and eyed the phone, then read the notification.

If you could travel anywhere, where would you go?

Despite myself, there came the smile.

We'd been texting little questions for the last few days. Ever since our date on Monday, he'd messaged me at least twice a day with a basic question—what's your favorite food? What's your favorite color? What was your favorite class in high school? What's the last book you read?

I couldn't pretend to dislike it. I loved hearing from him, and I anticipated those little questions and the chance to ask him one in return. Though a small way of getting to know each other, it felt like a big deal—like it showed me he really did want to know me, and didn't just want to... whatever I was so afraid of. Use me. Satisfy his curiosity. Who knew?

I readied my response. *Paris! Croissants! You?*

His reply came quickly. *Barcelona—probably. Choosing a favorite is hard—all kinds of qualifications for each favorite.*

He'd seen the world at this point—it made sense he couldn't easily choose just one. But Barcelona... huh. Somehow, I'd never thought much about Spain. My family's ancestry, like so many Americans, was an utter mish-mash, though funny enough, lots of people in our small town had a very clear sense of their history since such a small group of people had settled up here—mostly a handful of German-American and few Irish-American immigrant families originally, and then it had diversified a bit, particularly considering Utah's relative homogeny. But as far as I knew, the Paxtons had come because Gran had come, and I'd never been sure why she lived here—she hadn't grown up here like Jamie's grandpa and so many others in her peer group.

Hope you had a great day. Glad I got to see you for a minute this morning.

My heart kicked, and happiness warmed me. He certainly did a good job of making me feel like I had his full attention... that I held a special place in his life, even now.

I rolled my eyes as I set the phone down. I was definitely in trouble.

CHAPTER TWENTY-SEVEN

Jamie

I took a calming breath. No good would come from arguing.

"Da. I'm here, and I'll stay here through the summer. But please understand, I can't have you treating me like a teenager."

"Son, you're a grown man. Why would you even say that?" Da's voice came, all indignation.

I chuckled and shook my head—of course, he'd conveniently forgotten my trip in the fall when I'd gone to Salt Lake with Quinn and a few others and got back after hours only to find him *and* Ma waiting up for me.

"You remember in September? I was here for a week, and you both asked me every morning what I planned to do that day, never mind what time I'd be home."

A huff into the phone. "Just because you're grown doesn't mean we stop worrying about you. Frankly, having you back in the house brings some of that out more than it should, I know. But you've got to understand we parented you kids for decades—it's a hard habit to break, caring about your children getting home alive."

I sighed audibly. "And here it comes…"

"And someday, when you have your own children, you'll remember this moment, *this* conversation, and you'll come to me and say 'Da, you were right about all of it.'"

The tone, the delivery… identical to the many times he'd said the same thing all my life.

"All right, all right. I'll try to keep you aware of my plans if you and Ma try not to pry too much. I'm generally not out all that often anyway, especially since Bel's got to be up so early most mornings—"

"What's this? Bel Paxton?" Ma's voice cut in—I *knew* she'd been listening.

"Yes, Bel Paxton. It's nothing much yet, but I've taken her out once and we're going out again tomorrow."

Saying it out loud sent little bolts of nervousness through my gut.

"Wonderful! Why didn't you start with that news? Remember your manners and open her car door, and don't let your fans get in your face or hers especially. Don't talk about the famous women you've dated, and don't—"

"*Ma*, I'm good. I'm being smart with her."

The unspoken thought there that she could probably hear echoing in the abyss said just how stupid I'd been years ago. She didn't know everything that happened but she'd known something had since Bel had once been ever-present at the house, at family dinners, at any event we did. She'd always been invited because my parents had taken on looking after her since her parents were perpetually gone, plus she and Danny were glued at the hip until high school, and even then they were very close.

"You better be. You've messed up enough with her—"

"*Ma*. I love you, but please. I know I messed up, and I did some groveling, and I'll probably do some more. But while she's giving me a second glance that's not filled with dislike and mistrust, I'm taking the opportunity."

"Good. You should. I never understood why you ran away like that. She clearly liked you, and Danny would've recovered eventually."

The choking sound issuing from my throat must have tipped her off to how she'd surprised me.

"You didn't think I knew? I know you, Jamie. I know you think you've never fit, and I know something changed with Da's event. I know you're trying with us, and I'm glad you're trying with Bel. I just hope you know you don't have to *try* here. You just being with us is enough."

Her voice, impossibly gentle and yet stern like only her voice could be, had my response sticking in my mouth. I swallowed, cleared my throat. "Thanks Ma. Only problem is you're not actually *here* here, so..."

She chuckled and gave me their flight information. They'd return while I traveled for the concerts in June, but then they planned to stick around for a while. That meant I had about six weeks until they came to join the fun. I genuinely looked forward to seeing them, even if it meant reporting on my comings and goings for the first time since I was a teen.

After hanging up with my parents, I wandered into town and sent Bel her first message of the day. *What is a quality you find unattractive?*

There—right to the good stuff. I wanted to know if anything about me stood out as unlikeable to her. I'd become bolder with my questions, and why not? Messaging like this gave us both an opportunity to be honest while we adjusted to this new world where we didn't hide from each other. It usually only took a few minutes to receive a response. Sure enough...

Arrogance. Dishonesty.

Fair enough. I didn't like those either. I recognized the bad news though—good chance she saw me as an arrogant jerk. I'd played that up when I'd left, making her believe I'd dive into a string of women as soon as I got to LA instead of what really happened—I dove into work, felt my chest hollow out every time I thought of her face when I told her, and attempted to ignore the shroud of guilt I wore for hurting both her and Danny.

Very dislikable qualities. I can't deny owning a bit of the first, but I can promise to avoid the second.

Truthfully, I was arrogant. Confident, sure, but I knew I'd developed a healthy level of arrogance in the last while—that became practically unavoidable when people fawned over you, screamed your name, and begged for your attention. But I also saw it, and tried to tone it down. I'd done a good job of it here for the most part, and I made a special effort because being around my siblings helped remind me who I really was—not a world-famous rock star, but just a guy who'd wussed out and run away from his family and the girl he liked.

Obviously, that grossly oversimplified things, but the point remained that hopefully Bel could overlook my brand of arrogance. I'd attempted and would continue to make amends for the dishonesty that had come with the lies I'd told her, but since then, I hadn't lied to her, nor would I.

I don't expect perfection. I hope you don't either.

Her reply had me smiling as I strolled past the inn and

onto the path that led to Main Street—I'd taken the longer way in because I had nothing else to do, and so far keeping myself from barging in the coffee shop and grabbing Bel for a kiss had become a full-time job.

"So you make amends with your girl, and now I'm... what?"

Quinn's voice met me as soon as I stepped onto the sidewalk.

I smiled as I crossed the street to her and her daughter and greeted her with a high five as Cara jumped up and down and chanted "Jamie! Jamie!"

"You're still one of my best friends—no need to get sour on me. It's not like you've been pounding down my door to grab coffee." I gave her a look.

She smirked and grabbed Cara's hand as we all crossed back to the other side of the street. "True. We've been busy —haven't we, girly?"

"It's true Jamie, we have." Cara nodded solemnly, and I couldn't hide a small laugh at her sincerity.

"Everything going well for you two?"

"Of course. Homework, school play, music lessons, work for me... just real life. Six weeks until summer and we can start sleeping in!" Quinn and Cara slapped a double high-five, their signature move, and then Quinn eyed me again. "And how's it going for you?"

"Work's fine, though writing's going slow. A few other things in the mix moving along."

"And things with The One You Pushed Away?"

I frowned at her name for Bel and shook my head. Quinn had never been one to let me get off easy, and even though we saw each other maybe once a year and chatted via messages every few weeks or less, she clearly wouldn't start now.

"Going well. Big date tomorrow."

"First?" Quinn slowed as we approached the *Rise and Shine* sign.

"That was Monday. Longer one, a bit more involved, tomorrow."

At that, she gave me a genuine smile. "I'm happy for you, Jam. I hope you stay smart."

I peeked in the window, but Bel wasn't at the counter. A quick internal debate had me continue walking, so Quinn and Cara did too. I'd only make a fool of myself if I went in there. We had plans tomorrow, and I'd already stopped in yesterday. Smothering her wouldn't make her dive in with me, and it could very well drive her away.

I stopped at the crosswalk where I suspected Quinn and Cara might go—sure enough, we said goodbye as they continued toward the school, I assumed.

I waved as Quinn walked and Cara skipped farther down the street where they'd disappear around the corner before they arrived at the library, then a bit beyond, the school.

I shoved my hands into my pockets and rounded the corner onto Elk Street, debating where to go first. I'd been considering getting a haircut—just chopping it off and simplifying life again with shorter hair. *Maybe I should ask Bel.*

There it came—one of those moments when I wished it made sense to ask her. I wanted her to have a say about me —I wanted her to have an opinion, and share it. Maybe I could ask her after tomorrow.

That left the law office where I had a few documents to sign for one thing or another, which would definitely be open, so I stayed on that side of the street passing *Cut*, the salon, and the small sign that hung just next to the law office's door that indicated Liam and John's brewery space in the basement. I'd have to check in and see how that was going, but last I'd heard, he planned to hand off his manager's position by end of summer if things went well.

Before I entered the building, I took a minute to breathe in the bright, springy air I missed so much when I lived or toured anywhere else. I did love it in Silverton, even if I couldn't imagine being here all the time.

Out of the corner of my eye, I noticed Danny walking in the direction Quinn and Cara had just gone—interesting. Must be off to the library again, whatever that was about. Could it be one of those things he'd mentioned having in the works?

I thought of Quinn's send-off. Of course she wouldn't say something like *I hope everything works out* or *I hope it goes well for you* or *I hope she falls madly in love with you and can't bear to be without you.* No. Quinn hoped I stayed smart... honestly, so did I.

CHAPTER TWENTY-EIGHT

Jamie paced outside my house on the small stretch of sidewalk between the main walk and my door. He hadn't rung the bell.

The phone to his ear, occasionally he nodded, but he didn't speak much. At least not that I'd seen. I'd stopped short of pulling the curtains back and watching him, but knowing that on the other side of the door marched Jamie, a person I'd missed as much as I'd mentally cursed over the years, I couldn't simply ignore him.

When I saw him stop and stare at his phone, I jumped back, straightened my dress, smoothed my hair away from my face, and took a deep breath.

I'd spent the morning with Gran, as usual for my Saturdays. She had a cough developing, but when I asked her if she'd seen the doctor, she gave me *the look* and told me to worry about myself. She couldn't actually believe I wouldn't worry about her, but her tetchy response had eased my mind a bit.

The time with Gran proved to be a decent distraction from the date with Jamie. I thanked God more than once we weren't meeting at some ridiculous dinner date time like seven p.m., but instead at four, which meant I had just a few hours to eat up after arriving home from Gran's in the early afternoon.

I showered, washed and dried and styled my hair, and spent a solid half-hour trying on various outfits, hoping to find the perfect option for a date with a world-famous Rockstar to an unknown location somewhere up the canyon. That could mean anything—hiking, or a new restaurant, or... somewhere else. I honestly had no idea.

I'd landed on a simple cotton dress with short sleeves that hung to just above my knees, not fitted but not particularly loose. Kind of in the middle of everything, just in case this turned out to be a climbing adventure. I could still run, move, sit on the ground in this thing. I wore rubber-soled ballet flats, which I'd also road-tested for mobility and varied use.

After what felt like a small eternity, but had only been two minutes according to the watch I'd checked about twenty times in the last few minutes while Jamie paced my front walk, a knock on the door sounded.

I pulled it open, flutters of nerves whooshing through me at the sight of the man standing at my door. I already had my purse and a sweater in hand, so I pulled the door closed behind me as he stepped back and held the screen.

"Ready?" he asked, amusement in his eyes.

"Yes—but why do you have that look in your eye?"

"I'm used to waiting, I guess. I thought it might take you a minute to grab your stuff, or maybe you wouldn't be quite ready. I did say four o'clock, right?" He checked his watch with mock concern.

"I saw you pacing around, so I knew you were here. I figured I might as well be ready to go so we can get this show on the road." I trotted down the steps and out onto the walk as he let go of the screen door and followed.

Did he expect me to admit that I'd been waiting by the door for him? That starting at about ten after three, I'd been counting minutes, and sometimes aching seconds, until he showed up?

Not going to happen.

He could be the charming Rockstar, the too-good-looking date, all he wanted. No chance I'd let him know how much he affected me or how much I liked him. The deal I'd made with myself when I said yes to spending time with Jamie was that I'd walk away first—this was part of it. He couldn't know how much I already liked him. Nope.

He opened my car door, then hustled around to get in the driver's seat. He started the car but paused before putting it in gear, staring out the window for a moment, a frown on that beautiful mouth.

"Mind if we make a quick detour before we head to dinner?"

"Of course not. Is something wrong?"

He put the car in gear, and we hummed along in his old truck for a minute before he answered.

"I don't think so, no." He drove for a few more minutes, out of Silverton. "I'm working on something up here, and I need to check on it."

"Okay..." Vague. Also a bit mysterious. What would he be working on here?

I didn't ask any questions because he'd tell me what he

meant if he wanted to. Plus, seemed like we were heading to visit that project, so I'd know more any minute.

Before long, we turned onto a dirt road I'd never noticed before, though I rarely came east of town. The road followed a little creek and then rounded into a densely wooded area. Another minute, and we stopped in front of a towering home with a gorgeous stone façade and giant wooden door.

Jamie pulled into the cobblestoned driveway, parked, and got out. I still sat there gaping at the house, which seemed like it'd sprouted out of the ground since everything around us was just... nature, when he pulled open my door.

"What is this?" I asked, the wonder in my voice a bit embarrassing, but I couldn't quiet it.

A smile flashed across his face when I looked at him. "My house."

"Of course it's a house, I mean—*wait.*"

His smile grew.

I swallowed, concerned about the way my lungs seemed to have forgotten their primary role in the body's system. "Did you say *your* house?"

"Yes." His perfect teeth flashed at me again.

"I—" I had nothing. *He built a house here?*

He grabbed my hand. "Let's go inside. I need to check on some things."

I followed willingly, unable to enjoy the sensation of his warm hand holding mine thanks to the roiling in my belly. Hope, relief, fear, anger all swirled around inside me.

He opened the unlocked door and stepped inside. I took in unfinished wood floors, high ceilings, bare walls. He ran a hand over the carved wooden bannister that led up the stairs of the entryway and passed through into the kitchen.

What a gorgeous room. Marble countertops, a farmhouse sink, no appliances yet, but there'd no doubt be top of the line everything when the time came.

He picked up a stack of papers and leafed through them while I wandered into the living room with a gorgeous stone fireplace and a whole wall of windows that looked out first at trees, then off into the valley. Situated at the back of the house, the view overlooked part of the valley in one direction and looked straight up at Silver Ridge Peak in the other.

"This is incredible."

"It's getting there—another few months and it really will be," he said, his head still buried in the documents.

I walked the rest of the first floor until he came to find me and took me on a tour. Everything stood unfinished to some degree, but it already won the title of fanciest house I'd ever set foot in. Stone and natural woods dominated the aesthetic. Where walls had been painted, the colors were subtle but warm.

The master bathroom had a *grotto* for a shower. No lie—the door-less, deep red and brown stone-tiled space had enough room for a basketball team and benches in two places, plus he said the floors would be heated throughout the bathroom, including in the shower. A gigantic jacuzzi tub nestled into the far end of the bathroom next to a huge window that shared the same view the living room had, just from one story higher.

"This is my dream bathroom. I'm declaring it. Right now." I ran a hand along the marble countertop with double sinks. Even the lighting was good. Perfection.

I looked up to find Jamie watching me, an odd expression on his face. "What?"

He shook his head, just barely. "Nothing. I'm just thinking this is my dream bathroom right now too."

Heat lit his eyes, and my pulse rocketed. *What did that*

mean? Something. It definitely meant something based on the way his focus intensified and my insides tightened. I stayed right there, unsure of what came next. He pushed off the door frame and came to stand right in front of me.

As he reached a hand up to brush my hair over my shoulder, his gaze slid over me, eyes hooded just enough to make me breathe a little faster. He leaned down, close enough that if I stood completely straight, our lips would touch.

Instead of finishing that short distance, neither of us moved. His eyes flared just slightly as he grabbed my hand and finally did breach the space to give me a quick, soft peck. "Time to go."

If he hadn't taken me by the hand, I might have stayed right there, still stuck in the mesmerizing glow that was Jamie Morris' up close and personal attention. I'd never been immune to it—not when I was thirteen, or seventeen, and not now, at twenty-six and apparently desperate.

After a few minutes in the car, I couldn't hold it in. "So... can you tell me why you're building a house?"

"I've owned this land for years. I bought it after I made my first real money, even before my house in LA. I have a partner I'm working with who knows more about this stuff, but we're developing this land into a residential area, and we're working on getting all the requisite paperwork in order for a small airport to make it accessible to the right people."

His hands gripped the steering wheel, then loosened as he took the curves of the canyon between Silver Ridge Peak and one of the slightly smaller mountains.

"So you're developing an entire neighborhood for super-rich people?"

He chuckled. "Basically, yes."

My thoughts flashed to Jonas Bauer's questions the week before. Did he know about Jamie's project? "Does Liam know? Or... anyone?"

"No." His voice emerged surprisingly short.

I didn't miss the tension in his jaw when I glanced over at him. "Is it a secret?"

It might have been my imagination, but I could have sworn he sighed as he ran a hand over his hair. "Yes... no. I don't know. *Kind of* is probably the best answer."

"Why would you keep this to yourself? It's amazing, and Liam is going to be thrilled at the thought of having a bunch of wealthy people up here drawing more tourists. Not to mention Jonas Bauer, who is probably chomping at the bit for this kind of news."

He didn't respond right away. I'd grown used to this to some degree, but it frustrated me, and also made me question my sanity for agreeing to date someone who refused to respond. Just when I'd almost given up my resolution to give him space and taken the dive to prod him into speaking, he beat me to it.

"Liam doesn't want my help."

I watched his profile. His lips turned down, brow furrowed, he seemed to believe it.

"You can't think that..."

"It's true. I offered to help, and he denied it. I know it's not coming from a bad place, but he's said more than once he doesn't want this to be temporary. He seemed to think if I'm involved, it'll only be a temporary fix—cash infusion, or whatever. But I've been working on this development project for a lot longer than the resort has been in trouble— or at least a lot longer than I've known it was in trouble."

"This is different than just tossing money at it though, isn't it?" It seemed very different to me anyway.

"I think so, but Liam will hear this news better if I've got more than my own home and my partner's to show for it." He glanced at me, then back to the road. "I don't want him finding out until we've got permits for the airport and at least another few lots sold. Without selling the lots, there's no way to have a firm date on when we'll have more people up here."

"I guess I can see why you'd want all of that settled before you tell him. But for what it's worth, I think it's awesome, and I know Liam will love it."

Liam and Jamie had always had a good relationship. Even the angst and pain I remember Jamie expressing in terms of his family and where he fit had never extended to Liam. But his unwillingness to share this huge project with him showed that wasn't entirely true—he wanted to earn his place in the family, even with Liam, and he'd evidently determined this would do just that.

"Thanks, Bel. Now, enough of this. Let's talk about you."

"I'm pretty boring, I hate to tell you."

The car came to a stop in a small parking lot just off the shoulder of the slim mountain road. A tiny log cabin-style building sat at the Elk River's edge.

"Let's go inside. You can tell me all about how boring you are, and I'll decide for myself."

CHAPTER TWENTY-NINE

Jamie

I hadn't planned to show her the house, but seeing her in it made me glad I did. Now I had to pray she'd keep it to herself.

She walked in front of me into the restaurant, her long hair swaying behind her in caramel waves that were nearly irresistible to me.

I'd always liked her hair. She'd kept it long since she was little, and as far as I could tell, it was natural—at least, it looked the same as it had years ago. No summer-blond highlights, but still that pure golden-brown color and so soft-looking. The few times I'd touched it, I'd confirmed the look matched the feel.

We were seated outside at Bel's request—the place had a gorgeous little deck that hung over the river cutting through the back of the property. A small bridge led over the water to a little natural garden with a large tree featuring a swing. The place was ridiculous—idyllic in a rustic, mountain way, but also kind of magical, like so many things up here in these mountains.

The restaurant was surprisingly full, though maybe not such a surprise since it was a Saturday. I kept my sunglasses on like a jerk as we walked through the interior and outside, though any chance the teenaged host would recognize me fled when he caught sight of Bel. He'd been entranced as soon as she'd flashed her smile at him and hadn't stopped tripping over himself as he awkwardly pulled her chair out and handed her the menu, never taking his eyes off her.

I couldn't blame the guy. I knew how he felt.

"This place is so cute. I haven't been here in years, but it's just the same." She smiled across the table at me, and I felt for the young host even more—she was mesmerizing.

"This is where I wanted to bring you that very first time we ended up at *The Elk*." I'd wanted to get her out of town, have her to myself, but the place had closed for summer break and we'd ended up at the restaurant where she worked six days out of seven. Real smooth.

"I'd wondered. They'd just opened back then, right?"

I nodded.

"I came here a few years later for the first time. And I always—" She stopped abruptly, looked out at the river.

I leaned forward on my menu. "You always *what?*"

Her green eyes turned back to me, a slight blush on her cheeks. "I always wondered if maybe this is where you wanted to go."

She ducked her head, studying the menu carefully to avoid my response, I supposed. I kept the raging jump of sadness and victory locked inside—sadness because I could have answered that for her. I could have kept in touch and changed so much about the way these years had passed.

And victory, because that meant, even years later, she'd thought about me.

The waitress swung by, barely a blur, and dropped a basket of hot, fresh rolls on the table and a "be right back for your orders." As we tore through the bread and soft honey butter, she delivered on her promise, and if she noticed who I was, she certainly didn't care.

One more reason to love it here.

"So you were going to tell me how boring you are," I prodded.

Bel finished chewing her roll, then sipped water. "I work at *Rise and Shine*, then I visit Gran on Saturdays, church on Sundays, repeat. I see Leo and Wells every few weeks, and other than that, I'm at home with Squish or going for a run."

"That sounds nice."

Part of me would give my left arm for that kind of routine, especially lately. I loved touring, performing, even recording, but I'd been ready for this break and it had come at exactly the right time. I didn't have anything else in me without some recharge time, and I'd very rarely taken that since I started years ago.

She raised one eyebrow.

"What? It does. It sounds like a nice routine—predictable, full of seeing people you love, doing things you like. I gather you don't feel the same?"

She fiddled with the fork in front of her, then leaned back as the waitress set down our dinner plates and practically ran to the next table before she spoke. "I know it's nice. It's just not quite what I thought life would look like, you know?"

The sadness in her voice rang clear, and my heart hurt for her. Even in the short time she and I had been friends that summer, I'd known she wanted to travel, get out of Silverton, have some adventure. It'd been one of the many things I'd liked about her so much—that like me, she had ambition to see more than just this small town.

"What did you think it would look like?"

She focused on her food—a hulking spicy chicken sandwich with shoestring fries piled almost six inches off the plate, before she responded. "I guess I expected there to be... more. Not like I need more money or a bigger house or even more people in it, I just... I thought I'd have done more, seen more, you know?"

Those green grass eyes of hers locked on mine, and I couldn't look away. I did know, though in almost exactly the opposite way she meant.

"I get it, though for me it's the reverse. I've done and seen... everything, essentially. I've been to every continent, met people from all corners of the world, done all the things I set out to do in the industry, but I often feel like I'm still nineteen, trying to find my way around my family, love, who I am in relation to those things."

I shoved my giant burger into my mouth to stop myself from talking. A bit more true confessions there than I'd planned, but all absolutely how I felt.

"Sounds like we need to trade," she said, a small smile making the words light.

I swallowed down the urge to tell her no—not a trade. A partnership. I could give her the seeing and doing. She could give me the relationships, the meaning, the love.

Too much to put on a person, of course, but I wanted it, and in that moment as we sat chowing on giant sandwiches at this weird little roadside mountain hideaway with the Elk River running under our feet, I wanted that with her more than I'd wanted anything in years.

Ridiculous.

It made no sense for me to want that with her, a woman I hardly knew anymore, and yet there she was, prettier than she'd been at seventeen because she'd grown into herself. More guarded, yes, but still soft, vulnerable, appealing to the part of me that never had these conversations with anyone else. Not even Liam—not really.

We chatted about more surface level subjects for a while after that, both sensing we'd dived deep and needed to take a breath before any more heavy material came out, when I noticed Bel's attention snagging on something behind me fairly often.

"Something wrong over there?"

She didn't hear me, but the more I watched her, the more uncomfortable she became with whatever she was seeing, until finally her face was red and she jerked her eyes to her now-empty plate.

"Bel, what is it?"

She heard me this time, and looked up, her face a study in embarrassment. "Uh, the couple behind us is... uh... really going at it."

"What?" I turned, stretched to one side of my chair, then the other, just enough to peek around behind us and *wow*.

"Wow. That's... a lot."

She chuckled, covering her mouth to stifle the sound. "So much. So so much."

This couple, definitely teens, were full on making out in their seats, hands roaming, tongues, hair a mess... truly a demonstration of teen hormones at work with no regard for context or propriety.

"Do you want me to say something?" I asked, laughing

at the delightful ignorance of the kids, and at Bel's reaction to them.

"No! No, don't say a word. I should be able to block it out, but it's just... it's *right there* and I can't seem to look away." She tucked her chin to her chest and her shoulders moved, signaling her silent laughter.

"Let's go across the bridge before we leave."

I stood, grabbed her hand, and led her across the little wooden bridge. The river was rushing up here, the spring run-off only barely getting started, but compared to midwinter, it ran wild. The sky had turned all navy blue and wisps of orange now, dark enough from the setting sun that the restaurant had turned on their fairy lights that laced along the railing of the bridge and into a few of the trees in the garden on the other side.

Her hand in mine felt right—a bit smaller than mine, cool from the chill in the air, and *hers*. That's what made it right.

"Thank you. Apparently, I'm not mature enough to handle teens making out." She shook her head and wandered ahead, releasing my hand.

"To be fair, they were really going at it. I've really only seen that level of... action, at parties."

Her head whipped to me. "Big party guy, huh?"

Something in her tone told me that wouldn't be a winning quality for her, and luckily, I could answer honestly. I walked to where she'd just sat on the little swing hanging from a giant oak, standing right in front of her. "Definitely not. Don't you know I'm a bit of an introvert?"

I slid my hands down to cover hers where they gripped the rope.

"I guess I did know you used to be."

Quiet, intimate, her voice spoke into me.

"I'm still that guy. Obviously, I've grown and changed—that's necessary for a person. But the fundamentals about me, the things you knew, those haven't changed."

Her lips pressed into a thin smile. "Did I know you?"

One hand rose to her face of its own accord—I had to touch her, be connected, in this moment. The things I'd wanted to say for so long now open for discussion.

Yes. Yes. Better than anyone.

Before I spoke, flashes lit up the space around us and then it came.

"OH. EM. GEE. IS THAT JAMIE MORRIS?"

CHAPTER THIRTY

Bel

Two teen girls were screeching—truly, genuinely *screeching* about ten feet from us where I sat on the swing and Jamie stood just in front of me. I could see them through the crook of his elbow where one hand held the rope. His other hand, that moments ago gently touched my cheek and caused a riot of butterflies in my belly, had now dropped, though he'd stepped marginally closer rather than away when we'd heard the girls' voices.

To protect me? Hide me?

"Oh seriously, no *seriously* Jamie Morris, I am one of your biggest fans. Well my brother was for a long time and then I stole his iPod and started listening to your stuff and now I'm obsessed because you are gorgeous and hot and so so talented and I just can't believe you're literally standing in front of me right now—"

"Allison, chill. You need to breathe and let him

respond…" The other girl grabbed the hyperventilating one by the arm to stop her rant.

"Give me just a sec," Jamie said quietly, running his fingers lightly over my shoulder before turning to the girls. "Would you like an autograph?"

A squeak emerged from one of them, the other nodding enthusiastically, and Jamie sweetly took a pen from an outstretched arm and signed the scraps of paper.

"Also, um, a selfie?"

"Of course."

The girls took turns getting photos with Jamie, who smiled and dazzled gamely for each shot.

"Thank you so much! Is that your girlfriend?"

"She's gorgeous."

"She's sooo pretty."

"But so, is she your girlfriend?"

Jamie coughed into his hand, then glanced at me, a crooked smile on his face now. "Not yet, but I'm working on it."

As he turned back to the girls who were in alternating states of swooning and squealing, the bottom dropped out from under me. The swing rocked back and forth as I held on and focused on a spot at the base of a tree a few feet in front of me.

Not yet, but I'm working on it.

Could that possibly be real?

I'd been nervous and excited for our evening, but at no point had I assumed this would go anywhere beyond a few fun dates, maybe some kissing, who knew. But nothing serious, nothing with real emotions tied up. Calling me his girlfriend, or even voicing that he wanted me to be… Unexpected.

Couldn't be true, though. Surely, he was simply putting

on a show for the girls, and he found it easier to say that than say I was some girl he used to know who he was on a date that led to nowhere with.

And yet...

I couldn't deny the pulse of pleasure at his response. *Not yet, but I'm working on it.* Some sick, self-flagellating part of me wanted it to be true. Sure, I'd have to walk away from him—given. But wouldn't it be nice to actually have him—really have Jamie as *mine*, even for a minute, like I'd wanted to all those years ago, and like I'd so often thought about since?

"Sorry about that."

His voice sounded close when he spoke, and I looked up to find him standing right next to the swing.

"Don't apologize. I love seeing you with your fans."

"They're not always that easy to get rid of, but they seemed to want to make sure I succeeded in convincing you."

He settled his hands over mine on the swing and stood close enough my knees jutted to either side of his legs as I swayed to a stop.

"Succeed?" My voice had lost its surety, and someone had replaced it with a thin wisp of a thing, practically useless.

But he stayed *close*. And he smelled so good. And his jeans brushing against the inside of my thighs, his warm hands folded around mine, his head bending to speak to me with that voice that was veritable catnip for women the world over... *oh.*

His blue eyes focused on mine. "Yeah, I've got to talk you into being with me. How's it going so far?"

I pressed my lips together to hide the thrill that would have shown on my face. He had to know he'd win—there'd never been any competition for him, and there certainly wasn't now.

"I'd say pretty well. It's just..."

One eyebrow quirked up, and he inched closer so we shared breath.

I tilted my head up so we were an inch apart, feeling my insides melt at his nearness even as I fought for some semblance of control in the situation. I couldn't kiss Jamie here in this romantic, perfect spot. I'd never be able to come back to this place for the rest of my life.

That thought kept me strong—kept me from closing the gap and taking the kiss I wanted, restaurant audience or no. Knowing I would be back someday, and it'd be without him —that he'd leave, off to travel and perform around the world, and I'd be left here.

I leaned back just enough to give myself space to think, to breathe. "If you really mean business, you better find me dessert."

His eyes never left mine, but he moved away slowly, deliberately, unwilling to break the spell between us even though I'd given it my best shot.

Eventually, once my blood pounded in my ears just from looking at him right there in my space, he let his arms drop to his sides and held out a hand.

"All right then, let's go get dessert."

The waitress had kindly kept our table so we sat right back down and shared an unnecessarily large brownie à la mode. Whatever magic Jamie'd done to me as we crossed that little bridge hadn't worn off—he'd become more magnetic, and I could not stop thinking about kissing him.

It had become a problem. I could hardly focus on the words he spoke because I wanted, to near desperation, to feel his lips against mine again.

"Do you think?"

Jamie's voice cut through the daze I'd lapsed into as I watched his delectable mouth shape words.

"Uh... huh?"

He chuckled, and a smile flashed before he tucked it away. "Sorry, I changed subjects. I asked if you felt like you knew me before—that summer. Going back to what we were talking about before the girls came over."

My pulse jogged at his mention of before. *Before.* As though it divided the line of our history, and yet it clearly did. And now, even after just a few hours with him, it seemed so silly that I'd ever let myself get so torn up by him.

But it wasn't that simple. Because what'd happened with him had happened right in the midst of so much else, and I could admit, at least in hindsight, much of the hurt I'd experienced and blamed him for could be traced to my parents too.

Enough of that.

"I did think so. But I revised my opinion about that when you treated me like a groupie and left."

Pain sliced across his face, and he reached for my hand where it rested on the table. I let him take mine in his warm one, and watched his face.

"I was an idiot. I thought I was doing the right thing, and even if Danny hadn't been the primary issue for me, I wouldn't have wanted you to wait. I wouldn't have been able to manage a long-distance relationship—not because I was partying or hooking up left and right, but because that next year—really, years—were the most terrifying, stressful years of my life. Of course I couldn't have known that, but I don't regret letting you off the hook. But I absolutely—and please, believe me when I say this," he paused, those blue eyes boring into me. "I am deeply sorry for hurting you like that and for failing to make it right for so long."

He'd apologized before, and it'd felt good, but this felt like my heart doubled in size—my chest ached, and my lungs swelled with a breath as I took in his sincere voice, his intense face, the clutch of his hand around mine.

"Thank you. Let's have this be the last time you feel you need to address that. I feel thoroughly apologized to, and I don't want to keep going back to that. But thank you."

He nodded, his eyes not leaving mine.

"And I have to say, it wasn't all you. It's embarrassing to admit how hurt I was, but I know some of it was bundled up in the fact that you'd been there for me as my parents left, and when you left, I lost your support and soon after, I lost Danny. I'd never felt more alone, and when I left Silverton, I did it wanting to set fire to any bridge back except for Gran."

I remembered the crashing, crushing feeling I'd had as I'd driven away from the tiny town, really all I'd known, and let the bitterness and disappointment fuel my desire never to go back.

"But you came back, and you stayed. Do you ever wish you could leave again?"

I licked the chocolate-covered fork and set it next to his long-abandoned one. "I did. I'm grateful I did because I do love this place, and even though it wasn't my plan, coming back and reconnecting to people here was healing—especially with Leo, who'd never been my closest friend and is definitely one now. But yes. Yes. I want to leave, and see, and do, like I said. I just don't know how to."

The waitress came before Jamie could speak, and he

quickly paid before we wandered out to the car, the sky fully dark and clear so the big and little dippers poured out their light as we crunched onto the gravel lot.

I stood to the side of the passenger door so Jamie could open it for me—he'd done that habitually, and I didn't fight it. I liked the small gesture to show me he'd thought ahead about me.

But instead of opening the door, he placed a hand on either side of me and stepped closer, boxing me into the car as he dipped his head and took my mouth in a kiss so unexpected, sweet, and lush, I couldn't remember how to breathe.

I pulled him closer at the waist and neck, pressed against him and let myself forget we were in a parking lot where anyone could see us. We'd exited the building to an empty exterior, and the almost non-existent lighting created a false sense of privacy.

Heat shimmered between us as the kiss built, but he pulled away before I forgot how to stand.

"You can't spend all of dessert looking at my mouth and not get kissed."

CHAPTER THIRTY-ONE

Jamie

I shut her door and rounded the car to my side slowly—I needed a minute to calm myself before climbing into an enclosed space with her.

I could feel it happening—that slipping, sliding toward her I'd felt so long ago. Familiar and terrifying, it'd felt the exact same way the day we laid under the tree by the pond and I'd kissed her.

At twenty-eight, you'd think I could handle myself. Something about Bel Paxton threw me off my game—and not *game* like I knew what I was doing, but rather just my ability to keep composed, to keep myself tucked away. She drew me out and made me want to slice open my chest and let her dig out my heart before we'd even had a third date, or technically fourth, if we counted our first time at *The Elk* years ago.

We drove in silence for a few minutes before I gave in to

the thought prodding at me and turned off to the development.

"I'm taking you somewhere before we head home. You don't work tomorrow morning, do you?"

"No. Did you forget something at the house?"

I shouldn't have been impressed that she recognized the turn, but the darkness alone would've kept me from finding my way, let alone if I'd been a passenger. I had absolutely no sense of direction unless I drove or navigated—if I simply rode along, I was hopeless. That'd gotten me lost in my fair share of cities over the years until I finally admitted it.

Of course, Bel didn't have the same issue—her observational skills were excellent, and I supposed it made sense that directional awareness counted amongst her tool kit.

"No, I didn't forget. I want to show you something."

I parked at the house and pulled a blanket from the back of the truck—I'd prepared for this, just in case the moment struck. Bel didn't seem antsy to get home, so I followed my gut.

I led her by the hand around the outside of the house to the back yard, then through the trees on a path, then down stone steps the landscaper had already brought in—he'd warned that if we waited until the grass grew in, he couldn't guarantee he wouldn't tear it all up. While I didn't love that answer, it meant the landscape team had finished this feature of the house.

Bel gripped my hand tightly as she walked, though the moon and stars were bright enough we didn't need flashlights.

I heard the soft intake of breath, then "Jamie," almost whispered, before I turned to see her face.

"This is incredible."

No lie. The stone steps led down a steep path that met a

wooden deck about twenty feet by twenty feet—the first of three decks and the largest. An in-ground firepit sat surrounded by wooden benches built into all sides. Eventually, I'd put a table and chairs here. The deck essentially hung off the edge of a cliff—the hill's intense grade made it so no one else would develop the land anyway, but I owned everything that ran down and a bit into the valley underneath.

Julian's genius design meant we'd built two more decks accessible with wooden stairs—we'd hoped for stone steps, but the ground was too steep to make that work. Next came a smaller deck for sitting, or something—I hadn't decided— and then the last deck featured space large enough for a hot tub. I'd never been huge on hot tubs, but Julian had insisted I'd be glad for it, and I figured I could always remove it if I didn't like it. The tub itself had been installed, as had the electrical wiring right along with the decks themselves, but the whole thing wasn't up and running—I hadn't realized how much I'd wish it was until this moment.

I moved to spread the blanket on this first level of the three-tiered deck. "It's my favorite part of the house, other than the trees."

We sat on the blanket and stared out at Silver Ridge, rising from the darkness of the valley up into the glinting starlight, white snow still covering the mountain in a sparkling blanket despite the warmer days we'd had.

"Whose idea was this?" she asked, scooting closer on the blanket so our shoulders touched.

"I wish I could take credit for it, but this was Julian's brainchild. He insisted that every house have total privacy as we designed lots, and carefully considered the natural landscape of each one. Then he also sketched out special features like this for each house based on the lot."

He really was a genius, even if I hated admitting it because the guy needed to be told about his intellect like I needed to be told I was good at guitar.

"Is he an architect?"

Her hand inched closer to mine on the blanket, and while I didn't look, my body took note. My pulse picked up, eager to see if she'd make the first move for once.

"No. He's more of a tech guy who's too smart for his own good. Plus I think he fell in love with the area when he visited a few years back, so this is like his little baby side project he works on to relax."

"Wow... that doesn't sound particularly relaxing."

I chuckled. "Apparently when you're a tech billionaire, designing other peoples' back yards is a fun hobby."

"*Billionaire?*" She pulled her gaze from the stars to look at me.

"Yes. He's... doing quite well for himself."

She watched me, brows raised, until we both started laughing. "Yeah, I guess he's doing okay."

"He's a good partner, and a pretty good friend too, though if you ever meet him, you'll see what I mean when I say he's... odd."

"I hope I do meet him," she said, looking back out at the view.

"Me too."

That simply, I felt my ribs ache with the truth of it. I wanted her to know my world. I wanted her to be the person who knew all my people, and who knew *me*.

"Bel, I—"

Her hand on my chest stopped me. Despite the thin sweater between us, her fingers resting against my pounding heart, now gripping the material like she wished it'd disappear, set fire to my lungs. The look in her eyes did nothing to quell it—the green of her irises dark, somehow heavy and purposeful in the moonlight.

I waited. I wanted her to the point of pain, but so far, everything had been up to me. She responded, but I needed her to show me her interest wasn't passive.

She hesitated, like she had something to say, but must have thought better of it because then she leaned up just as she pulled on my sweater, bringing me closer, and pressed her soft lips to mine.

All I needed—check! My hands found her jaw, her hair, fingers sliding over her delicate neck, and just when I had the thought, she must have too, because she pulled me with her as she lay down. I laced my hand into the hair at the back of her head to cushion her, holding her up as we rolled down to lay on the blanket, then combed gently through the strands once she rested against the deck.

She overwhelmed me, looking up with glittering eyes, moonlight shining in her hair spread out over the blanket.

"God showed off when he made you, Bel."

I gave her no time to respond. We crashed together, and everything in me tuned to the note that Bel struck.

Each kiss, each touch, wound us tighter together, 'til we felt each breath, each heartbeat of the other. What years of silent longing had built up now released between us—no amount of careful planning or measured steps could stop the wildfire lit between us.

What I did resist, what I miraculously did not say because it was far too soon, pulsed there in my chest, blazing away right with the heat between us. I kept it locked down, just that one thought, even as my lips and hands and body told her everything else.

CHAPTER THIRTY-TWO

Bel

Jamie's kiss tingled on my skin, the chilled mountain air cooling each place his mouth had traced as he move from my jaw, to my neck, to the line of my collar bone...

Buzz.

His fingertips glided along my side, inching upward in teasing circles—

BUZZ.

My eyes flew open, and I blinked against the bright light of what must have been morning—I very rarely woke after the sun had come up except in summer, and even then only just after sunrise.

I scrubbed a hand over my face as I sat up and grabbed for my phone. Ten after eight—*wow.* I couldn't remember the last time I'd slept that long.

Granted, I'd been up later than I had been since New

Year's Eve. After several hours enjoying the view, *amongst other things*, he'd driven me home after one a.m. We'd hardly spoken at my door, but he'd given me a quick kiss, a long hug, and said he'd call today.

Speaking of calls. I flipped to the missed calls in my phone's log and saw not Jamie's name, which made some sense since he'd probably sleep in, but rather, Gran's. I must've been sleeping so heavily I'd slept through several calls before this last one woke me.

A spike of alarm shot through me as I hit the call button. "Gran? I'm sorry I missed you. Is everything okay?"

"Ms. Paxton, we're calling to let you know we're going to admit your grandmother to the hospital in town. We're transporting her now."

"What?" I jumped out of bed and began pulling on clothes with shaking hands. "Are you—what's wrong?"

"Her cough has developed into a possible chest infection, and we don't want to wait too long and see this develop into full-blown pneumonia."

This person's ability to stay calm on the phone impressed, and I tried to absorb some of her calm.

"All right, good... which hospital? I'll be right behind you guys. Tell her I'm right behind her and I'll be there soon."

I hung up and ran to the bathroom to take care of the basics as quickly as I could, grateful I'd been too wired to sleep and had showered last night before bed. I dropped food into Squish's bowl and gave him a pat on his head as I rushed out the door, only to run into Jamie on my front walk.

"Hey, what's wrong?"

"It's Gran. They're taking her to the hospital. I'm

leaving now so I'm right behind them." I pulled keys out of my purse and kept walking.

He'd turned to follow me as I walked, and kept up. "Let me drive you. You shouldn't drive right now anyway. I've got plenty of gas—get in."

He shoved a bag under his arm and opened my door. Before I could think better of it, or protest, or anything, he'd handed me a tray with two drinks in it and a canvas bag I knew too well, and closed the door after me.

I told him which hospital, even though it'd be forty-five minutes until we made it down the mountain to the first bigger city, Ogden, and he grabbed my hand.

"She'll be okay. We'll get you there safely, and she won't be alone for a minute."

I took a slow breath, then let it out, slamming my eyes shut against the coming tears.

"There's coffee and pastries for you. Did you eat already?"

I opened my eyes, my gaze landing on the two to-go mugs from *Rise and Shine* and the bag he'd handed me. I peeked inside to find a pile of flaky croissants.

I cleared my throat, swallowed against the surge of sadness and sweetness that sight brought. "Thank you. Their phone call woke up me, so I basically threw on clothes, brushed my teeth, and ran out the door."

"They're getting her settled in the room and then you can go in and see her," the representative from Silverton Springs explained, completely unperturbed, professional and put together despite the crazy morning.

"Thank you. Thanks for calling and getting her here so fast." I'd be forever thankful for their attentive care of Gran.

"It was all thanks to your grandmother. She let the staff know she's been ill and we'd planned to check in this morning and evaluate. I hate to say it, but it likely would have been another eight or twelve hours before someone noticed if she hadn't spoken up. Even though we have great caretakers, our clients have to help us by communicating. Your grandmother is never shy, never afraid to advocate for herself."

The woman—Lorraine—who I'd met for the first time when Gran had been so sick years ago and had only seen once or twice since, smiled approvingly at me. I had nothing to do with Gran's self-advocacy, but I felt glad for it.

"Well, thanks for the way you run things there." I glanced around, ready to take a seat and wait as my small talk capabilities waned.

Jamie's hand rubbed a comforting circle between my shoulder blades, though he didn't speak.

"I'm sure you can take a seat and they'll call you when ready. I'm going to check on another client who's over in ICU. I'll be back in a few hours."

I slumped into the nearest chair, exhausted by the drive and the worry. I kept picturing Gran in this same place when she's been in the hospital and so sick she'd lost fifteen pounds in two weeks. She'd looked so tiny and frail and *old*, something I'd never seen her look until the day I blazed in here to find her. I prayed silently that this illness wouldn't progress into pneumonia, wouldn't take her from me.

"She'll recover, Bel. She's tough, and it sounds like they're catching this early." He took my hand in his and laced our fingers together.

"Thank you. Part of me knows that. The other part feels

so guilty for not bugging her more. I could tell she hasn't been quite right, but yesterday, I barely paid her attention at lunch because I was thinking about our date, and I should have noticed. I should have made her call the doctor, or something else—"

"But she did. She told them she might need help, they saw her, and they got her here. It sounds like she did exactly what she needed to. Don't get bogged down in guilt, especially not if there's nothing to feel guilty for."

He tucked a flyaway behind my ear, and I leaned over to rest my head on his shoulder.

"Thanks. I get that in theory, but I struggle not to feel responsible for anything bad that happens to her. She did so much for me as a kid and even these last few years... I just want her to be okay." I shut my eyes, willing away the tears that threatened.

A nurse in blue scrubs approached. "Ms. Paxton?"

I shot out of my seat, and Jamie came to stand next to me. The nurse smiled at me, then at Jamie before her smile faltered and her eyes widened. *Ah.* She must have recognized him.

"Um, uh, the room—you can go see your grandmother now. Room 106." She whipped around and walked back to the desk where we'd checked in as Jamie and I searched the hallways.

"I'll be right out here if you need me," he said, a little grin for encouragement on his face.

I moved around the door to find Gran all hooked up with an I.V. in her wrist and an oxygen tube in her nose.

"You needed an I.V.? And oxygen? Why didn't you tell me something was wrong yesterday—"

"Stop that, and come sit by me." Gran never did tolerate my spiraling, and I had to thank her for it. "I'm just fine, and

I didn't say much yesterday because I wasn't feeling so bad. But the night was a long one, and my cough got worse. The I.V.'s got the medicine to treat this chest infection so it doesn't blow up into pneumonia, and the oxygen is just because I was a little breathless after getting settled and having a coughing fit. I won't need it long but they're being cautious because... you know." She grimaced.

The look on her face melted me. I should have slunk into a puddle of love for her, right there at her hospital bedside, because her sass could not be tamed, not even when she was sick. Goodness, I loved her for that.

"Because you're *old?*"

She pursed her lips in disdain and nodded once. She hated the realities of aging and bemoaned them often, but when she was sick, she became particularly enraged by it, especially when things were done *because* of her age. All the while, she understood that treating geriatric patients like her and her friends was different than treating younger people with perfect immune systems and easier bounce-back, but still. This little slice of her spunkiness made my heart pulse with all the love I had for her.

"Jamie's out in the hallway. Do you mind if he comes in?"

Gran's eyes lit up. "Oh he is, is he? So last night went well? Did he come from your house?"

Sly one.

"Yes, very well. And no, he did not. He brought me croissants just as I left the house." I ignored the slight blush that rose to my cheeks.

She smiled, full-out. "Excellent. Yes. I do believe I'd like to see young Jamie in the flesh. It's been years, after all, and one never knows what kind of editing the news photos do..."

I hid my eye-roll at that comment and leaned out into

the hallway to find Jamie standing encircled by a half-dozen nurses and several people who must have been patients.

"Jamie?"

His eyes darted to me. "Be right there."

"Need help?" It must be overwhelming to be surrounded like that, but no one touched or crowded him too closely.

"I'll be fine. Be there in just a minute."

CHAPTER THIRTY-THREE

Jamie

Bel disappeared back into her Gran's room just as one of the nurses standing near me tucked something into the back pocket of my jeans. I moved to grab her wrist, but she didn't linger, thankfully. They didn't always remove their hands so quickly.

"Is it a family member, Jamie?"

"Don't ask him that!"

"Are you on vacation here?"

"When are you going to play Salt Lake again?"

The crowd chattered away as I smiled for photos and made small talk, careful not to answer any of the personal questions. Normally, I easily avoided sharing personal details—after this long, I'd conditioned myself accordingly, but I always found it challenging when my real life and my professional life ran into each other like this. It made those boundaries much more difficult to identify, especially without Bobby or Mac, my security guys, keeping people away.

Soon enough, a stern-looking head nurse arrived and shooed the group away. "I'm deeply sorry, Mr. Morris. Please excuse this breech in privacy, and I assure you it will go no further than here."

"Thank you."

Her ignorance at the way people behaved was admirable in that I could almost guarantee some gossip outlet would know I'd been here within an hour once one of the people I'd just chatted with tagged me on social media, but in the end, it didn't matter. It was a blip, and I could ask my assistant to post something of me in LA to counteract it in twenty-four hours if it became an issue.

I knocked twice and Bel poked her head out, then reached out a hand. The feel of her cold fingers in mine calmed the frustration in me. I loved meeting fans, but the number of times a woman had slipped her hand into my pocket was innumerable at this point.

I wanted to pull Bel into my arms and keep her there, warm her up and take solace in her while she did the same with me. But right now, I had to face down Bel's Gran, who was as much a force to be reckoned with as my Grandpa Will.

"Jamie Morrison, you've grown."

Ella Paxton sat straight in her hospital bed, three pillows propping her upright, and no amount of tubing or pallid skin could diminish her.

"Good to see you, Mrs. Paxton." Not my finest greeting, but at least I hadn't said *I hope you're feeling okay* like I'd been about to, as though she hadn't just been in an emergency transport to the hospital.

"Just call me Gran. You're dating my granddaughter."

Her tone was only slightly softer than severe, but the look on her face was all pleasure. She'd never been one to appear too serious.

"Yes ma'am, I am." I squeezed Bel's hand. She squeezed back, then pulled away to sit in the chair closest to the bed.

"And how's it going?"

I coughed just as Bel said "Gran!" but the woman in question did nothing except flutter her eyes and make clear she expected an actual response.

"Uh, well, that's probably a question for Bel, don't you think?" I looked to Bel, who'd tucked her lips together to hide a smile, her cheeks blazing, and realized she wouldn't be much help.

"I already know what Bel thinks. I want to know how *you* think it's going." She ran a weathered hand across her lap to smooth the sheet, then arched a brow at me.

I choked on a laugh, not at all surprised that this woman had a way of soliciting information I hadn't said aloud. "I think it's going really well."

Bel's eyes found mine, her smile bright, and my heart beat faster in my chest at the sight. Even worried, stressed, and tired, sitting in a frigid hospital room, she was the loveliest thing I'd ever seen.

"Good. I'm glad. Bel honey, can you get me some juice?"

Bel straightened. "Uh, sure. Jamie, do you want—"

"He'll stay and keep me company." Gran's green eyes pinned me to the spot—I got the message. She had something to say and wanted to say it to me without Bel in the room.

"Of course. We'll be here when you get back."

I leaned in to kiss Bel on the head as she passed me, unable to keep myself from touching her. She grasped my wrist as she went, then released me reluctantly, her hand sliding down my arm and past my fingers as her eyes stayed on mine.

"'kay. I'll be back."

When the door shut, I turned back to Gran.

"Have a seat."

Something in her tone had me wary. I might have been a bit nervous already, but I'd known Bel's gran for most of my life, and she'd always seemed to like me. But the hardness in her voice, the insistence on having me alone... only an idiot wouldn't be apprehensive now. I sat straight in the chair, my weight forward and my hands resting on my quads.

"Everything... all right?" My voice sounded younger, small.

"You tell me. What are you doing with Bel?"

Her brows canted down and gave her a more menacing look than I'd ever seen on her pleasant, usually very open and kind-looking face.

"Dating her. Getting to know her again after years without seeing much of her."

Gran's head bobbed slowly up and down, almost in slow motion. "And when you leave, then what? I assume you'll go back to LA or on tour or *somewhere* and leave Silverton behind again."

Leave Silverton behind again. A dagger. She couldn't possibly know the amount of shame I held for avoiding it for so long, let alone how poorly I'd left. But her aim was true. She'd identified not only the thing I felt worst about in my past, but also the thing I'd tried to ignore and shove away regarding my future.

I let out a breath. "I'll have to leave. I can't stay in

Silverton forever—I'm not ready to retire from music just yet."

"And Bel?"

How could I explain this? And how had I gotten myself into a situation where I spoke of these things with Bel's *grandmother* before we'd ever had the conversation ourselves?

"That would probably be up to Bel."

A brow rose again, and green eyes watched me. She must have been waiting for something—a sliver of doubt or maybe some sense that I didn't mean it. But no. Because after last night, even as premature as it was, I wanted Bel in my life. If things kept going the way they were, and I hoped and prayed they would, I'd want her with me all the time. Whether she'd be willing to brave what that meant, I genuinely didn't know yet.

Finally, she nodded, one definitive gesture that left her still staring me down, but with a pleased glint to her eye.

"Good. That's all I needed to know."

"What did you need to know?" Bel asked as she closed the door behind her.

"Just that Jamie values you, and he's not going to run away like he did last time."

Bel's head whipped to me as I chuckled, not entirely surprised Gran had found a way to throw me under the bus without actually revealing what we'd talked about. Crafty lady, that Ella Paxton.

I hopped up to give Bel the chair and slipped my hands in my back pockets to avoid sliding my hands through her hair or pulling her into a hug. I didn't know how Bel felt about PDA, and I certainly had never felt the desire for it, until now.

My fingers grazed the paper the nurse had slipped into

my pocket so I pulled it out and tossed it into the trash can near the bedside before moving away, but must have missed.

"Ready when you are." Bel's voice sounded hollow as she read the bright Post-It.

"Sorry. That's nothing. Chuck it." I didn't like the look she gave me—confused, a little hurt.

"Is this from one of the people you met in the hall a few minutes ago?" She held the paper between her index finger and thumb, barely touching it.

"Yeah. I'm sorry you saw it—it's garbage."

"You're sorry I saw it? What do you mean?"

I sighed, the pit in my stomach swallowing my calm. This was the part most women couldn't deal with. "Can we step outside a minute?"

Bel nodded, her expression moving more toward hurt and maybe angry as the door closed and I crowded her enough so I could talk as softly as possible. The hallway wasn't an ideal place for this kind of conversation, but I didn't feel like having it in front of Gran, no matter how close she and Bel were.

"This happens. All the time. I don't typically look at the notes because they mean nothing to me, just like I didn't look at that one."

Her eyes moved back and forth between mine, searching me.

"Do you believe that? Because if not—"

"I do. I trust you. I get that this won't work at all if I don't." Her expression didn't lighten though, and I wished I could pry into her head and see what thoughts had her mind running so wild. "I guess I should say I'm *learning* to trust you, and I trust you about this."

"Good."

I'd take that. Better than no trust at all—than the blatant

mistrust she broadcasted every time I'd seen her over the last few years until weeks ago when we'd started to settle that part of things.

"It's just..." she trailed off and turned to look both ways down the hall. "It's pretty weird. It's easy to forget that you're... *you* now."

The sinking feeling tugged at me, but I pushed it away. "Bad weird?"

A smile pulled at her lips before she let it loose. She rested one hand on my chest and reached up with the other to pull me to her, but stopped before we touched. "No. Not bad. Just weird. But I'm weird too, so it works out."

CHAPTER THIRTY-FOUR

Bel

Gran insisted I go home that afternoon. I didn't want to leave her, but I couldn't deny the small part of me that felt a raging relief at the thought of sleeping in my bed that night rather than the chair in her room.

Jamie had stayed the whole time. I'd told him more than once he could leave, but he'd insisted on staying. The doubtful, worried part of me said it was only because he knew I had no other way home, but the hopeful, rapidly falling for a guy I knew I shouldn't fall for part said he stayed because he cared.

Hard not to believe that. He'd gone to get us lunch, done whatever Gran asked even to the point of the ridiculous, which she'd done when she asked him to write a song for her. He'd chuckled and sung out a rhyming little verse that had had her blushing in no time.

As I lay in bed that night, I should have been thinking of Gran. The doctors said she'd likely be home tomorrow, just one night in the hospital, and she'd threatened my life if I came to visit again the next morning since she claimed she knew for a fact she'd be back in Silverton by dinnertime.

Maybe that's the reason I couldn't keep my mind on her. Instead, my brain ran through a flip book of all the small moments Jamie'd cared for me that day, starting with bringing me croissants and coffee that morning.

He'd waited with me. Rubbed my back. Held my hand. Humored my oddball boss of a Gran. He'd gotten us food, fetched drinks. He'd played with my hair as we listened to the doctor, until, as though he hadn't realized he was doing it, he'd jerked away and stuffed his hands into his pockets. He'd driven me home, offered to stop by the grocery, offered to make me dinner, offered to tuck me in...

Heat rose to my cheeks at the memory, and I smiled into the dark room. It'd been the perfect way to lighten a heavy kind of day—a long hug and sweet kiss at the door, and that offer—*"You know, I'd happily tuck you in if you need help getting to sleep."* But there was no fire behind it, no pressure, not even any real inuendo other than enough for comedic effect. We'd both laughed and I'd kissed him again, so very glad I hadn't spent the day without him, so thankful that he'd chosen to be with me.

I lifted my head and let it drop back into the pillow. *What am I doing?* I hadn't planned on feeling this much for him this soon. I'd thought I'd be able to extract myself, clean edges intact, but this would be messy. This would leave me limping for a while, even if everything went my way.

With a terrible night's sleep under my belt thanks to the sweet and sour thoughts about Jamie and a few worries about Gran, I stumbled into *Rise and Shine* and went through the motions until nine when I took an extended break to attend a meeting at Silver Ridge Lodge. I'd been summoned by Liam via voicemail the day before, and fortunately no one minded if I slipped out for an hour that late in the morning since things had died down. Sadie would be in the back still if Garrett needed help.

The skeleton crew version of the meeting today made me think everyone felt similarly bedraggled. Jamie hadn't made it, and even though I'd known he had a meeting with someone related to his property development project, I still deflated a bit when he didn't show. But Liam had energy to spare somehow, Jonas Bauer took his usual seat and gave off absolutely no sense of what he was thinking, and Leo vacillated between total, irritated silence and brilliant ideas for the upcoming summer celebration.

"You have all the design done, right Bel? We'll start soft promos in the media in about six weeks so I want to make sure we have everything perfect."

Liam's enthusiasm had increased exponentially the closer we got to summer. I wondered if it was more due to Jonas' increasingly large role in things which seemed to free him up bit by bit, or if it stemmed from the not-so-secret promise he'd made himself to hand off the resort if the summer season and celebration in August went well.

By the end, we'd identified due dates for all final design and marketing materials, we'd assigned to-do lists, and just before Liam dismissed the group, Danny rushed in, ruddy-cheeked and smiling as usual, and apologized for being late. Though his primary obligations were focused in the winter months, his summer and fall jobs around the resort tended to be cutting and maintaining trail so the summer hikers enjoyed their time, at least as far as I knew.

"You're heading up talking with local sponsors, right Dan?"

Danny nodded, and I eyed Leo. She made a face that said she was surprised and impressed too—Danny wouldn't usually take on something that big.

"I've got a list, but you can help me. I'm going to try to get commitments before mid-April because I know a lot of the early summer events already have people lined up. This one's a big deal so I feel like it shouldn't be too hard, but you never know."

Danny leaned his elbows on the table and got that Morrison look—that's the only way I could describe it. Each one of the Morrisons right up the chain to Grandpa Will got that look—determination mixed with a kind of elation at finding a situation that required it. I hadn't seen it on Danny's face much, to be honest, but he'd get it sometimes when talking about a ski run he wanted to best back in junior high or something like that. A thrill ran through me at seeing him like this—for him, and for Leo, who often bemoaned him *wasting himself*.

Before long, Liam adjourned the meeting, and I turned to Danny. "You're taking on a lot."

He smiled. "For once."

I winced, and he chuckled. "Go on—you can say it. I've begun to realize just how easy I've had it, but how unsatisfying that is, in the end."

"That's amazing. I'm glad for you, Danny."

He beamed back at me, that bright, genuine smile just as captivating and endearing as it always was.

"Anything you'd credit for the change?"

I'd been wondering about him for a while now—between what Jamie'd told me about his discussion with Danny weeks ago, to the way he'd been physically present at most of the meetings, to this kind of thing when he'd open up about being less than engaged in the past, I'd definitely noticed something had changed.

Like always, Danny's face flushed, his cheeks downright raging red.

"A front row seat to Liam's near-break-down these last few months has been a contributing factor. Burying the hatchet with you and Jamie has been another." He gave me a close-lipped smile.

I nodded, urging him to keep talking since we so rarely did anymore, plus I could tell there was something else.

"And also... I think it's time for me to grow up. Everyone else has, or is working on it, and I've been stuck. I thought I wanted it that way, but I'm finding... other things I want."

That smile tugged wider, and he blasted me away with his toothy charm yet again. His happiness radiated from him, absolutely a thing to behold.

"I'm glad for you."

"Ms. Paxton, could I speak with you for a moment?" Jonas stood between where Danny and I still sat at the conference table and the wall.

"Of course." Everyone else had left the room.

Danny popped out of his seat and patted Jonas on the shoulder with a mumbled *"see ya man,"* as he left, shooting me a nod and wink, while I gathered my things and then stood to find Jonas had stepped back to allow me space to scoot out my chair and exit without bumping him.

"How can I help?"

He came to a stop before we reached the door of the conference room and stood straight, strict as always, his eyes wandering for a moment before they settled on me. I'd thought we'd talk as we walked, but evidently, he wanted to stay in the room.

"I need information."

Hmm. "Um, what kind of information? I can send you the slides I did—"

"About Mr. Morris' project."

My mouth went dry. Jonas was intimidating enough, but he clearly wanted some news and had decided I knew about it, despite my making clear I had no idea what he was talking about the last time he mentioned it. But now, I did have it. And from what I understood, I shouldn't share it.

Jonas prodded again. "I know he's working on something. It'd be a huge help both for the development here and for reassuring the investor that he's not the only one engaged in improving the area and bringing more traffic. It'll dignify all of this, and encourage even more investment on his part, possibly. Knowing a few details, even, could make a fine difference."

I exhaled through my nose, my teeth clenched against speaking. As much as I disagreed with Jamie about keeping this all under wraps, and as much as I knew for a fact Liam —and everyone else for that matter—would rejoice once they heard Jamie and Julian Grenier were working to culti-vate the high-dollar neighborhood and small airport, Jamie'd made clear he didn't want anyone knowing about it. I could understand Jonas' perspective, and his expertise on the matter was glaring, but I acknowledged the knot in my stomach and knew saying anything would be a mistake.

I folded my arms tightly at my chest around my laptop and notebooks. "I'm sorry. I don't have any information for you."

Truth. I lived by a no lying if at all possible policy and felt better about this answer. I couldn't outright deny knowing about the project, but I could definitely say that I didn't have information for *him* since Jamie didn't want me telling anyone... even if it made no sense to keep such a positive, exciting thing under wraps.

Jonas' eyes flickered back and forth between mine for a moment, and the air went heavy. I thought maybe he'd ask again, keep pushing.

Instead, he nodded once. "Thank you for your time," and he was gone.

How long he'd let that answer lie, I couldn't guess. Jonas' persistence stood out as one thing we'd all come to admire about him, and I had a feeling this persistence might very soon be directed at me.

CHAPTER THIRTY-FIVE

Jamie

el, Bel, Bel.

All I thought about. All I dreamed about. Definitely all I wrote about—which, hey, at least I'd been writing. The first few weeks back had been utter silence, but lately the songs tripped out of me.

Funny enough, sitting by the giant oak near the swimming hole where we'd first kissed, I remembered all the times I'd written songs about Bel. Not all that many had made it to recording, but a few had, and all of them were my more angst-filled, brooding ballads. Very popular with the ladies—apparently the lovesick, heartbroken Rockstar appealed to the masses.

But now, the songs about Bel had nothing to do with brokenness. They had everything to do with a sense of grace, of wholeness, and hope. The pairing of being *home* and beginning to feel like I did actually belong there, at least part of me did, and getting to sew up all the wounds that'd been gaping for too long... the sweetness of this reality provided the perfect fuel for writing.

Both happiness and misery were excellent muses. Today as I sat in the shade with a notebook and my guitar, a cool spring breeze rustling the newly sprouted buds on the trees and the mountains towering around me, I could easily say I preferred happiness.

Especially when that happiness came from all angles. I didn't have closure with the family—I hadn't gotten there yet, but I could feel it coming. Julian had called to let me know he had a small party of interested buyers coming to see lots as soon as we got the airport fully approved, and he expected that to be in the next few weeks. I had no idea what strings he'd pulled to make that happen, but there would be a nice influx of tourism, regardless of our neighborhood planning, if high-end skiers could charter flights in and out during the season.

I strummed along aimlessly for a while, grasping for a melody that was just out of reach, but my phone jarred me from the song.

"Hey Chad." My manager, of course. He hadn't checked in this week.

"Jamie. When are you done there?"

I shook my head and implored the sky for patience even as I said, "End of summer, as you know."

"Not homesick? Your house in LA is ready any time you come back."

"I'm good, Chad. What do you need?"

No pause, no shift, and fortunately, no attempt to talk me into coming back early this time, or so it seemed. "I'm confirming studio time. Have you in late August, yeah?"

"Yes. I'll be there then—send Katie the dates exactly so

she can book a flight back a few days before so I'm not dehydrated or tired."

After four albums, the prep for recording had become automatic. I'd tried to jump off a plane and dive into recording the next day, and it had never worked. Even a short flight like SLC to LAX would kill my energy and had the potential to spoil the first day or so—no sense in rushing it.

"But remind me—you're still doing a few festivals, right?" The impatience in his voice rang clear.

"Yes. I committed to one in Germany and one in the UK in June, I think. You should know. I'm doing two shows each, and I'll bridge between them so I'm only gone for a week or so altogether. Make sure the band is scheduled to arrive at least forty-eight hours before so we can practice—"

"Is this my first rodeo? Are you my first client? Did you just barely start, or is this Jamie Morris, my client of almost a decade, the kid who I've grown and nurtured into an international star?"

He had an outburst like this during any given conversation, particularly if I questioned him or insinuated in any way he might not automatically do something.

"I know you're good at this, and you've got the bases covered. That's one of many reasons I can take this big break, and I'm thankful, Chad. But this is also the longest I've ever gone between concerts—practicing isn't something we normally schedule out, so I thought—"

"Just stop. I am fully aware and partially horrified that you'll be going something like six months between concerts. You'll go perform at these festivals and choke on stage over my dead body."

I scrubbed a hand down my face. Chad handled the

stresses of the job well, but his flair for the dramatic could be exhausting. "Great. Thanks for looking out for me."

We said our goodbyes just as Bel walked up.

"How are you doing?"

She wore what she must have worn to work—jeans and a white T-shirt—nothing spectacular, but when those very basic items were on Bel, they made magic because she was.

I'd spent time in rooms full of the world's most beautiful people, but I'd never felt for anyone what I felt for Bel. Never once. Not what I felt before, and not what I felt now. There's just no comparing anyone to her.

I hopped up and set my guitar down just as she reached me. I wrapped her in a hug and indulged in small kisses from the collar of her shirt to her ear, breathing in her sweet scent as I went. "I'm perfect now."

She touched her forehead to my temple. "Are you sure? I don't want to interrupt you."

I pulled back to level her with my most sincere look. "I want you with me all the time. I absolutely and with all certainty do not want you to leave, nor do I think of you as an interruption."

She swallowed, and her lashes fluttered. Something like wonder, or maybe just surprise, crossed her face. "Okay."

Was it that surprising I wanted her here? She must not have any idea how much I felt for her—clearly she didn't. I'd have to rectify that. Maybe right now.

"Bel, you know, what we're doing here... for me, it isn't just for old time's sake." I pulled her to stand in front of me in the shade, my back against the giant tree.

Her green eyes—more bright emerald today thanks to the leafing trees and sprouting grasses all around us— searched my face. Smooth eyebrows arched down as she studied me.

"What are we doing here, Jamie? Dating? Just having fun? Biding our time 'til you leave? I've been trying to figure it out."

My pulse rocketed in my veins—now? I hadn't planned on a discussion like this today, but here came an opening I couldn't deny. *Should I tell her now?*

I lifted a hand and let my fingers sweep along her jaw, my thumb brush over her cheek. I could feel her breathing where she now leaned against me. "I—more. It's more for me, anyway."

She swayed closer, now chest to chest, and touched her lips to mine, retreated. Then again. A trill of need arched through my body, and I hugged her closer, my hand in her hair, at her jaw, my arm a bar against her lower back urging her closer. She kept up with me, her hands seemingly as eager as mine, but far sooner than I would have chosen, she pulled back.

Her gaze heavy on me, eyes moving over me, her chest rising and falling almost dramatically, she then closed her eyes and let out a sigh before slipping out of my grasp and pacing away.

I scrubbed my hands over my face and walked in a small circle next to the tree, working to find my breath and steady my thoughts. She scrambled my brain just by being near me, let alone touching me. Add any kind of intimate contact, and my ability to reason or form words disintegrated, apparently.

When I finally stopped and looked up, she stood waiting for me, arms at her side and face calm, but serious.

A warning sounded in my head. I'd thought she'd pulled away because the kiss had grown into a bonfire yet again and she didn't want me to start stripping her clothes there in the daylight on a fairly well-trod path, but no. That thought couldn't have brought this look to her face.

My slowing heart rate spiked again... had I gone too far? Had telling her it was more for me mere days after our second date this side of our age-old drama ruined any hopes of her eventual reciprocation?

CHAPTER THIRTY-SIX

Bel

I couldn't make the words form on my tongue.

I couldn't make anything happen—nothing worked but my eyes, which greedily took him in standing ten feet from me. His hands on his hips accentuated the muscles that corded every part of him. His golden skin looked warm—was warm wherever I'd touched—in the sun. Lips curved down into a somber arch. Brows pinched in the middle.

Eyes... frantic. Wild from our kiss, but now subdued as he took me in just as I did him, wary.

He didn't seem to realize I couldn't return the sentiment—I couldn't say this meant more to me than something casual. I couldn't verbalize those feelings no matter how much I felt them. If I did, I'd give up any shred of power I might still have, and if I did that, I'd never be able to walk away.

He hadn't declared his love, but the thought that this was anything more than dating meant we were on the road to getting there.

No way to deny it—we had too much history, and our lives had intertwined too much, even with our time apart. Just the few weeks together with him had shown me that. We wouldn't need months on end to fall in love—no. I wouldn't.

I swallowed that thought, pushing it down and away from the forefront of my mind.

"You okay?" His voice came tentatively.

I moved to him. I didn't want him to worry, and the more distance I placed between us, the more likely he'd realize I hadn't said I felt the same, and might ask. If he asked me, point blank, could I lie to his face?

Would I?

"Of course." I took his hand in mine—I loved that left hand, its fingers just a bit more calloused than his right from years forming chords on the frets of his guitars. I willed a smile, something small and light. "If you kept kissing me like that, we'd be in trouble."

He studied me, clearly unconvinced that my concern centered on the kiss, but must have decided whatever I was thinking didn't need pushing right now. Thank goodness.

"My sincerest apologies. I will only offer you smiles and handshakes from now on." He took his hand from mine and made a dramatic old-timey bow.

I laughed. "If you must."

My head fell back against the couch, and Squish's purr escalated. That small movement of my head bumping into something in his vicinity perked him up—fortunately this time, it was a purr and not a swatting tail. I smoothed a thumb over the fur between his ears and his pleased cue intensified, a little box of furry thunder.

"That's all you get, or you'll go crazy on me," I whispered, knowing another second or two and he'd be forced by his feline nature to punish me for paying him so much attention.

I'd hugged Jamie, kissed his cheek, and left him to his writing. That had been days ago. Since then, we'd messaged, talked on the phone, and he'd joined me for my lunch break in the little garden behind *Rise and Shine*.

I'd worried things would be strained since my reaction the other day had been strange—I could admit it. I'd asked him the question—what were we doing? When he'd answered honestly, it had set me ablaze. But just as quickly, I'd recognized the absolute wretchedness that would come if I let myself hop, skip, and jump down that path like I so desperately wanted to.

He'd let me go, buying my excuse that I had marketing work to do, and I'd left. I'd felt terrible the whole walk home, but the reality that I did have marketing work to do had helped. I wanted to spend all my time with him, but down that path lay danger.

So I'd trudged home feeling too many things to land on —elated that he saw us as *more*, but destroyed because as much as that sounded lovely, he couldn't mean it. Exhilarated to have him want more even if it didn't make sense, then crushed knowing I couldn't let myself feel the same and survive our inevitable ending.

Fortunately, the work for the library and Silver Ridge Lodge took hours, so I'd genuinely been busy every day after my time at the coffee shop. By Wednesday, Jamie had asked if he could bring me dinner while I worked, but I'd been knee-deep in projects and wanted to power through. I wanted to see him, but knew it was best to take a breath as I let my heart settle a bit before I saw him again in any intimate setting.

He'd insisted on a date that weekend, saying he'd come and go with the setting of a timer if that's what I needed. It was what I, for some reason, never expected from him—sweet. Thoughtful. Considerate. He demonstrated it over and over again, yet it continued to surprise me. Perhaps I'd spent so long thinking poorly of him that now accepting he had been and still was *sweet* had become difficult. It almost defied logic that he *could* be sweet at his level of stardom.

I agreed we'd spend Saturday after my lunch with Gran together. By the time I arrived at Gran's after getting to a stopping place that morning, I knew I'd have to confide in her about Jamie. I couldn't see him that afternoon with this pent-up feeling.

Gran sat at her small dining table, a glass of iced-tea next to her, a book in her hand. She glanced up, took one look at me, and arched a penciled-in brow. "Spill it."

I set the big bowl down in the middle of the table, pulled off the plastic wrap, and dished out the salad I'd made us for lunch, then set hearty multi-grain rolls from the shop on our bread plates. I filled my glass with water, and since she already had tea, sat down and placed a napkin in my lap.

When I looked up, she sat ready, waiting.

I exhaled dramatically—Gran really brought that side of me out, even though I liked to think it was a fairly small side.

"Jamie said he thinks of us as more. I don't understand why he'd say that even though I was glad to hear it."

Her lips twitched.

"What?"

She let out her smug little smile. "I knew it. I knew this would happen, and I'm so pleased."

"Knew *what* would happen?"

She sipped her tea and took up a fork. "I knew you'd fall for each other. Now you just have to get over the logistics."

I ignored the falling for each other part of her comment. "The logistics are exactly the problem. He doesn't live here. I do. He travels the world constantly, and I stay in one place. And honestly, I have no interest in being in a long-distance relationship indefinitely."

Gran finished chewing, swallowed, set down her fork. "That's a very pretty excuse you have there, Isabel, but I'm afraid I can't let you go on thinking it's anything but an excuse."

I opened my mouth to respond, but found it void of words.

She continued. "You can go anywhere, do anything. Just because life hasn't looked that way to this point doesn't mean it shouldn't look that way now."

My time at Gran's had been short. Her words had shaken me from my frustration and impressed me with a kind of ponderous quiet as we finished eating and I left to get ready for Jamie.

Just because life hasn't looked that way to this point doesn't mean it shouldn't look that way now.

She thought it that simple, didn't she? That I should just change everything for this man who, yes, I'd known all my life and yet hadn't even dated more than a month? And honestly, that all assumed he wanted me beyond the here and now. Yes, he'd said it was more to him, but what did that really mean? He could very well be thinking that yes, he felt something for me, and it was more than just casual dates, but that meant nothing in terms of commitment, a future, *anything*.

I'd tortured myself with those thoughts for the two hours between leaving Gran and Jamie's knock on my door. By the time I pulled it open and saw him, broad shoulders blocking the bright sun to the west of the house, one strand of hair hanging down into his eyes, I'd decided—I would figure out a way to have this discussion sooner than later. *Tonight.*

Yes, tonight, I'd bring it up. I'd get him to say what he wanted, and how long he wanted it. Then I could put my concerns to bed—he'd say while he lived here this summer, and I could wash my hands of all these swirling emotions making me read more into what he'd said, everything he did, the way he looked at me now like he'd been waiting months just to set eyes on my face.

CHAPTER THIRTY-SEVEN

Jamie

Julian would be here in ten days. I needed to write at least three more songs before he showed up and took over my life with his expectations and whoever he planned to bring with him beyond Jack McKean, who Julian had at the top of his list. If everyone else was like Jack, we'd be fine, but I had a feeling it'd be a long list of high maintenance fancies. My parents would be home not long after that, and then I'd be off to Europe for the festivals.

But first, Bel.

I had to figure out what had happened the other day.

I'd stopped by her work and we'd had lunch—pleasant. Delightful, even, considering just being in her proximity without all that angst that'd hung over us for years made me feel lighter, happier, than I had in many years.

Except for the nagging feeling that she'd lied to me after

we'd kissed days ago—or if not lied, then shied away from being fully honest. I'd *felt* something there—some drop in the atmosphere that meant big things were about to happen, and yet she'd sauntered over and acted like it had been all about the intensity of the kiss.

Like an idiot, I'd promised her I'd only smile and shake her hand, and aside from giving into kissing her on the head and cheek when I'd seen her at lunch, I hadn't touched her otherwise.

This, a small form of torture.

But I'd always wanted to make sure Bel chose me without pressure, without obligation. Part of me worried that our history created a kind of obligation. Yes, we had chemistry enough to power a jet engine, and I would bet the attraction I saw in her eyes when she looked at me came naturally.

I wanted her to want me the way I wanted her. I wanted her to show that to me. And I'd realized, only after she'd left me alone to strum aimlessly on my guitar like a perfect little cliché, that she hadn't said what she thought we were. She hadn't said she thought we were more, like I had—nor had she said we were only dating, biding time 'til I left, etc.

And that had created my agenda tonight. I couldn't be sure she'd avoided me all week, but I knew, at least in some small way, that had played a part in her being so busy she couldn't even take an hour to have me drop off food one evening.

Honestly, a large part of me liked that about her—she wouldn't cow to me. She wasn't impressed by me. She wouldn't clear her agenda for the foreseeable future in order to cater to me, my needs, my schedule. I'd had plenty of opportunity to be with women like that, and it'd never become more appealing. Whit Grantham's life had been just as insane as mine, and maddening as that proved to be, it'd been a relief not to find a woman I'd dated a handful of times virtually waiting by her phone for my beck and call. If only Whit and I had been right—but we simply weren't anything more than friends.

The other part of me felt a kind of madness at being denied Bel. Didn't she realize we were on a timeline? Didn't she know I had shows to play and obligations elsewhere, and our time *now* was all we could bank on?

The ugly truth. I both delighted in her refusal to be amazed by me, and yet, frankly, it drove me insane. I could have used just a bit of her being willing to do what I wanted, to accommodate me, so that we could get into whatever was bothering her, and then past it.

So, by the time Saturday afternoon came and I stood on her doorstep, the grip I had on my emotions slipped when she opened the door—all the wanting, the longing, the frustration waited for just a glimpse of her.

She swung it open just seconds after I knocked, and her caramel hair fluttered in the warm breeze that blew past me into her house. I stepped up, over the threshold before the door opened fully, and my hands were in her hair, my eyes staring into her green ones, before she could speak.

"Please tell me I can kiss you." It wasn't a question.

"Yes, please do."

I took the kiss—branded her with my mouth, my touch, right there with her front door wide open. Someone would see, but no one would care—or if they did, so be it. *I* didn't care anymore.

I pulled back, intending to close the door and continue, but she jumped a bit and laughed as she touched a hand to her cheek.

"Good to see you too, Jamie."

I shook my head as I stepped fully inside after her and closed the door. She stood in her living room watching me, maybe wondering if I'd kiss her again. I wanted to.

I desperately wanted to.

But first, the words.

"Bel, I think we need to sit and talk through some things."

Surprising that I didn't flinch at my smooth delivery there, or at my easing into the subject. But the long week between real interactions, between honest discussions, had propelled me to this point. I'd started to feel the ticking clock of my schedule and I wanted... certainty.

"Let's sit." She gestured to the couch.

I sat at the edge of a cushion, not even feeling the pull of the cat sprawled belly up on the back of the couch. Bel sat next to me, back straight, knees pressed together and hands resting on them.

Where to start? I knew where I wanted to go, but how to begin?

"Do you have some specific things you wanted to discuss?"

I could hear a small quaver in her voice—a little blip that told me I'd made her nervous with the pronouncement and then my subsequent unwillingness to actually talk with her.

I cleared my throat and pushed the hair out of my eyes, attempting to tuck it behind an ear, but it was too short—the one random strand that wouldn't fit all the way into the bun I wore every day.

"I'm not sure where to start."

Bel's lips pressed together, likely stifling a smile. Good grief, she killed me with those hidden smiles.

I chuckled at myself, letting some of the odd tension in my shoulders go with the laugh and ran a hand through my hair again. "Sorry. I just got nervous."

"Why would you be nervous? I can't imagine that's a very common feeling for you anymore."

"True. Not professionally anyway." I raised a brow at her and gave her an embarrassed smile. *Good Lord man, just start talking!*

I scrubbed my hands over my face and shook my head, feeling ridiculous and young and inept. A hand on my quad had me looking up.

"Jamie, what's going on?"

Her lovely face was pinched with worry now. I'd done an excellent job of drawing this out and making it as painful as possible. *Great.*

"Sorry. I'm sorry—I know I'm making this weird." I took a deep breath and covered her hand, still on my leg, with mine. "I want to talk about where we're going with this— you and me. I told you last week that for me, this means something, but I'm not sure what you think or want and... I hope you'll tell me."

She paled, visibly and immediately, and my heart sank.

"I... I care about you, Jamie."

Not a bad start. Not bad news... but her voice, her whole demeanor seemed regretful.

"Good. I care about you too," I confirmed, yet again, and wondered if she could tell how feebly the phrase *care about* described my feelings for her.

She pulled her hand to her lap and folded it together with her other one, all her attention on her hands and no longer on me. "I just... I guess I don't understand where this *can* go."

A fissure that had opened when I'd realized she hadn't

reciprocated last weekend cracked wider. But she didn't say she didn't *want* it to go anywhere else, but rather that she didn't know where it could.

I could clarify. I could fix this rapidly derailing train.

"Bel, baby, look at me." I took her hands to cradle in mine, wanting to pull her to me, hold her, close this dreadful gap between us, but I couldn't do that yet.

Her green eyes found mine, and my pulse ticked up again at the sight of the sadness, the uncertainty there.

"I want to be with you—not just here and now. All the time. *All the time.*" I let my focus press into hers, willing her to understand, to see, to believe.

"How?"

A sliver of relief snuck in then. She wanted this—she did. She just needed to know we could make it work. We could be together even though we hadn't been for so long.

"I'm here most of the summer—I'm only gone about two weeks in June, but then I'm back 'til August. After that... we'll see. What you want to do, and what feels right, but..." I swallowed back the nerves. "You could come with me."

"I—" She stopped, all kinds of indecipherable emotions crossing her face. "In June?"

"Yes, absolutely."

I said it automatically, but *yes*. That would be amazing. Having her with me would be a dream—not so lonely, and we could swing through Paris—I could buy her fresh-baked French croissants and kiss her at the Eiffel Tower and show her all my favorite little parts of the Left Bank.

"Yes. You can take time off, take a trip. As long as you don't mind me having to work, it'll be amazing. I'll actually have a fair amount of free time because I only play a few shows, it's just not worth flying back and forth."

She stared at me now, mouth slightly open. I watched as

the idea took root and her disbelief and surprise turned to joy, her lips curving up as a laugh emerged.

"Uh, okay."

"Okay? You'll come with me?" I pressed her hands closer to my chest—could she feel my heart thumping under my skin?

She nodded, laughed. "Yes, I'll come with you."

She pulled her hands away and threw herself into my lap, arms around me, face pressed to my neck.

My eyes closed as I savored the feel of her there, the sense of home and peace and release that settled in my whole being when she relaxed into me like this over-whelming everything but the twinge of worry I pushed away.

It didn't matter that she hadn't said anything about after the trip in June—maybe that was too much, too soon. I could understand that. We'd take it slow, go easy. She'd get a great vacation. And I'd show her what life could look like all the time.

CHAPTER THIRTY-EIGHT

Bel

Leo and Wells sat across from me, identical expressions painted on their faces.

"He asked me to go with him."

Brows raised, mouths slightly open, they must have looked just how I did when he'd said it.

"He asked you to go with him on his trip to Europe in less than a month?" Leo leaned forward, hands pressing into the table.

"Yes, he—"

"Here we go ladies. Anything else we can get for ya?" The waiter at *Basta* set down our dishes, each piled high with steaming, fresh, glorious pasta.

"We're fine, thanks." Wells offered a kind smile, no doubt in order to counter Leo's glare. Leo tolerated an interruption about as well as a root canal.

"You were saying..." Leo nodded, twirling pasta onto a fork.

"He asked me to go with him. He's there for like ten or twelve days, but then he only has like four shows or something. I'm not totally sure but he said he'd have more free time than a regular tour." I inhaled a steaming breath. "Am I crazy for considering this?"

Wells piped in. "Absolutely not. I think you'd be insane to miss it."

"Agree. But... what then?" Leo shoved her mouth full of pasta—some kind of spicy shrimp fettuccini I couldn't recall the name of.

Of course, Leo would be the one to verbalize what I'd been thinking every minute for the last four days.

"I don't know. He keeps trying to talk about it, and I just... I don't want to. I don't know why I can't face it. I've already made up my mind about how things are going to go from my end anyway, so it doesn't even—"

Leo jumped in. "What does that mean?"

I stuck a forkful of whole wheat penne into my mouth to avoid answering right then, chewing methodically as my mind raced through whether I should tell them the agreement I'd made with myself.

"Bel, what do you mean you've decided how things are going to end?"

Wells wasn't one to push me—she seemed to have an innate sensitivity to pushing, probably because she'd been pushed so forcefully in her previous relationships. I'd always love Liam for being a man who didn't push her in that way.

I swallowed the delectable pasta, though sadly, the flavor dimmed in comparison to how delicious it usually tasted. After a sip of water, I told them.

"I can't be the one to be left this time. It hurt too much, and for too long last time...every time," I said quietly. "So when I accepted Jamie's suggestion that we date, I decided I'd only let myself do it if I ended it before he could. I'd always planned to end things before he left on that trip—clean break, give us both time away."

Wells looked thoughtful, while Leo looked... scary.

I continued. "I don't want to hurt him, of course I don't. But, especially before we spent time together, I couldn't believe I *could* hurt him. And I know he cares for me, but I'm still not sure I could. But..."

I couldn't admit any more. Not now.

Leo put her hand on my shoulder and leaned forward to lock me in her gaze. "It's understandable, Bel. You're the only person who can take care of your heart, and as much as I love Jamie and don't believe he'd ever want to hurt you, I know he *has* hurt you and his life isn't here."

Daggers to the heart... Leo knew just where to stick them.

"Yeah." My voice came out watery, subdued.

"So next time there's a chance, mention that you're looking forward to the trip, that it'll be great to make the memories, and then let that be that. You'll have a few weeks back here, and you can use those weeks to step back so by the time he leaves, you're in the clear." Leo patted me where her hand rested, then withdrew it and returned to her meal.

"That's the plan," I said, feeling less and less enthusiastic about all of this as the conversation went on.

"Topic change?" Wells offered.

"Yes please—"

"For the love of everything good in this life, yes." Leo and I spoke simultaneously.

We all chuckled, and Wells took the floor. "I've contracted someone to come walk the Eastern property and then draw up plans for a hotel."

"What?"

"That's amazing!"

"When?"

Wells' smile beamed. "June. He's coming in June, and then we'd work on breaking ground next summer if I can get all my ducks in a row. I never thought I'd be ready for this so soon, but I've got an insanely busy summer, and with the work everyone is doing on the mountain, I think we'll be ready. Jonas said he thinks—"

"Oh, not you too! You're a fan of Herr Bauer?" Leo's voice whined as she spoke, and the sound of it jarred both me and Wells.

"Uh... yeah. You remember I knew him and Karla Ritter from before I moved here. He's amazingly smart about all of this business, especially for towns just like ours. He's basically been consulting on this for me pro bono, and I'd be crazy not to accept it."

That surprised Leo, to say the least.

"*Pro bono?* Huh. I guess you can't pass that up... I just didn't see him as the type." She said this to no one, staring into her pasta.

"Why would you say that?" Wells verbalized my thought well.

"He just... doesn't strike me as someone who'd do much for free. I see him as more of a shark, out to get what he wants and make money."

Wells sat back, stunned. "You really haven't interacted with him much, have you?"

Leo scoffed, shoving a piece of pasta into her mouth and chewing aggressively before she answered. "You know as well as I do *interacting* with Jonas Bauer is a combination of awkward and painful I try to avoid in my life. He may be doing good things for the lodge, which I take issue with as it is, but that doesn't mean I have to be his friend or like that he's some nameless investor's puppet with a questionable motive."

Wells and I sat silenced by her tirade.

I cleared my throat. "Good to see you're keeping a neutral opinion of the guy, Leo. That'll serve you well these next few years he's around."

Leo waved off my comment, and eventually we found less stressful points of conversation—the small trip Liam had planned for him and Wells after the anniversary fest, Danny's new interest in the library and wondering if Mia's presence had anything to do with that, Gran's health and Grandpa Will's latest chess shark scheme at the retirement community.

When we parted with hugs, the banished thoughts of Jamie and our future returned, unavoidable for longer than a few minutes at a time even with the best distraction.

He'd been so pleased when I accepted his offer to go on the trip—I wanted to. But after a few minutes of talking, I could tell he would jump back into discussing the slightly more distant future if I let him. I couldn't do that.

And worse, what if he'd meant I should come with him all the time? What if he wanted me to drop my life here and be his little roadie groupie, or whatever it's called. I had a life here. I had a job and friends and a house and a cat and Gran, who I couldn't possibly leave.

I sighed, leaning against the inside of my front door, glad to be home where I could let myself sigh and pine and wander around aimlessly for a bit before I got in bed. I thanked God for Friday tomorrow and knowing I could sleep in a few hours on Saturday.

When I slid into bed, I let the real fear rise to the surface, inevitably when everything else cleared away and I couldn't ignore the concerns closest to my heart.

What if, in the end, he had only meant he wanted me to go with him on this trip, and had no intention of anything beyond his time in Utah? Even though I'd made that my plan—enjoy the time, revel in the butterflies and kisses and attention, and then leave—the shattered feeling in my chest when I thought about him saying goodbye without a second glance come August told me I was already in too deep.

CHAPTER THIRTY-NINE

Jamie

Julian looked good.

He'd brought his usual bulldog attitude with him, which I could've lived without, but it was good to see the guy in the flesh after more than six months talking over phones and e-mail, and even better to see his pleasure at the progress on the neighborhood.

"I'll be happy when I visit here and can stay in my own home and not an inn where everyone knows my business," Julian grumped, glancing each way across the street as we walked from lunch at the *The Elk*.

"You realize you've chosen to develop this neighborhood, and outfit a home for yourself, in an extremely small mountain town where everyone knows everyone's business?"

His eyes cut to me, and he slowed. "Not everything, or everyone, would know who I am and what we're doing."

I crossed my arms and nodded. "True enough. Only Bel knows, and otherwise I assume everyone thinks you're a friend or someone who works for me."

Julian scoffed at that, and I hid a smile, pleased my baiting had worked. He was an odd enough bird to begin with—partly introverted, partly just awkward, but fully genius. But he also seemed to feel threatened at the thought of being employed by me. I had no idea why except that he also seemed to disdain fame to any degree. He refused photo ops and interview requests regularly. I'd never been able to pry him open far enough to learn where all that came from.

As for me, I loved to poke at him and get a rise—I suspected no one else who interacted with him dared do such a thing.

"Is this woman who knows all your secrets somewhere nearby so I can put a face to the name?" Julian's voice cut through my musings, sharp and impatient—so, totally typical.

"In fact, she is. She'll be working at *Rise and Shine.*"

"Is she the baker? Is she the one who makes the bread?"

Julian's voice quickly transitioned to one of awe—not a sound I'd heard very often at all. In fact, the only other time he'd spoken in that tone in my hearing had come at the sight of the mountains on his first visit here, and then as he plodded around the acreage that would eventually become our development.

"No. She manages the place. Sadie Miller is the owner and the woman responsible for the food."

Before I'd finished, Julian marched ahead and tore open the door to the coffee shop. I caught the panel before it shut completely and watched as he continued his mission right up to the counter where he thrust his hand out to Bel, who stood behind the register ready to take his order.

"Bel Paxton. Julian Grenier."

Bel's eyebrows jumped, and a grin appeared before she met his outstretched hand with her own. "Nice to meet you."

"Likewise. Good to put a face with a name." Julian withdrew from the handshake and his hands dropped to his side, his weight shifting from side to side.

Odd.

Bel's gaze flickered to meet mine, and we shared a perplexed smile. "Hi, Jamie."

"Hello, lovely."

I said this low enough likely only she and Julian could hear. A small group of women sat at the long tables at the front left of the store, but they were talking and laughing boisterously enough they couldn't have heard.

Her smile glowed a bit and I reveled in that, my heart feeling that incessant relief and longing whenever I came near her. Nothing had gone to plan in our interactions lately, but it was all so roundly *good* I hated to think of it as anything but that. She'd made it clear in the way she'd steered our last serious conversation that she didn't want to go back to talking about what happened when I left for good.

Fair enough. But we'd talk about it soon. We'd have to. And in the meantime, I'd make my plans for showing her some of Europe and getting her to fall for me so by the time we were in Paris, I could actually confess my feelings and she wouldn't be scared away. I could do that in three weeks, right?

"Ms. Paxton, may I ask—"

"Please call me Bel, Mr. Grenier—"

"Oh, well, then please call me Julian... errr, could you tell me whether the owner is in?" Julian stretched his neck to peer past Bel, apparently trying to see through the walls and into the kitchen with his genius X-ray vision or something.

"I'm sorry, no. She gets an early start as she's also the master baker here, so she's usually gone before noon unless we have a special event."

Julian nodded. "I'll have to try to meet her another time."

"Sure... I'm... sure she'd like that."

Bel gave him an easy smile even though her voice didn't match. She and everyone else in town knew very well Sadie would like nothing about meeting Julian as she largely didn't talk to people. Or, we could assume, considering she didn't talk to the people in the town she'd grown up in and known all her life.

I lingered at the front while Julian tromped back outside, his mission evidently complete.

Bel raised a brow at me.

"Told you. He's an odd one."

"It's fine. I like weirdos. I'm friends with your sister, after all."

I chuckled and took her hand, kissed her knuckles while looking in her eyes, and watched the blush creep in at her cheeks. "I've got to go. We're heading up to the property and then prepping for the meeting to petition for the airport permits tomorrow at the county building."

"Will I see you again?"

"You say when, I'll be there. Julian's only here 'til tomorrow."

He never stayed very long, never stayed beyond the necessary and scheduled period. He simply didn't have time

—he made my schedule look like an unemployed slacker's, and that was true even during tours and busy seasons.

"Then come over when he leaves. Any time after four."

"See you tomorrow."

I didn't actually skip out the door, but I felt like it. Having her initiate still blew my mind, and having her want to see me that soon fell on the right side of rewarding, for sure. I'd expected her to say Saturday, which had become our go-to date day since she got to sleep in and I never had plans, but Friday came a day sooner. Obvious, but for me, that small thing had me bouncing by the time I reached Julian, who stood outside of *Odds*, the odds and ends store just next to *Rise and Shine*.

"How does this place stay in business?" He nodded with his chin to an eclectic window display ranging from vintage books to hardware, and what looked like an old buck shot-riddled stop sign.

"You know, I have no idea. I don't even remember who owns it—it changed hands a few times when I lived here, and the contents have gotten more and more diverse, it would seem."

"Someone needs to buy it and make it something useful," Julian said as he turned to walk.

"Well, maybe someone who moves in to the 'hood will want a small hobby business and—"

"Mr. Morris, good to see you."

Jonas Bauer stopped in front of us, his attention falling immediately to Julian, who Bauer would recognize was dressed in a bespoke suit and Italian leather shoes. Doubtful anyone else in the town cared, but this man would.

"Mr. Bauer, good to see you too. This is Julian Grenier." I gestured to Julian, who stuck out his hand. "Julian, this is

Jonas Bauer. He's partnering with the lodge to revitalize and is a liaison for our primary investor."

I prayed Julian remembered me mentioning Bauer, but Julian had no desire for the details of our project to be uncovered yet, just like I didn't, so I could safely assume he'd keep any details under wraps.

"Is this a visit for business, or pleasure?" Bauer asked.

I could have sworn his gaze sharpened as he eyed Julian.

"Visiting an old friend, seeing the sights. I'm sure you can see the appeal. I'm staying at the charming Silverton Inn, where we're headed now." Julian nodded to the sidewalk ahead, and Bauer stepped to the side.

"Please, don't let me keep you. Say hello to Ms. Bryant, if you would. She's doing an excellent job with the place."

We said our goodbyes even as we started walking, and Julian and I said nothing until we reached the end of the long path where we could see the inn and no longer feel Jonas Bauer's laser eyes at my back.

"He's the one asking questions?" Julian said, hand on the gate at the edge of the inn's property.

"Yes. He's far more observant than anyone else, and for some reason I've caught his attention. I don't think he's put anything together, but he's exactly the kind of person that would take what we're doing and run with it in order to exploit it for attention, and maybe even investors for the lodge. I can't fault him for that, but you know as well as I do—"

"We agreed. Until we fill half the lots, have airport permits, and are ready to break ground there, no one knows but us."

CHAPTER FORTY

Bel

I'd talked myself into and out of spiraling about seeing Jamie like ten times.

What would I do if he wanted to talk about _the future?_ (Cue dramatic music.)

How would I avoid that without seeming like I was?

My thoughts swirled around and around, mixing and tangling with the plethora of emotions that hounded me at all times. Jamie made me feel _everything_. Happy, excited, sad, lonely, important, expendable, worthy and worthless, confused...

Maybe I couldn't lay all that on him, but this situation certainly had me feeling all those things and more. But tonight, I didn't want to sit down in the mire of that writhing pile of emotions. I wanted to enjoy Jamie. Because however this played out—me walking away, or him, or both of us—this would come to an end. And when it did, I wanted at least a handful more memories to sift through and savor.

The doorbell rang just after five. I smoothed the silky white dress over me. No, summer hadn't yet hit, but it'd been a warm day, and I'd wanted to look good. I'd decided yesterday that we'd stay in at my house—I wanted Jamie to myself, and even though I accepted the fans as part of his life, I wanted privacy.

But I also wanted to look good. He made me breathless and a little dizzy almost every time I looked at him—both because he was *that* good-looking, and because the reality that he wanted me, even in a small way, overwhelmed me.

I wanted to do that to him. Maybe this exemplified pettiness and I should be ashamed, but I'd so rarely wanted to make someone feel this way. In fact, that last time I had, it'd been him.

Jamie stepped through the door holding a large pizza box in one hand and a bag in the other, then stopped just inside when I closed the door behind him. "The pizza guy was out there so I grabbed it and—"

His eyes burned into me, sliding from my hair in waves to the thin straps holding up the material over my shoulders, and farther down to where the dress stopped mid-thigh, then to my bare feet—I'd forgotten shoes, but there's the plus of staying in.

"Hi," I said, my voice all breath since my heart had begun pounding out of my ears the moment he set his eyes on me.

He shook his head, his chest visibly rising under a perfectly fitted shirt with the top two buttons undone. He brushed past me into the kitchen, leaving me to stare after him for less than ten seconds before he returned, hands free, and stalked toward me.

"What are you trying to do to me, Bel?"

His voice melted over me, rich, dark, maybe even dangerous.

"Just... I—I'm not trying anything."

One side of his mouth kicked up, and just that fraction of movement sent heat whirling through my chest, racing to the tips of my fingers and toes.

He dipped his head and ran his nose and lips along my neck, jaw, then hovered at my ear and said in a near whisper, "I don't believe you."

His lips then touched just below my ear.

A sigh escaped as he set his hands at my waist, the silk separating my skin from his calloused hands. I wrapped my arms around his neck and nudged him so he'd lean back, give me the chance to look into his face, but instead he set small kisses along my jaw until he found my mouth and *took*.

Jamie knew how to kiss, and it seemed he was determined to demonstrate just how well in this moment. Soft kisses gave way to the intensity I felt whenever he lay his full attention on me.

The doorbell rang. It rang again. The only thing that stopped the rising heat between us was my concern something had happened with Gran and they'd come to tell me in person—a chilling thought, and enough to make me pull back, set my hands at Jamie's chest, and urge him away just a bit.

"Just ignore it. Who cares? They can come back another—"

"I have to get it, just in case. I'm yours tonight, Jamie... there's no rush."

Heat rose to my cheeks as I said that, surprised at my ability to verbalize something so direct, but glad I had. We didn't have to pack all of our physical interaction into the first ten minutes, and I didn't have to wake up early, so we didn't have a work-induced curfew.

I pulled open the door to find a teen boy holding another carboard box —somewhere in my mind I knew his name, but my brain felt like mush, so I'd blame it on that.

"Sorry. I totally forgot your breadsticks."

I reassured him, then shut the door, and found Jamie sitting on the couch cradling Squish, his eyes on me and the fire in them only marginally diminished.

"Breadsticks," I said, holding up the box and moving toward the kitchen.

"Oh, well that's worth it then." The sarcasm in his voice, and maybe... maybe something else—hurt?—clear.

I set the box on the table and spoke as he moved to the sink to wash his hands.

"I'm sorry. I thought maybe it was something about Gran. They have these procedures where they come in person if certain things happen, or if they can't get a hold of you. My phone is in my bedroom, and I just... I can't imagine ignoring something like that."

He turned to me as he dried his hands on a towel and hung it back on the hook. "I get it. And you're right. There's no rush. I don't want you to think that's the only reason I'm here."

I didn't, of course. But at this point, he'd ruffled his tail-feathers enough I had to provoke him a little. "No? Well what else are you here for?"

He set a hand on my shoulder, slid a finger under the thin strap of my dress, sending a shiver through me, then smiled with hooded eyes. "The pizza, of course."

~

The steamy beginning to the night gave way to more lighthearted fare, and I thanked God for that. I could only take so much of his intensity and attention in *that* way before I'd spontaneously deconstruct into a pile of limbs.

I regretted my choice of white dress for eating pizza, but shamelessly tucked a kitchen towel into the front of the bodice to protect it. This may have proved more revealing than the garment regularly would have been, but in the name of not murdering this dress with pizza sauce and breadstick grease, it happened.

We laughed and joked, and he caught me up on his time with Julian.

"He's clearly a fan of Sadie's bread. I'm betting when he puts his mind to something, he gets it... she's going to have to meet him, isn't she?"

He nodded as he finished chewing. "Afraid so. There's likely no getting around it."

"I wonder if I should warn her." I took the last bite and wiped my hands carefully, then untucked the towel and set it aside.

"Nah. I know she's an introvert, but she'll be fine. You met him—it's not like it'll be a prolonged interaction. She'll survive his introduction, whatever praise he'd like to lavish, and then he'll turn and disappear, much like he did yesterday when he got his answer."

I chuckled, remembering Julian's abrupt departure after I told him Sadie wasn't in. "I guess that's a good point."

We worked on cleaning up as we talked.

"He doesn't seem like someone who'd *lavish praise* though." I couldn't picture Julian Grenier praising anyone— he seemed too uptight and in a hurry.

"Despite appearances, he's an incredibly generous person. The first time we met in person, he extended his hand and said 'your talent is ridiculous as is your dedication to your music and your fans, and you are the prettiest man I've ever seen.'"

I turned from where I'd been wiping the table, my laugh loud in the small kitchen. "Really? I cannot imagine that."

Jamie shrugged and grinned. "It's true. He's direct and expedient like that in all things. If you can learn to handle it in the day to day, it pays off in his other qualities. He's not someone I would have guessed I'd be friends with, but he's been loyal and incredibly helpful in some tough times."

I gave him a look that asked the question for me. Jamie let out a sigh as he set the last plate in the dishwasher and closed it.

"When that woman broke into my house, he helped out. He knows someone in private security who found out it was my security firm who'd allowed it to happen and... well. It's fine now. But I'm not sure how many more break-ins I would have had if it hadn't been for Julian's tenacity in finding out who should take the blame."

I moved to him, wrapped my arms around his waist, and hugged him to me. "I'm glad he did."

"Me too," he said, holding me just as close.

I leaned back to look at that gorgeous face and tucked the errant strand of hair behind his ear. I smoothed it away from his face when it fell in front of his eyes again.

"This little piece just won't cooperate, will it?"

"It won't. Should I cut it?"

He searched my face, and I straightened when I saw he meant the question in earnest.

"Cut your hair?"

"Yes. It gets hot in the summer, especially when I perform. Plus I'm just... I don't know. Tired of the man bun thing." He patted the back of his head where said man bun resided and made a face.

I gripped his wrists. "But... no! I haven't even gotten to enjoy it. I mean, I just, I haven't—" I swallowed, stopped, not sure how to say what I wanted to say.

Mischief lit his eyes. "You haven't gotten to *enjoy it?* How do you plan on doing that, Bel?" His voice had dropped to that delectable, silken tenor that made me feel restless and hot.

"I don't know. I just... haven't gotten to yet."

I squeezed his wrists, then let him go, feeling oddly embarrassed by my admission that I hadn't gotten to *enjoy* his hair. I didn't even know what I meant, but the thought of him cutting it before I'd ever even seen it down in person gave me a ridiculous feeling of loss.

He reached for me as I walked away and hooked his arms around my waist, then pulled my back to the front of him. He leaned in to speak softly, his breath tickling the shell of my ear. "Maybe we should work on that tonight."

CHAPTER FORTY-ONE

Jamie

My shoulder slammed into the wall, but I managed to cushion Bel from the same impact. Luckily, we'd pulled back just before hitting the surface. She laughed, her hands around my neck, my arms around her back.

She rose to her toes and kissed me, pressed against me so every part of us touched, and as if they weren't already, my nerves lit and sang. If we kept bumping and stumbling our way down this hall, I knew what we'd find—a soft, inviting bed where I could lay Bel down and... I swallowed against the new flood of heat at that thought.

"Maybe we should slow down. It's getting late—I'm sure you're tired after being up early for work..." I suggested, feeling my heart, my vision, and my mind scattering in all directions.

She stopped, let her hands slide down to brace against

my chest, and looked at me in the dim hallway light. "I *am* tired, but I don't want you to go."

Her hand between my pecs must have felt the beat of my heart race at that, as though it hadn't already been sprinting.

"You don't want me to go." I repeated it, like saying it aloud would decipher the meaning.

Was that a wistful thought—a *gosh, I'm sorry you have to go, wish you could stay?* Or was that *I don't want you to go, please stay?*

I looked for clues in her face, but all I could see were her eyes, those green glass charms just killing me with their loveliness. She swallowed, nodded, but I couldn't take that for confirmation.

"Bel, baby, I know what I want you to mean, but I need you to be clear."

If desperation filled my voice, I couldn't be blamed. The situation felt desperate—my love for her, my need for her, this weird separation I'd felt on and off for the last few weeks and my desire to banish it—desperate.

She bit her bottom lip, that sly little attempt to hide a smile making me want to take her mouth again, but I didn't.

"Jamie Morrison, please stay with me tonight."

I woke with daylight shining in my eyes, a numb arm, and a weight on my shoulder. The ensuing smile came like the sunrise—inevitable after the night. I rolled my neck to stretch, wishing I could move my arm, but unwilling to dislodge this heavy head from my shoulder. Bel's hair spread across my chest, around my neck—everywhere.

Her quiet breaths made her back rise and fall, the calm

sound giving me a sense of peace I couldn't remember feeling at any other time. This woman... I'd loved her before, in the way I could at nineteen and barely knowing her. I loved her now at twenty-eight. Some unearthly part of me knew I'd love her at forty and sixty and ninety, should I be so lucky.

Now, how to tell her. How to make her see. How to help her understand we could have a life together, despite the obvious obstacles.

She wouldn't have asked me to stay if she didn't feel the same—I knew that in my gut. Whether she'd admit it, and would be able to say the same... the gamble rested in that. She'd been cagey any time I brought up the future. But maybe what kept her from being able to share those feelings stemmed from her lack of surety about *me* and how I felt. I could understand that, and had hesitated to tell her my feelings because of that very reason.

We'd stayed up late into the night talking, and the words had been on the tip of my tongue so often I'd had to bite it to keep from making my confession. Maybe I should have told her last night, but for some reason, I'd wanted to wait until the daylight came and everything felt more real. So much of the night before had felt surreal, like a dream.

I couldn't wait any longer for this conversation. I'd thought I could wait until we were traveling—maybe bring it up in a romantic moment in Paris. *No.* Today.

But first, breakfast. I couldn't think very clearly yet—not with Bel soft and sleeping against me, not with the memories of the night before, not with my stomach growling like it had any say in this day's events.

I extricated myself from the tangle with Bel, miraculously not waking her, and dressed quickly. If I jogged or walked fast, I could retrieve coffee and pastries before she even realized I'd been gone. I hated the thought of not being next to her when she woke, but that would come. Hopefully, it'd come every day, indefinitely.

In winter, Silverton would have been bustling by seven on a Saturday—skiers would be breakfasting in preparation for the lifts to open at eight, and businesses would have been operating already. In summer, the town adopted a lazy start thanks to no pressure from the mountain's schedule, but the sun rose early. Anyone in town for the Memorial Day weekend break had come to hike, kayak, raft, and slow down, and the hikers were probably already on the mountain if they planned to be gone all day.

This morning, hardly anyone roamed Main Street, and *Rise and Shine* sat quietly anchoring the street at its middle. I hustled in, the bell ringing behind me, startled to see one of the high schoolers behind the counter even though I knew exactly why Bel didn't grace that space.

I smiled at that thought. I liked knowing where she was, and that I got to return to her.

I ordered coffees, croissants, and a few other pastries, and half a quiche. I couldn't speak for Bel, but I'd awoken with the hunger of three men.

I felt like whistling on the way back. In fact, a song was building in my chest, that one that'd been out of reach. Maybe I could grab a few hours today while Bel visited her gran and get it down on the page. I still needed three more songs before we left on the trip in two weeks or I'd end up having to rush the rest of the album and not have anything to choose from come recording time, which I hated.

I snuck in the front door, moving as quietly as I could in case she'd managed to stay asleep.

"Hey." Bel's voice came from down the hall. "Wasn't sure where you'd gone."

I peeked around the corner to find her combing through wet hair, jeans and a T-shirt in place, feet bare.

"Had to go get us breakfast—I thought maybe you'd sleep through and I could surprise you. I should have left a note or something, sorry."

"Never apologize for bringing breakfast." She sent me a smile and disappeared into the bathroom again while I arranged the pastries on a plate and poured our coffees into mugs I took a minute to warm with hot water from the sink first. Everything cooled down faster at this altitude, and pouring hot coffee into a cold mug only accelerated the process.

"Thank you for this," Bel said as she sat, her hair now dry.

Had it really only taken her, what... could it have been five minutes, even? To dry her hair?

"You dry your hair impressively fast. If I remember right, Leo's would take like fifteen minutes." I set the plate of pastries between us and handed her the mug with her coffee.

"It's not completely dry but it's enough that I won't get cold and it won't get crazy." She smiled as she perused the pastry selection, looking completely pleased.

"How do you not get sick of the pastries from the shop?" I wondered.

She chuckled. "I don't eat them unless I'm with you, really. Sometimes, I take some to Gran and indulge then, but pastries aren't a daily feature of my life, despite how amazing they are."

"Oh... would you rather have something else? I did get quiche—in fact, it's in the oven staying warm—"

She set a hand on my arm before I could stand. "No,

Jamie, it's great. I love them... really. And I love that you brought them."

Her warm smile calmed the part of me that thought I'd messed up, that boy who lived in me and tried to keep me small, doubting, anxious.

"Good." *And speaking of love...* ha. Right. I needed a better transition. "So, two weeks until our trip..."

Her mouth full of food, she raised her brows and nodded as she chewed.

"Did you have any trouble taking off from the shop or anything?" I'd been meaning to ask her, but we really hadn't seen each other all that often—not nearly often enough in my opinion, and when we did, I didn't want to talk about logistics.

"No problem at all. I'm actually part owner of the shop —just a quarter, but I do all the hiring and scheduling so it's really up to me to shuffle as needed. It's perfect since school is out by the time we go, all the kids working afternoons and weekends are looking for more time, and we have a few people from college who've gotten back this month once the semester ended so we've got good backup."

"Sounds perfect. I'm glad. Also, that's amazing that you own part of the shop—when did that happen?" She'd never even hinted at having a larger hand in the shop than simply managing it during the week.

"About a year after I moved back and started working there, I guess? Sadie needed someone else to have a small role, and honestly I think she needed someone who could take meetings and deal with some of the more personnel-focused things. I was already managing schedules and ordering, so I guess she felt confident we could work together and that I understood her. I'd saved plenty during college with scholarships and work, and since I don't pay rent on the house, I had some cash to invest."

I took a bite of a delectable raspberry Danish—damn, Sadie knew what she was doing. Perfect pastry, perfect night, perfect morning... "That's brilliant. So if you come with me in August, you could totally swing it."

"Uh..." she dragged the sound out.

Not the way I'd planned to bring it up, but now or never, right?

"Yeah, I've been thinking. I don't want us to be done when I leave here. I care about you too much, and we shouldn't have to be over because we live in different places. So... you should come with me."

Her eyes were wide, the portion of croissant in her hand paused midway to her mouth.

Maybe she needed more information. I could give her that. "I'll head to LA in August after the fest, then after we record, I have another tour starting late October. You can come with me on that too, which will be awesome, and then we can come back here during the break at Christmas. I've been better about scheduling in time off during holidays, even for Euro and Asian tours, because I want to make sure I'm coming back at least once a year."

Her lashes fluttered, and the hand holding the croissant dropped back to the table. "Jamie, what are you talking about?"

CHAPTER FORTY-TWO

Bel

He looked genuinely perplexed by my question.

I quelled the riot of confusion, excitement, and irritation in my chest. "We haven't discussed me going with you. What would I do about my job?"

"What do you mean? You just finished telling me you're part owner and you arrange everything. You have the freedom to leave. You have more than two months to get things all settled..." He leaned away from the table and folded his arms.

"But my life is here, Jamie. I work here. I have a home here. Gran is here. My friends are here. And Squish."

"I realize that, but... *I'm* not here. Not often, anyway. And you have flexibility. You work at a coffee shop—that's an easy fix. You can do that anywhere, if you really want, or obviously I'll support you. Your gran lives in an assisted living community with thirty of her best friends. You'll see friends when we visit, or I'll fly them to you, whatever you want, and—"

"So I just up and leave? Just follow you around like a groupie and you pay all my bills like, what? A mistress or something?"

The look on his face said I'd offended him. Cute, considering he'd just belittled everything about my life in one swipe of his hand.

He straightened in his seat. "No, not like a groupie or a mistress. Like a girlfriend and friend and someone I want to be with all the time. I don't want to do long-distance. I've tried it, I hate it, and I don't want to do it. I can't change my life—not in the way you can, Bel. This isn't news."

I stayed quiet, breathing, nothing but pressure in my head and chest filling my mind.

He scrubbed his hands over his face. "I thought you'd be excited about this. I know we haven't talked about it, but I'm offering a solution to us having a drop-dead date. I realize you'd have to change your life—I get that, and it's no small thing. But your life is... it's..."

I wrapped my arms around myself, feeling the need for a shield against this conversation that had unraveled in a completely unexpected way. "What, Jamie? What is my life?"

His eyes shot to the ceiling, and I could see him taking measured breaths before he spoke to me again.

"It's... small. *No.* Not small." He made a pained, grumbling sound. "It's changeable. You've been stuck here for years, and you don't have to be. All you have to do is decide you can change it. I'm giving you a way to do that, and I'd hoped, a really good incentive to want to."

I sucked in a breath, feeling my chest hollow out.

I'd never thought of my heart as a structure before—vessels, chambers, valves, sure. But in this moment, I pictured it like a perfect sheet of shiny tinfoil, never touched but for an accidental bend here or there, until this moment. Jamie's calling me stuck, calling my life small and changeable and essentially saying my life meant less than his... that took my shiny tinfoil sheet and crumpled it into a tiny ball. I knew, even if I managed to flatten it out, it'd never be the same.

I could feel him watching me as I stared at my plate, my hands, out the back door—I looked anywhere but at him.

"Bel, please... what—"

"I think you should go for now, Jamie." The tremor in my voice made me grit my teeth, knowing it signaled tears weren't far behind. I felt them coming—I wanted them, and I wanted him gone when they came.

"I'm not leaving until we clear this up. I wanted this to be a good thing, and somehow, I've just hurt you and it feels like I've ruined everything. I don't want to leave right now." He put a hand on my wrist and searched my face.

"I need some space. You gave me a lot to think about. I'm not going to freeze you out, I just need time to myself to think. I've been on my own for a long time, and I just..." I cleared my throat, clenched against the flood of sadness and hurt rising. "Just need some time, okay?"

He looked truly upset, which should have been some consolation, but all I could hear were the things he'd said, the way he'd made everything I'd built since college seem like an accident, like it had come from my being too scared to live my life.

"Yes. Of course." He stood, nodding rapidly, like the action might calm him or me. "Can you please call me later, or text me at least?"

I avoided his eyes but knew failing to agree to that small term would mean he'd stay and fight—for what, I couldn't tell. But he'd stay, and I wanted him gone. I offered only an *Mmhmm*. I sat at the table as he gathered his things, not moving until I heard the front door shut. I immediately locked it, then went to my room. I had three hours until I had to be at Gran's... maybe I could fall back asleep and forget all about this.

Yes. I could forget about how this man I'd fallen for had just taken my life, the one I'd come to terms with, and made it seem like nothing. I could shove it aside and ignore the pain shooting through my chest, the gulping, drowning feeling as I tried to breathe. I could block out his suggestion that everything I had could so easily be left behind and that I must have chosen to stay *stuck* for so many years because I must be, in his estimation, a complete coward.

I crossed my arms over my chest, assuming a modified fetal position, pulled the comforter over my body, and closed my eyes.

Gran could always tell when something had gone wrong, and this visit proved to be no different than so many like it over the years.

"What happened?"

I slumped into a chair at the table and set down the takeaway Mexican I'd bought from *Guac*. I couldn't get out of bed and make myself cook what I'd planned to for our lunch, so I'd called in lunch for us—guacamole could soothe all manner of wrongs, right?

"Jamie asked me to go with him back to LA in August."

I'd delivered it like the bad news it was, but Gran clapped her hands together and brought them to her lips.

"That's perfect!"

I straightened in my seat and eyed her like the alien invader she'd apparently been snatched by. "In what universe could that possibly be perfect?"

She looked at me like I was the crazy one. "You can ride off into the sunset with a man you've been at least partly in love with for most of your life—how could that *not* be perfect?"

"I—" I shut my mouth, unsure what I'd started to say. How could she be *happy* about this? "Doesn't it matter to you that I'd be leaving? I'd be gone. I wouldn't see you every week. I'd be in LA, and then going with him on his tours to who knows where. I wouldn't be visiting Utah but maybe once or twice a year."

That thought quadrupled my heartrate. If I was running, I'd be nearing a sprint, based on my pulse. Anxiety officially had hold of me.

When I looked up at Gran, her face was all pity. I cringed against it.

"Bel honey, you cannot make your decision based on visiting me."

She said this like it made sense—like it should be obvious to me.

"I'm not. It's not just that. I have a house. I have a job here. I have a cat. I have friends, a church, a library that's just getting revitalized..." Maybe I'd stretched with that last bit, but didn't she see? Didn't Jamie see I couldn't just... *go*?

Gran reached for the bag of food between us and began unwrapping the foil-covered containers. "You do have those things here, that's true."

Good. Finally. Someone could see what I meant.

She set the lid to the side and dove into the dish with her fork, took a bite, chewed quietly. When our eating came to a natural pause, she spoke again. "But do you think you could find those things somewhere else, too?"

I sipped water, searching for words to explain. "I understand that I can reinvent myself, but the way he said it... it was like he didn't see anything I have as valuable. It's like everything about my life is disposable so I should just throw it away and run off with him. How can I be with someone who doesn't see how much these things matter to me?"

Gran sat back in her seat and poked at her food for a minute before finally leveling me with her grassy green eyes. "Do they matter to you that much?"

My grip tightened on my fork, grasping at something to ground me. "How could you ask me that? Of course they do! I love you more than anyone in this world. I love my friends. I love living in the house you gave me."

She tsked, her head tilting to one side to examine me like she used to do when I lied and she wanted me to tell the truth before she asked me for it. I shut my eyes against the look and hunched under the weight of my frustration and fury.

I spoke without looking up at her. "They do matter. You especially."

"And Jamie? Does he matter? Can you let him go and continue living here without any regrets? That's really the question you need to ask—what matters more?"

Her voice would have been soothing, except those words cut.

"It's not that easy. It's not as simple as what matters more. This is my whole life!" The heat rose in my cheeks as I practically shouted. I'd hardly ever raised my voice at

Gran and felt another little ping of mortification and sadness at that realization. "I'm sorry."

"No, get mad. That's good. You've let yourself trot along without confronting your life for too long, and I've failed you by not pushing you on it. It sounds like Jamie is finally doing what I should have done years ago." Her voice shook with the conviction of her words.

I searched her face, so familiar to me but downright foreign in this moment. "Done what?"

"You never should have stayed here, Bel. You wanted to live in the city, travel, see the world. You wanted a bigger life than this."

"I don't—"

"—Listen, please. First, I must tell you that your parents left you too soon—they failed you. I know you claim to have made your peace with that, but darling girl, they hurt you deeply. I want for you to own that and know that their leaving had nothing to do with the amazing, special woman you are."

I choked back a sob, shaking my head. I didn't want to talk about my parents. Not on top of everything else.

"I think it's possible that their leaving you—their *abandoning* you—has made it hard to trust anyone else. I hate that for you, and I hate even admitting that might be the case, but my son and his wife made the wrong choice and have continued to fail you these years."

I pushed a breath out my nose. "I'm not worried about them. They may or may not have failed me, but at this point, I've accepted it. Their move when I was in high school is not—"

Gran tilted her head in a kind of plea, that action cutting me off. "I know you say you've made your peace with it. I admire that, and I hope it's true. I'm afraid I should have acknowledged their failure a long time ago so you'd know—you'd *know* it wasn't you..."

"I know that. I know." My voice came out watery, weak.

"And honey, I love Silverton. I moved here more than fifty years ago and I don't regret a day living here. I can see why you'd love it too. But *you... you* Bel, should not have stayed. I'm afraid I became an excuse, and then I loaded up more excuses—encouraging you to work while I recovered and giving you the house so you felt tethered here. Please... *please* don't overlook this chance to get out, see some things, and be with a man who I suspect loves you very much."

I looked at her, this woman who'd raised me, who'd loved me all my life. I saw the love she had for me there in her face, in the way her hand held mine—when had she taken it? I knew she had my best interest at heart, but that *you should not have stayed* rang in my head. Was this just like my parents, just like Jamie before and Danny and probably what Jamie would do again—was this her saying she'd leave me if she could, but since I stayed, I needed to leave her?

"I don't know what to say." It's all I could eke out before I jumped up and left.

CHAPTER FORTY-THREE

Jamie

Bel didn't call me that day.

Or the next.

By six that Sunday night, I couldn't take it. I knocked on her door, ready to hash out whatever we needed to in order to clear the air and move forward. No way could I wait until tomorrow and corner her at work—this just wasn't a conversation to have in public.

Obviously, I'd made a mess of things yesterday. I'd spent every waking moment thinking about my words, about hers... and trust me, there'd been plenty of time to examine them as I'd only slept a restless four hours.

I hadn't meant to make her feel bad, or for it to seem like I thought her life was small. It's just I saw my life as fairly inflexible—I currently lived the most flexibility I'd ever had, and because I'd taken the time away, I'd have to pay for it when I returned to reality.

I knocked again a few minutes later, the pit in my stomach growing at the thought she might not answer. She'd said she'd talk to me, but maybe it'd just been a way to get me to leave.

"Hi."

The relief at seeing that door swing open and her behind it swooped in, releasing with it a gust of air. "Hi. Can we talk?"

She stepped back to let me in. She wore light gray sweats and a T-shirt, her hair pulled back into a messy ponytail. Dark circles ringed her eyes, and I had a sinking suspicion they were red and swollen from crying.

"Sorry I didn't call yesterday. Gran and I had a disagreement and I was just too upset."

She hadn't really looked at me yet—she sat petting Squish who took up his usual position on the back of the couch. I'd let her get away with that... for now.

"I'm sorry to hear that. Are you still upset?"

"It's complicated. I told her about your... offer, and she thought it was great."

Thank God for Gran. "Oh?"

Her head whipped to me. "Don't sound smug."

I held up my hands in a sign of surrender. Clearly, we were not yet on solid ground. "Let's talk about it then, please."

I sat next to her on the couch—close enough she couldn't avoid looking at me, at least part of the time, but not so close we were touching. Clearly, she needed space to process and express her thoughts.

"I'm sorry for saying your life was changeable. That came from a place of thinking mine *isn't*. I'm here because I've been planning this break for almost two years—ever since Da's heart attack. I won't have another months-long break like this for even longer. I can't live here in Silverton all the time, but it seems like... if you wanted to..."

Now that I was in the same room with her, I couldn't say it again. She clearly still felt hurt, and based on the way her shoulders hunched in, maybe even ganged up on thanks to Gran's agreement with me.

"I don't see how I can."

A flash of irritation bolted through me. I clenched my teeth to keep from speaking, knowing nothing good would come out of that.

She wiped under one eye, then the other, her head ducked. Were those tears?

"Bel..." Seeing the tears snapped me from my irritation, my pulse pounding at my temples and in my neck at the sight. I hated hurting her. I'd done it enough for one lifetime and hated that I'd done it again.

"Jamie, I don't know what to tell you. You and Gran and everyone else in town may see my life as a joke, but I don't. It's *my* life. I can't go with you." She stood, walked to the door, and opened it wide. "Not in two weeks, not in August, not ever. I wish there was some other way to make it work, but I know there's not. I hope you'll understand."

My throat burned with frustration, anger, sadness. I cleared it as I walked through the door, turning once I was outside so she'd know I didn't intend to stay since she so clearly wanted me gone. "I get it. Sorry I pushed you."

Have a nice life.

In the next two weeks, I wrote fourteen songs. Impressive, right? Maybe, but they were all depressing as hell, and I hated every one of them.

I didn't want to be the guy who wrote these kinds of songs anymore. I didn't want Bel to be the girl who still inspired them.

Ma and Da came home a few days after what I'd been thinking of as our break up, but I'd also come to terms with the fact that maybe Bel thought we'd broken up the day before so my showing up that Sunday was just a pathetic last attempt to talk her into seeing me as worth the effort when she'd already made it clear I wasn't.

My God, that stung. Not just stung—hurt. I didn't shy from the shredded feeling I had in my chest, like a wolverine or mountain lion or some other wild creature had happened by and taken claws to my torso.

I'd thought through my conversations with her a thousand times in the last two weeks and I always arrived at the same place: if she didn't see me as worth the risk, there wasn't anything I could do to change her mind. If she didn't want to change anything about her life, whether for me or better yet, herself, then she wouldn't ever change it. She hadn't seen fit to do that since she'd landed here five years ago after college, so I shouldn't have been so surprised she wouldn't do it now.

But damn, was that a repeated bludgeoning of the heart. Lungs. Spleen. Kidneys. Internal organs in general.

All of me ached. Everything hurt, and thinking about her made it both better and worse, so I kept thinking about her, unable to extract her from my mind.

I thought about her in circles. I thought about our history, distant and more recent. I thought about my future, gaping wide without her.

I hadn't come back to Silverton with the purpose of falling for her and talking her into being mine. I'd only come for the family, the project, but once here, I'd committed to easing that problematic dynamic between us. Then Danny had come along and planted the idea that she'd been waiting for me all this time.

Damn you, little brother.

I'd promised Quinn I'd meet her for a margarita at *Guac* the night before I took off—that worked well because I knew I couldn't have more than one and still wake up early enough for Liam to take me to the airport. I felt like drinking all the drinks they had and testing out whether tequila was as good a memory eraser as it used to be for me, but so far, I'd resisted the literal drowning of my misery. Might as well keep up the streak.

I walked in the door, glad to be out of what was a very warm afternoon, and ran right into Bel. Just *right* into her.

"I'm so sorry—sorry. I wasn't looking—"

"No, please, it's my fault, I wasn't either. I'm waiting for Leo and Wells and I—"

"Are you hurt? Are you okay? You look really pretty." She did. I couldn't help but say it with her standing there.

Her blush came immediately. "Jamie, I'm—"

"Hey you! Thanks for squeezing me in before you go." Quinn gave me a side hug and smiled at Bel. "Hey Bel."

"Quinn, hey. You look... awesome. Wow. I'm—I'm just going to go wait outside   "

"Bel, can we..." Before I got the full thought out, she'd left. Out the door and down the street enough so I couldn't see her.

Quinn squeezed my arm. "Yikes. Pretty rough, my friend."

I clamped my mouth shut, not wanting to take out my crap mood on her, even if I was most definitely having an internal tantrum.

Why wouldn't Bel listen to me? Why couldn't we just talk and repair things? "You know what, I'll be right back."

"Take your time."

Quinn's voice followed me out the door. I stomped down the stairs and looked right, left—ah. My heart raced as I approach Bel where she stood, attention on her phone.

"Please talk to me." Despite my pounding heart and the adrenaline racing through me, my words felt slow, my mouth dry.

"I think we've said everything, haven't we? It's not that I don't want to be with you, but it just won't work." Her eyes were mournful and lovely at the same time.

"We haven't said everything... not *everything*." My hands became fists at my sides, the determination building. This couldn't possibly be it—not after so long at odds and finally getting to something good.

"What's left?"

"What's left is I love you. I think I've always loved you. I'm in love with you. I don't want to be apart from you."

I reached out to her, but she winced when I did, the shock on her face, the rigidity of her body, making clear my touch would be unwelcome.

The leftovers of my heart, what hadn't been crushed two weeks ago, withered. The look of utter disbelief, of... horror, told me more than words could say.

No words remaining—I'd given them all to her.

I turned and left. Quinn would understand. I couldn't be anywhere near here. Not now. Maybe not again.

CHAPTER FORTY-FOUR

Bel

I love you. I think I've always loved you. I'm in love with you. I don't want to be apart from you.
I love you.
I think I've always loved you.
I swallowed hard, my lips trembling.
"Hey girl! Where's Leo?"
I'm in love with you.
"Bel? What happened?"
I don't want to be apart from you.
A hand on my arm jerked me from the replay of Jamie's words in my head, his face, his voice fleeing from me as I startled to find Wells looking at me, expression all concern.
"Bel, why are you crying?"
"I'm not. I'm... I—" I couldn't figure out what had happened.
I stared at an elaborately drawn chalk taco talking to an

avocado on the sidewalk—lots of the businesses did sidewalk chalk murals during the summer season.

"She's not talking. Any ideas?"

Leo came into view, pulling my attention from the sidewalk to her bright blue eyes. She searched my face, looked over my person, and squeezed my upper arms where she gripped me. "What is it? You have to give us some words."

"Jamie just told me he loves me. We broke up weeks ago."

Leo reared back. "You broke up, and he told you he loves you. I think I need more than that..."

I couldn't do this—I had nothing to give them. "Sorry, I'm just going to head home. I'll catch you guys next time."

Wells gave me a quick hug, and Leo nodded. I walked home in a daze, all the misery I'd felt for the last two weeks expanding and multiplying in my whole body. Once inside my door, I slumped onto the couch and buried my face in a pillow. I could feel I'd been crying—my face was wet and Wells had commented on it. I lay there, breathing in stifled air through the pillow, certain I should turn my head so I could breathe comfortably but unwilling to actually make the move.

"You really need to learn to lock your door behind you."

Leo's voice right next to me gave me incentive to shift my head—some small place in me rejoiced at not being alone while another stomped its foot and begged for solitude. My face had to convey the sadness and pathetic state of my mind because she frowned as she took me in, my body curled in on itself.

"I think it's time we had a talk, Bel."

Leo's voice had never been particularly gentle because she spent most of her time being so direct you couldn't help but hear that honest, bare truth in it. But now it was both—

honest, gearing up to destroy me, most likely, but also gentle in a way I desperately needed.

I waited, ready for her to lay it on me.

"Why does it upset you that Jamie said he loves you?" She petted my hair back from my face and I was grateful to her now that I could see her better, even if it meant I'd lost my shroud.

I pushed myself to sitting upright and pulled my knees to my chest. "Why did he tell me now? Why didn't he tell me before?"

"I don't know."

I huffed. "What does he want me to do with that? It doesn't change the fact that he lives in LA and travels the world, and I live here."

My voice broke on the last word, and I pressed my lips together to keep the threatening sobs at bay.

Leo gave me a regretful grin. "Doesn't it?"

I studied her face at that. "What do you mean?"

Her eyes shifted around the room and came to settle back on me. "Doesn't it change some things for you if you know that Jamie loves you?"

I shook my head, not understanding.

"You've lived half a life here, Bel. You've kept yourself from dating, you've huddled into yourself whenever he comes into town, you've refused opportunities at companies out of town... how can that possibly keep you here?"

I drew in a breath slowly, my throat tightening. "Half a life? How dare you? I'm not the one stomping around in a temper tantrum because I won't just be honest with my brother about what I want. I've chosen my life here, and I've made peace with it."

Leo's face twisted, her jaw clenched. "Yeah? You've made peace with it? That's why you're always looking around longingly, working at a dead-end job, tethering your-self to your gran like she's an invalid you're solely respon-sible for?"

I gasped at her harsh words. "Wow. Good to know what my best friend thinks of me."

Leo scrubbed her hands over her face and smoothed back her hair—those Morrisons were all alike.

"Dammit, I'm sorry. I didn't come here to fight. But this is something I should have said a long time ago." She stood up and walked to the door, then let out a big sigh. "I love you, Bel. I think you're making the biggest mistake of your life if you let my brother leave here and you don't tell him how you feel too, at least. I get you have a life here, but I think you've stayed because you're scared. It sucks to hear that, I know. I also know I have my own crap to deal with—I'm not saying I don't.

"But right now, we're talking about you, and you're the one looking in the face of something I know you've wanted all your life, and you're running. You're stronger than that. If you don't believe me, talk to your gran. She knows you best, and she's known you longest, and I know for a fact she'll agree with me."

With one last look, she turned and left.

And me? I buried my face in my pillow and sobbed.

Ten minutes or an hour or half a day later—at this point I'd lost track of time, I called Gran. Because it'd become clear to me that some of what Leo'd said, and some of what Jamie'd said, and some of what Gran had said weeks ago, held an alarming amount of truth. My heart writhed in my chest at the thought that any of the things they'd said might be true, but the sinking in my stomach signaled the truth that I couldn't just ignore them.

Maybe Jamie, if I wanted to be stubborn, because he'd

only just come back into my life. But not Leo, who'd been close to me for six years and a friend in one way or another since I moved to Silverton at eight years old. And I couldn't ignore Gran... no.

"Bel? Are you all right?"

Gran's voice held a note of concern, which made sense. We rarely talked on the phone because I saw her in person every Saturday, and in between, we messaged each other.

"No." My watery small voice tipped her off, no doubt.

"Tell me."

"Have I wasted my life here?" Just that, and the tears came again, not that they'd fully stopped at any point since Jamie had walked away. "Have I used you as a crutch?"

I heard a long exhale from Gran.

"Oh, honey. You've built a nice life here, and there's nothing to be ashamed about. I told you this the other day— I love it here. The problem is, I don't think you love it like I do, or like your Danny and Leo do. You've always wanted to leave, and in that, I do think..."

"You do think..."

A sigh. "I do think I've become an excuse."

I stared at Squish who stretched and sauntered up to me. He leaned up on my knee and sniffed at my nose, then butted his head against my leg and wandered to the kitchen.

My heart constricted, feeling squeezed, pressed in a vise. "An excuse."

Gran stayed silent for what felt like a full minute, but I had no sense of time so it could have been seconds.

"Honey, I'm not your responsibility."

"I know that."

"Do you? Do you really?"

I shoved off from the couch and began pacing the living room, restless energy filling me. "Of course I do. You always took care of me. I just... I want to do the same for you."

Gran tsked. "That's the problem, darling. You don't owe me anything. And I'm not sure if you've noticed, but I don't need all that much care-taking. That's one reason I moved here instead of staying in the house. You don't have to watch over me."

"What about when you're sick?" Panic rose at the thought of coming back from somewhere far away to find her deteriorating like I had after college.

"Oh, Bel. I love your sweet heart. I love that you want to be there for me. But you cannot keep yourself from doing what you want—maybe even what you're meant to do—for my sake. I'm old and I've gotten to make a million choices. You should have that time now. I want that for you, and I don't want to see you holding yourself back because you feel you owe me."

At this point, I could hardly speak through my tears. "But there's no one here for you. Mom and Dad are gone, and if I'm gone—"

"Bel, you are not responsible for me. I love you for how much you care for me, and how present you are in my life. I'm afraid your parents leaving has made you feel it's your job to look after me. Hear me when I say I love you and I'm not saying I don't treasure our time together, but please, *please* don't stay here for me."

CHAPTER FORTY-FIVE

Jamie

Nothing like a long night wallowing in the memory of the woman you love's face twisting in horror when you tell her you're in love with her.

Neat.

I'd said my goodbyes to Ma, Da, Danny, and Leo the day before. I'd be back in two weeks—even if now, my plans for the rest of the summer involved me never leaving my parents' property except when I had to.

I heard Liam's car pull up outside, and I slipped out the door, duffle and backpack in hand, and shut it quietly after me. Six in the morning had come quickly, but I felt nothing but relief to be leaving.

I needed space.

I needed time.

I needed...

Bel! my stupid heart screamed.

Hadn't it learned its lesson?

I dumped my bags in the back seat and got in the passenger side. "You know I could have had a car service get me."

Liam gave me a bored look, then put the car in drive and off we went. But something about that look seemed off. I ignored it for more than an hour of the drive, but when the mood in the car didn't shift and still felt weird for some reason, I had to ask, especially before we got to the airport and I had to have that swirling around in my mind pestering me for the next two weeks.

"What's up?"

Had he heard about my meltdown confession on the street last night?

Liam's low chuckle made my hackles rise. Yep. Something's up.

"What's up is you've been secretly plotting to rescue Silverton and the lodge with your high-class land development and airport deal." His mouth pressed into a stern line.

I swore under my breath. "How did you find out?"

He gave me a long glance before he returned his eyes to the road. *Bel.*

Was she so angry with me she'd told my brother just to spite me? It didn't sound like her, but damn if it didn't seem like that's exactly what she'd done.

"You know as well as I do we need more developments—"

"It'll be great. It's amazing. What I don't understand is why you've kept it from me like some dirty little secret. It makes no sense and honestly really pisses me off."

I shut my eyes and let my head drop to the headrest. This wasn't the way I'd wanted this conversation to go, obviously enough. "I thought it'd be better to tell you once I had everything lined up, all the buyers arranged. I wanted it to be so far down the line it couldn't be something else for you to worry about."

Quiet filled the car as he drove. One minute. Three. Finally, he spoke.

"I've told you before, you can't just dump money on us and save the day. The lodge and town have to become sustainable on their own, or there's no longevity."

"This is why I didn't want you to know until it's done. I'm bringing in infrastructure, high-income clients for the town and lodge, even property taxes for the county. It's not me *dumping money* and that's what I *knew* you'd say, even though this is something I've dreamed about doing for years. I finally have the tools and a partner with even better ones, so I'm doing it."

I wished we could have had this conversation face to face. I wished it could have come on my terms.

As I watched his hands tighten and loosen on the steering wheel, the frustration burned brighter. "Liam, it was never to swoop in and play hero. It's because I've owned this land since the day I got home from my first world tour, and because Silverton and Silver Ridge are mine too."

Liam pulled to the curb of the passenger drop off. *Perfect timing.*

"Li, I'm not getting out until you talk to me." I didn't want to go two weeks with him stewing about this.

Liam rolled his shoulders and shifted in his seat so he could look at me. "I hear you. I'm not happy about the way this looks but I get that it's a good thing. I'm just... angry you didn't feel like you could tell me."

We eyed each other for another minute, then we both got out. I grabbed my bags, and he gave me a rough hug before I pulled a hat low on my head and made my way into the airport. A few minutes and I'd be tucked away in a special lounge, my security team would join me, and I wouldn't be alone again until I checked into my hotel in Germany. A few minutes and I could grab a drink, stifle the fury that had now laced through all the hurt and disappointment I'd been feeling.

I made my way through VIP security, each step taking me further from Bel, further away from what I'd felt so certain of just weeks ago.

As I sat in the lounge, my phone buzzed. Maybe Liam had decided to call and hash things out while he drove. Surprisingly, I didn't feel as upset as I thought I would at his reaction—he'd get over it, and probably be excited. It hadn't gone as planned, but that couldn't be blamed on Liam.

But Bel? That was the part I couldn't get over. She'd been too scared of change to be with me, too scared of risk to love me, and now she'd essentially betrayed me.

She'd messaged me. I hadn't expected to hear from her, especially not after finding out about her telling Liam, and undoubtedly Bauer while she was at it.

I know you leave today. Can I please call you? I have a few things I need to say.

I snorted where I sat, swirled the ice in my glass, flipped the phone over. I did it all outwardly, ignoring the inward singe around my busted heart. What else could she have to say, after doing and saying nothing for weeks, and then saying the only thing I'd asked her not to?

I responded before I lost the courage. *I have nothing left to say to you.*

CHAPTER FORTY-SIX

Bel

Jamie had been gone from Silverton for close to a decade, but his absence the last two weeks had been more painful than all those years combined.

He'd sent one punishing sentence in response to my plea to speak with him, and though it hurt, I understood.

If he could set aside the fact that I didn't reciprocate his feelings when he told me—if only he knew how so much of me had wanted to—then there lurked another issue. As he'd stood there confessing his feelings, my mind had circled around the conversation I'd had earlier that very day with Jonas and Liam.

"Ms. Paxton, I happened to discover that Mr. Morris' friend Mr. Grenier is returning to town with several rather prestigious guests in the coming weeks. I wonder if Mr. Morris mentioned anything to you about this—have you met Mr. Grenier?"

He'd caught me off-guard. Jonas Bauer had a way of doing that, but I'd been ready to flee the premises and avoid any run-ins with Jamie, not that I'd seen him since the night he'd left my house, and me.

The meeting checking in about the sommerfest had gone smoothly, and the one bright spot of the last few weeks shone clear: without the distraction of Jamie, I'd generated a huge amount of work for the lodge, the library, and even a few other small businesses in town.

But Jonas had waylaid me here, just before I turned down the hill to walk into town and then hide away until dinner with Wells and Leo.

"Hmm, Grenier? I haven't heard of him. I don't know all of Jamie's friends though."

This came from Liam, and I winced. Of course he wouldn't know about Julian.

"Have you met him, Bel?"

The forced smile Liam offered showed me he understood questioning my involvement with Jamie's friends fell on the far side of ideal considering we'd broken up and he knew it. Whether Jonas did, I had no idea, but the towering German-American man didn't strike me as one to *not* know everything.

Their attention on me, the possibility of ducking out of the conversation or escaping evaporated. I cleared my throat, admiring the sun still high in the sky thanks to the long June days, and wished I didn't feel as though all my emotional strength and defenses had been battered into oblivion.

"You know, I think he's a business partner of some kind." I craned my neck as though to look down the road, hoping to avoid their questioning eyes.

"Any idea what kind of business?" Liam prodded.

I cleared my throat. "Uh, he's some guy from California, I think."

I braved a look back and the two men stood ready for more information. I had to get out of there.

"Bel, if you know something about this, it would be really helpful to have a bit more information. I know Jam's been working on something here—some kind of side project. I thought it was music-related, but if there's something else he's got going, I'd love to support him in it."

Ah, Liam. He always had been the consummate older brother—even to me. I pushed against the natural desire to tell him everything—he'd find out soon enough anyway, right?

"Ms. Paxton, anything Mr. Morris is involved in is likely to be incredibly beneficial to the town, the lodge, and to assuring our investors of progress and the good standing of their investments. I won't speak to Mr. Morris again until he returns from his trip, if even then, and I have a mid-month report to the investor in a week. I'd appreciate being able to include some new information, if there is any."

I swallowed against the pull to tell them. I could feel myself readying to speak. They could use the information, and it would help things. It could even mean getting Liam closer to his goal of leaving the manager's position and brewing full time. It could mean the investors weren't breathing down the board's necks. There were so many positives to it, and only one downside—disappointing Jamie.

But I'd already done that. I'd done it in spades. I'd done it in every color available in my crayon box, no going back now.

Liam grabbed my hand. "Bel, I know you know. Please just tell us."

His blue eyes begged me, but in the end, I couldn't. If I

could do one last thing to keep from completely ruining Jamie's estimation of me, it meant me staying quiet. "I'm sorry. I—"

Jonas held out a hand and dismissed me with a wave. "Don't concern yourself, Ms. Paxton. It's my understanding Mr. Morris preferred this project to be completed without fanfare or interruption."

"You—you know about the development?"

"Of course."

My face must have reflected my surprise, but relief welled up in me. "That's great news. I wish you'd said something sooner. Did you talk with Jamie?"

Jonas didn't respond directly, but his eyes sharpened. "I can only assume Mr. Grenier is returning in order to..."

I nodded along. "They wanted to get a few more lots sold before they told anyone, but Julian must think these people are good prospects. That'll help push the airport through too."

I allowed myself a small grin, feeling a little burst of pride at what Jamie had created up there.

Liam set his hands on his hips. "Bauer? What is this?"

"Mr. Morris evidently has a development in the works." His eyes cut to me, then back to Liam.

"And... an airport?" Liam's voice vibrated with surprise.

And my heart sank.

Evidently?

"Wait—he didn't tell you?" My attention split between them, my mind screaming.

Jonas spoke first. "I've learned enough independently. All I required was confirmation. For that, I thank you, Ms. Paxton."

He sketched a slight bow, as though this all fell under

the rules of engagement for whatever he had up his sleeve, all completely acceptable and congenial.

I made a sound—unintelligible, a little wild, maybe.

"Good day to you both," Jonas said, and excused himself. Then he disappeared, back to whatever diabolical corner of town he spent his time in.

"Why didn't he tell me?" Liam asked, his quiet betraying hurt, disappointment.

I shook my head. "He was going to, he—I shouldn't keep talking. I've already..."

He patted my back quickly and flashed me a forced smile. "No worries, Bel. I'll see you soon."

I'd felt sick to my stomach the rest of the afternoon. I'd decided I should tell Jamie that I'd blurted it out to them—that I'd take a few hours to attempt getting my head on straight to even speak to him, I'd go to dinner with Leo and Wells as planned because they always made me feel better, and then I'd do it.

But then, there he stood, just inside the door of *Guac* and looking as stunning and heartbreaking as usual. And for some reason, he'd chosen that moment on the street to tell me he loved me and maybe always had. How could I tell him *anything* after that? I'd been poured out and emptied in the last weeks, and my betrayal of him that afternoon had left me adrift, unsure of who I was or what I wanted. Maybe I hadn't meant to, but the fact remained that I'd given up information I shouldn't have—that Jamie had specifically asked me *not* to share.

Jonas Bauer's manipulation of me aside, I'd betrayed Jamie.

First Jamie, then Gran, then Leo, then Gran again—they'd all pressed the idea that my sense of duty to stay in Silverton was misplaced. It'd infuriated me when Jamie suggested I could simply change my entire life at the snap of my fingers. I'd never felt more small and pitiful—until Gran suggested I'd held myself back for her. Then Leo came along and delivered the brutal blow of her opinion that I'd basically settled for a mediocre life.

What got through all my self-pity and resistance to these people who loved me telling me something hard, in the end, were Gran's words. *You are not responsible for me.*

Had I truly believed that I bore the responsibility to take care of her? I'd asked myself that question more than once, at first rejecting the idea, then accepting it as an honorable thing, and finally, after much soul-searching, coming to terms with the fact that *yes*, I'd felt my parents had abandoned me *and* Gran and it fell to me to be there for her.

I'd had more conversations with Gran than I could count. I'd visited her almost every day—she'd gotten sick of me, and had said so.

Somewhere along the way, I'd gotten things so messed up. Much of the last few weeks since Jamie left had been spent in a kind of mourning—not over him, but for myself. For the girl who'd come back with intentions of leaving again and became too scared, too guilty, too stuck to leave.

But not anymore. Isabel Paxton would no longer cower in the shadows and let the clouds cover the sun just waiting to shine onto her life again. I was done with living that way. It was time to be me, to emerge out of all the hurt and heal the bleeding my heart had been subjected to for the past nine years.

I'd told Gran as much, and she'd sent me off on a mission today when I left her, two weeks and two days since I'd betrayed Jamie, since he'd told me he loved me.

"Go get him."

Just that, but it'd become my mission. He landed sometime today. I didn't know who would go get him, or how it would work, but I had to see him, I had to apologize, I had to tell him how sorry I felt for hurting him and revealing his project to the very people he'd begged me not to. And if he could hear me through all that, I had to tell him I loved him.

I'd always loved him.

CHAPTER FORTY-SEVEN

Jamie

I'd performed so many times in so many countries, I could hardly count the number. Someone probably had that stat—shows played, countries visited on tour, etc. etc.

My focus had never been so poor as it had been these last two weeks. In many ways, I felt the attendants of my concerts in Germany and the UK should be given refunds. Between not having performed in months and feeling like I was walking around with a gaping chest wound where Bel had ripped my heart out, nothing felt real. I hadn't really been there for them, and I hated that.

When would I get back to feeling normal?

No one seemed to notice but me—or so they said. Chad clucked and pounded me on the back as though I'd hit a home run. The band seemed pleased and upbeat, and they were probably the only honest barometer around. Even if they'd planned to blow smoke and pretend a bad show had gone well, their energy would have told me the truth.

So it'd just been me. I'd felt like I'd played the concerts underwater. I'd been separated, removed, almost out of body.

No matter what I did, my mind stayed locked on *Bel*. If only that wasn't as familiar to me as strumming my guitar. Would I ever escape this cycle?

"Listen Jamie, I think you need to talk to Bel."

Liam's voice cut through my messy thoughts.

I glanced over at him, not bothering to move my head from where it rested on the seat. We were ten minutes from Silverton, and he'd left me in peace until now. "I have nothing to say to her."

"I know you're mad, but I think she has some things to say to you."

I sniffed, dismissing the notion. She'd had plenty of time to say what she needed to say, hadn't she?

"Don't act like you're over her. I know better—everyone does. *Bel* does. You don't confess your undying love for someone and move on two weeks later just because you left town. That's a waste of energy. At some point, you two are going to stop running from each other and sit down and hash things out, and I suggest it be *soon*."

"Sure. Sounds easy. No problem." My falsely sunny voice told him exactly how I felt about that.

"I get it—at least some of it. Especially the part where she let spill about your project. I hope you know Bauer and I pressured her, and she fell into the trap he laid out for her with his baiting comments. She gave very little detail, and her entire demeanor changed when she realized you hadn't told us anything first."

My eyes cut to him as he pulled up onto the road that lead to Main Street. "What does that mean?

"It means she clearly felt terrible and she practically ran away from me after she told us. I'm not saying that excuses it, but I'm saying she didn't do it flippantly nor was it a calculated move to hurt you. *Talk to her.*"

∾

By four that afternoon, the prospect of sitting at my parents' house and managing to stay awake proved impossible. I'd launched out of the house when my well-meaning Ma had offered a cup of warm milk like I was a child suffering from nightmares.

Like a fool, I'd ended up where I so often did when I came home—the swimming hole. Sure, this place held a lifetime of memories, but those closest at hand were always the ones starring Bel.

I could remember one time she and Danny and a bevy of their friends sat around laughing and talking. I'd wandered up the path from town, taking the short cut through the woods instead of sticking to the main road so I could benefit from the shade. I think I was around seventeen so Bel had to have been fifteen. She swung off the rope swing after a running leap onto it, then came up laughing. I'd been struck by how free and brave she'd seemed. Honestly, I'd been halted by how perfect her laugh was— open and big, even though she'd always seemed quiet to me.

I sat down in the shade of the tree—the same one where I'd held her when her parents had left. The same one where I'd been sitting before I'd crawled over to her and kissed her for the first time, satisfying years of longing.

"Jamie."

My head snapped up to find Bel standing directly in front of me. I scrambled to my feet and shoved my hands into my pockets—my first instinct had been to grab her and hug her, to hold her to me and beg her to end my misery and just be with me and we'd figure it out.

I strangled that desperation with clenched fists inside my jeans and looked at her coolly, thankful for the many years of training to seem unfazed in front of crowds and fans. "Bel."

She twisted her fingers together in front of her, and my heart lurched, that small movement calling out to me and demanding I hold her. But I wouldn't.

"I'm sorry. I'm so sorry. You have no idea how sorry I am. I knew you didn't want them to know and I just—I failed you and I'm sorry."

Her brilliant green eyes pleaded with me to believe her, and that small tremor in her voice, the threat of emotions spilling over, battered my ribcage.

"I wish you hadn't told them."

She winced. "I know. Me too. I am truly sorry."

I ran a hand through my hair and crossed my arms, searching for words. Before I found them, she spoke again.

"Can you forgive me?"

This full assault proved successful. "Of course. I hate that you did it, and I'm frustrated, but from what Liam said, you didn't mean to. It definitely set him on edge with me, and I haven't even seen what the fallout is going to be with Bauer, or Julian for that matter, but I believe that you didn't do it maliciously."

"I would never do anything to purposefully hurt you."

I laughed—it sounded bitter, I could admit.

She moved closer, set a hand on my arm where it

crossed over my chest. Her eyes found mine, and as I looked back her, I lost my breath.

"Please, Jamie. I'm sorry. I'm sorry about the project. I'm sorry for not being willing to look at my life and see how we could make this work. At first, I saw it as you being a jerk, honestly. I saw it as you thinking you were more important because you're a rock star and all that."

"That's never been the way I thought—"

"I know." She squeezed my arm and set her other hand on me. I pulled my arms free, and she took my hands in hers. "I've done a lot of thinking in the month since that first conversation. Honestly, it's been... rough, to say the least. But I can see I've let myself get stuck here, and I can also see that—" she swallowed, her eyes searching back and forth between mine. "I can see that there's nowhere I want to be more than I want to be with you."

My heart rioted in my chest, a rush of sound in my ears.

"I love you, Jamie. I have loved you since that summer you first gave me a second look, and I'm afraid I'll always love you." Her eyes glittered with a layer of tears, and she pressed her lips together.

Everything around us froze with her words. If I'd stepped outside my body, I would have seen the river stopped in its path, the birds caught mid-flight, the little wisps of cottontail arrested on the now-dead breeze. And me—my mind, my soul, that had ached for this woman, stuck in place, too shocked, relieved, amazed, to act.

Fortunately, my body reacted when my mind couldn't. I pulled her close, guided her to me with hands at her smooth cheeks, and kissed her.

I kissed her like it was our first and last kiss. I kissed her like I'd wanted to for years, like I'd done not nearly enough these last few months, and I kissed her like I hoped I would every day for the rest of my life.

"I love you," I said, because all of my being needed her to know it.

"Thank you. Thank you for loving me," she said between kisses.

I shook my head as I pulled back from her, still holding her head in my hands, her hair spilling over my arms and all around us. "Don't thank me. Loving me is likely not going to be easy. But if you're going to do it, I hope you'll do it for good."

She laughed at that. "Obviously, loving me is *incredibly* easy, so..."

We smiled at each other in a heart-burstingly surreal, too-perfect moment.

"And for the record, woman, I'd given you plenty of second glances before that summer."

CHAPTER FORTY-EIGHT

Bel

Jamie and I spent the next few weeks in a bubble.

He told me about his trip, and my heart ached at missing the time with him, and how he'd described feeling so removed from all of it because things were so undone between us. The only salve for that—the very settled feeling between us now.

We'd been quick to make plans since I finally wrapped my head around the fact that I could leave Silverton and the world wouldn't come crashing down. I couldn't pretend it didn't make me nervous and that I didn't still battle the feeling that I *should* be here, but I knew that with time, I'd adjust.

Wells also suggested I talk with a therapist, and I'd started that the week she mentioned it. I wasn't so deluded as to think I didn't have baggage that needed a professional's help sorting through, and I wanted to be healthy so I could enjoy what lay ahead, whatever it looked like. I wanted to move beyond feeling stuck, either physically in Silverton, or mentally in the guilt and shame I had for being left by my parents, or leaving Gran.

Jamie's support had been unwavering, and it felt like our love grew and burst and multiplied by the day. I'd be ready to leave with him by the end of the summer... I hoped. He'd suggested I plan to come back in October for the *almabtrieb*, and then that we'd come at Christmas. That eased the pre-emptive ache I already felt when thinking of leaving. Squish would travel with me to LA and I knew he'd provide me comfort when homesickness set in.

But along with that ache came a sense of anticipation more vivid than I could have asked for. I'd be with Jamie. I'd get to see somewhere new. And fortunately, I'd continue doing my work for the lodge, and several other local clients. The reality that I already worked from home most of the time hadn't sunk in until Jamie suggested I ask Liam how he'd feel if I continued to work for the lodge remotely.

Liam had laughed, looked at me like I was crazy, and said, "I assumed you would."

Oh. Okay.

Leo had demanded a full run-down of everything that'd happened from when she saw me crying on the street in front of *Guac* to the next time she found me, as she described it, *wrapped around my brother like a scarf.* I'd never seen her so angry on someone else's behalf, but when she heard how Jonas had led me to tell him about Jamie's project, I could've sworn her eyes actually sparked with flame. I'd hate to be Jonas Bauer when she confronted him about that. For my part, since Jamie had forgiven me, I decided I'd let him be the one to deal with Jonas' trickery, and he assured me he had.

For now, I could relax for the next few weeks until the big sixtieth anniversary celebration for the lodge. And better, I could spend every non-working moment with Jamie. He made a point to work on his song-writing and schedule his meetings with people during the hours I worked at *Rise and Shine* so we could spend as much time together as possible. He'd warned me his schedule once back in LA wouldn't be as flexible, particularly during recording.

I could handle it. I'd explore and do my own work. I'd revel in this next phase in my life.

We lay on a blanket on that top tier of his deck. I wondered if we'd do that in years to come whenever we came back to Silverton. No, we hadn't talked about what exactly all that looked like, but I knew we both wanted the future, too.

And tonight, I'd savor this man who'd stolen my heart so many summers ago. He leaned over me, the stars an embarrassment of jewels behind him, and kissed my forehead, my cheek, my chin.

"Bel."

I smiled against his lips as he kissed me. I should record him saying my name so I could listen to it whenever I wanted—the sound was pure decadence.

"Jamie."

He pulled back, and the small smile on his lips faded, his eyes growing serious. The air seemed to shift with a warm summer breeze. The smells of dewy grass and clean mountain air swirled around us.

"Bel, I love you."

My smile brightened. Hard to imagine that declaration getting old.

"I'm in love with you."

I leaned forward to steal a kiss. "I'm in love with you too."

"I don't want to be apart from you."

Familiar words. I wondered why he'd repeat them now. "I feel the same way."

He paused, swallowed, and I felt it. In my bones, I knew what was coming.

"Will you marry me?"

I pulled him to me, crushed him to me with my arms around his back and my lips pressed to his. I kissed him thoroughly.

"Is that a—"

"Yes. That's a yes, Jamie."

The end. (For now.)

I hope you loved Bel and Jamie's story! They are truly one of my favorite couples. **You can grab Danny and Mia's story today** and see a little more of Bel and Jamie, too! Keep reading for a sneak peek of Danny and Mia.

Patrolling for Love at Silver Ridge: Silver Ridge Resort, Book 3

Fire and Ice at Silver Ridge: Silver Ridge Resort, Book 4

The Back to Silver Ridge Series

Almost Perfect, Book 1

Almost Real, Book 2 - 2022

Almost Sure, Book 3 - 2022

Almost Home, Book 4 - 2022

The Rambler Battalion Series

Sweet Military Romance

Where You Go: The Rambler Battalion, Book 1

As You Are: The Rambler Battalion, Book 2

Don't Stop Now: The Rambler Battalion, Book 3

Home With You: The Rambler Battalion, Book 4

All of You: The Rambler Battalion, Book 5

The OCONUS Bonus Series

Sweet Military Romance Overseas

The Problem with Planning Love, Book 1

Livie Anderson's got a plan for her life and she's on track for her next step. The last three years traveling Europe and working on a US Army base helped her experience all the adventure she wanted before she settles down in one place and stops the nomadic life. Now, her deadline to return home and start a family is fast approaching and there's a wrench in her perfect plans. Colonel Eric Wolfe came into her life and it's getting hard to picture leaving this world behind—but the Army life is the opposite of what she's always planned for.

Eric can't deny his interest in Livie, which is monumental in itself considering his total disinterest in everyone since his divorce three years ago. Despite his efforts to remain just friends, he can't resist Livie's pull—her joy, love for life, and genuine way of dealing with people. But he can't see a way to be with her without subjecting her to the military life that ruined his first marriage, and Livie's leaving anyway, so why can't he bring himself to let go?

Their lives are too different, and their plans don't match. They definitely shouldn't date, and they certainly shouldn't develop feelings. Too bad neither one of them can seem to stay away.

Finding Happiness in a Hoax, Book 2

Learning to Fight after Flight, Book 3

The Bright Side of Brooding, Book 4

Holding On to Hope, Book 5

ABOUT THE AUTHOR

Claire Cain lives to eat and drink her way around the globe with her traveling soldier and three kids, but is perhaps even happier hunkered down at home in a pair of sweatpants and slippers using any free moment she has to read and cook. Or talk—she really likes to talk. She has become an expert at packing too many dishes in too few cabinets and making houses into homes from Utah to Germany and many places in between. She's a proud Army wife and is frankly just really happy to be here.

You can also join Claire's facebook reader group for exclusive content and fun: https://www.facebook.com/groups/clairecain/

Website: http://www.clairecainwriter.com

E-mail: Claire@ClaireCainWriter.com

Newsletter sign-up for new releases, exclusives, and freebies: http://www.clairecainwriter.com/newsletter

ACKNOWLEDGMENTS

Thank you to the readers who've been looking forward to this book! It certainly gave me the push to finish during the last crazy months of pregnancy.

Thank you to Christy for always being up for an early read.

Thank you, Emma, for being an amazing supporter, friend, bookstagrammer (Check out her gorgeous feed @wordsfromworlds), and essentially my romance writer pimp. You are a delight and I am so thankful for you!

Thanks to Jamie for calling, chatting, cheering, commiserating, and generally being one of my favorite humans.

Thanks to Zee Monadee for the edits, insights, and for not laughing too hard at my confusion over grin. So glad to partner with you!

To Meme Hernandez, thanks for sharing your craft with me for this cover.

Thanks to my crazy kids, all three of them! I love you so and hope we'll get back to our beloved Rockies soon. Thanks especially to Millie for being a baby who makes me want to create. Matthew, I love you, and thank you for helping me carve out time to write in the midst of the madness.

Thanks again to everyone who read the book—I know there are a million other things you could be doing. If you have a minute, please review the book wherever can—reviews are immensely helpful to indie authors!

SNEAK PEEK: PATROLLING FOR LOVE AT SILVER RIDGE

Danny Morrison gets his chance! Read on for a sneak peek. Now Available!

I kissed Kai's curved little cheek, felt a pang at the ever-present realization that the curve was smaller as he became more a *kid* and less my little boy, and sat back down with my laptop, ready to pay bills while he enjoyed a playdate. I sat there for no more than two minutes before I raced around the house gathering supplies, then charged out the door in my shirt, shorts, and hiking boots, only a small pack on my back—and a fully charged cell phone because I'm not a complete idiot—and jumped in my car to get to the trailhead.

I loved the library, but between getting settled in the house and working, I was constantly inside. Nothing wrong with that, except part of what I wanted when I chose Silverton (though admittedly, in many ways it felt like it chose me), was the proximity to the mountains.

And now, here I sat on a rugged little stump at the side of the trail, gripping my ankle and praying I hadn't broken it when I rolled it moments ago. I wouldn't cry, no, because I'd given birth and nothing would ever compare to unexpectedly birthing a child without medication on the pain scale, but I clenched my jaw and had to blink away the moisture gathering at my bottom lids as I pictured a fissure in the bone of my foot and a doctor frowning at me saying "it'll never be the same."

Perhaps I had an active imagination. I liked to think it aided me in my job, my parenting, and also in my rather lonely interior life.

I ducked my head and breathed through my nose, then attempted to flex my foot. The sound that emerged from my mouth could only be called a yelp.

I shut my eyes and tried to calm my rapid pulse, feeling the panic rising in me. If I couldn't flex my foot, then I couldn't walk down this path, even though I was only a half mile or so from the bottom. I'd hiked for hours with no issues, but now the solo trip was catching up to me—*of course*. I'll be the ridiculous new woman in town who had to call 911 because she rolled her ankle.

I attempted to pull in a slow breath but a sob interrupted it. I clamped my mouth shut, unwilling to give in to the panic, knowing the panic didn't give a crap whether I had plans to give into it or not.

"Whoa, you ok?"

My eyes flew open at the sound of a man's voice, and then, there he was, *him* of course, crouching in front of me, shucking his pack, lifting his sunglasses to reveal those brutal blue eyes.

"Ma'am?"

I didn't cringe at his calling me ma'am. Never mind that

he had to be close to my age—he'd likely been trained to address people formally as a ski patroller. That I knew exactly who he was and he clearly didn't know me... well. Story of my life in Silverton thus far.

"Uh, yeah... hurt my ankle." I could hear the pain in my voice as it eked out, thin and watery.

"Ok. Can I take a look? I'm a ski patroller, trained for this kind of thing. I work for the lodge. If we can stabilize it I can help get you down."

Those lovely blue eyes assessed me head to toe, then zeroed in on my mutinous left ankle.

"Sure. Of course."

He kneeled and placed a warm hand behind my calf, his large hand soothing and a little rough. If I hadn't been in this particular situation, I might have been captivated by the feel of his hand sliding along the curve of my leg, though there was nothing sensual in his movement. Just his touch...

I winced and stifled a gasp of pain when he shifted my booted foot to one side.

"Sorry." His face showed he meant it, his dark brownish-red eyebrows knit together, a frown on what I could now appreciate, even in a ridiculous amount of pain and no small measure of embarrassment, were surprisingly full lips. "Just need to get a sense of what we've got here. I'm hoping it's just a sprain and not broken—shouldn't need an evac."

I nodded, not sure I could find words as a bolt of fear rocketed down my spine at the word *broken*. I didn't have time for a broken ankle. I didn't think my insurance would cover much more than basic x-rays, and it certainly couldn't be cheap to have an *evac*, whatever that was.

He eyed me as he moved the foot one way, then the other. When I jumped, he nodded like it was good thing. "I'm sorry. But this is good. Pretty sure it's just a nasty sprain. Best thing to do is keep it in the boot to stabilize it, and head down. You're going to be fine."

I wondered what it'd look like to get down this mountain, but couldn't pretend I didn't feel hugely relieved not to be on my own with this.

He shuffled a few things in his pack, took a swig of water and suggested I take one from mine with a nod toward where it sat next to me, then stood and set his pack in front of him. Every one of his movements was certain, steady. "Ok. We're going to get you up. It's going to suck, but if you can give one good jump, I'll do the rest."

"Uh—"

He leaned over, his face alarmingly close to mine. "Arms around my neck, and when I stand up, put your weight on your good leg. Then I'm going to turn, and I need you to hop if you can, and I'll get you up."

"Uh—"

He placed my arms around his head, and my hands seemed to know to lock at the back of his neck where they met.

"Ok, now." He stood, and I pressed up on my thoroughly exhausted good leg, and found myself flush against Daniel Morrison.

"Ok?" He searched my face, and I nodded, breathless from exertion and definitely not his proximity.

"'kay, I'm going to turn, and you're going to jump, then I'll grab you under your legs and hike you up."

"Wait. Wait." I tightened my arms around his neck so he couldn't turn. "You're going to carry me?"

"Yeah. Piggy-back." A sweet little smile and wide eyes showed me he had no idea why that might be surprising to me.

"You're going to carry me the entire way down the mountain?"

"Yeah. Or, did you want to take the car?"

Oh, ok. Sarcasm. "No, I don't—that's fine, but I'm pretty heavy."

His gaze flickered over me again and he shook his head. "Nah. We'll be fine. Ready?"

I couldn't tell whether my heart felt like it might pound out of my chest because this guy I'd never even talked to before planned to haul me on his back and hike down the rest of the mountain with my full, dead weight draped across his impressive shoulders, or if it came down to the pain still pulsing in my foot and the mild freak out I'd been having as he arrived.

As much as I didn't relish being *carried* down, there wasn't another option unless I wanted to one-leg it, and I didn't. I swallowed and took a deep breath. When he bent down into a deep squat, I hopped up as best I could. His hands held my bare legs at my hamstrings and he sort of jumped me up to get a better grip. I silently winced at the jostling of my leg.

"Sorry. Just want to make sure I have a good grip." Then he reached down and somehow, in a move I didn't comprehend nor could I really see from my vantage point at his back, looped his pack over his chest. "Ready?"

"Yep. Just let me know if I get too heavy." I ran my hands along his shoulders searching for a place to grip—his very muscular, defined shoulders. Could I actually hold on without hurting him? I pulled my hands back quickly, then dove in and grabbed on since essentially caressing his muscles probably wasn't the way to go here.

"It'll be fine. You maybe should tell me your name though. I'm Danny."

Danny. *Adorable.*

"Right. I'm Mia. I work at the library. I think I've seen you a time or two."

"That's right." He snapped, like he should have known. "I saw you a week or two ago when I stopped in. Meant to come say hi but you were surrounded by a group of people." He trotted down the path like I weighed nothing more than his pack.

"Why would you say hi?" My voice bumped along with my body, my chest hovering a few inches away from his back to save us both from that discomfort, even if it made me feel like I might fall off. I tried to keep my core strong so I wasn't too useless, then wondered if stiffening up like that might make it harder for him. My cheeks burned as I tried to keep a sturdy grip on him without strangling his neck where I held on.

"Why not? You're new in town, and you're taking over as the new head librarian, right? An important woman to know."

I wished I could see his face. I could hear a smile in his voice, and would've loved the distraction. His clean, woodsy scent calmed me as if this whole being carried by a stranger with a busted ankle thing didn't still threaten to push me into panic.

"That's nice. Not many people think that way." It would've been nice if more people did. I felt awkward introducing myself and forcing my way into the community, but so far I'd done it when I had to.

"Silverton isn't a terribly insular place, but I admit people are a bit slow to welcome newcomers because of all the seasonal worker we get. But you're here for a while, I'm guessing?"

Hmm. *Insular?* Was he trying to impress me, or was

that just him? A little flare of attraction shot up into my mind as I recognized how naturally he'd said it, and the odds of him having a good vocabulary if he read a lot, which it sort of sounded like he did. "Yes. Indefinitely."

He moved quickly down the path, slowing to tiny steps on steeper grades, taking larger strides where the trail inclined. We stayed quiet for a while, only the sounds of the mountain and his breath, only occasionally audible, our soundtrack.

"So... do you hike alone a lot?" He asked as we hit the last narrow, rocky decline of the path.

"No. Not usually. Not after today, for sure." Relief that he'd come along swooped in. How foolish I'd been, especially now that I knew my phone didn't have service up there.

"But... do you normally?"

I could hear the concern in his voice—not judgement, just wariness on my behalf. "No. Really. Before I moved I had a group I went with when I could make time. I just don't really know anyone who's into hiking here." Good thing he couldn't see the humiliation on my face.

I felt silly enough for getting hurt and need his help, and let's not even talk about the fact that he'd now been carrying me for close to twenty minutes *on his back*. But admitting I didn't have anyone to hike with—essentially admitting I didn't have friends? I shut my eyes against the embarrassment.

He looked to the side—like he wanted to look back at me, but since I clung to his back directly behind him, he had no way to see me. "Not hard to find people who like to hike around here. But you're new—you've only been here a few weeks, right?"

"Uh, more like two months."

"Really? How have I not seen you yet? This town is tiny." He sounded genuinely baffled.

I chuckled, forcing myself to project a lighthearted tone even though my ankle had begun to throb and my thighs felt raw where they rubbed against his hips and the waistband of his shorts. Where he gripped under my legs would be red, maybe even bruised, though I could tell he held me as lightly as he could.

"It is pretty small. I've been behind the computer or in the back office at the library the vast majority of the time I've been here, so that's likely why, even if you come into the library fairly often." Those first weeks of transition were full of accounting reviews, volume reviews, funding request reviews, schedule reviews... so many things to review. I had a headache every night for weeks after staring at the computer, no doubt hunched like an old crone over the keyboard, neglecting good posture, hydration, and any effort at eating normal meals during the workday as I tried to meet Mrs. Stanton's deadline for her exit from the job.

"Guess that explains it. I definitely would have noticed you." An audible swallow—not quite a gulp—followed.

Did he realize he'd said that—and...

What?

My mouth opened like I meant to respond, but I had nothing. What did that mean? Did I look that obviously out of place? Sure, I was new to town, but I'd lived in the valley, was born and raised in the state. It wasn't like I'd transplanted from the East coast. My heart sped up for the umpteenth time in the last hour.

"I must not be blending in very well." My words were thick in my mouth.

He cleared his throat, did that futile backward glance

thing, and hiked me up on his hips, then mumbled "I doubt you ever could."

"*What?*"

He couldn't be referencing my race, could he? Utah wasn't a particularly diverse place, but Salt Lake had a decent cross-section of culture and I knew a fair number of fellow Filipinos. I was only half, technically, since my father was Caucasian—maybe one reason we hadn't been tapped into the community and I'd been left alone when they passed.

That's enough of that.

I worried Silverton would be a little pocket of homo-geneity, especially based on the town's roots with German- and Irish-American settlers, but so far I hadn't felt out of place or like I stood out. In fact the bigger problem, maybe, was that I didn't. Or so I thought.

"I said, 'seems like you're doing good.' I just mean it seemed like that group of kids and parents were really happy and excited to be talking to you the other day. And Jake was psyched as ever to be working with you."

I smiled at that. "I think Jake is psyched about everything."

"All the time. Yep. He's the most roundly enthusiastic person you'll ever meet." He nodded his head even as he walked.

We settled into that quiet again, and I focused on breathing through my nose. Jostling around behind Danny had given my brain a scrambled egg effect. I had the strange thought I'd like to lean against him and rest my head against his—luckily I wasn't that desperate. He'd probably think I was a crazy person.

We reached the parking lot and I directed him to my car. As he squatted down to get my good foot closer to the pavement, I slid down his back in a rather intimate way considering I'd only met him an hour earlier—less—and yet I'd been riding on his back for close to a half hour, so I supposed we'd crossed at least one normal physical barrier already.

I balanced, one hand on his shoulder, one hand on the roof of my car, and he spun around. He grabbed my wrist to steady me as I wobbled, my feet pinging with the pins and needles sensation after dangling so long.

"You ok? Let me get your keys." He reached for my backpack and helped me remove it, then found the keys where I'd hooked them inside the front pocket. He unlocked the car, and as I hopped to get out of the way of the door, he reached around my waist and lifted me out of the way.

It would have been an entirely inappropriate move, again, if I hadn't just been *on* him. But I couldn't get used to his ease with hoisting me about, despite the recent trek.

"Elevate, ice, anti-inflammatory. If it swells a whole lot more than it is when you first get home, head to the ER. If your foot gets cold, head to the ER. If you just can't stand the pain and the ice and elevation and meds don't help—"

"Head to the ER, got it." I gave him a close-lipped smile.

"Good. Yes. I'm really sorry I can't escort you home and get you set up myself, but I have a meeting that started about ten minutes ago."

Horror struck. "Oh no. I'm so sorry to make you late."

He smiled wide, and his brow furrowed as he touched my wrist gently. "I didn't say that to make you feel bad. I just wanted you to know I'm sorry I can't help you."

I let out a laugh. "You have helped me—you've gone above and beyond. Really. Thank you."

"My pleasure, Mia." His blue eyes pinned me there,

made me forget, for a minute, how bad my ankle ached and how miserable the weekend would be as I tried to keep Kai entertained on one leg. He seemed so purely genuine and capable and happy to help. That paired with those sky-blue eyes sparkling back at me, that smile, that scruff-covered jaw...

I shook off that train of thought, refusing to acknowledge the butterflies flitting around my belly. "Thank you. Again. Please go so you're not any later than you already are."

He smiled a moment longer, then nodded. "See you around soon, Mia. Take care of that ankle."

Grab Danny and Mia: **Patrolling for Love at Silver Ridge: Silver Ridge Resort, Book 3**

Then read Leo and Jonas: **Fire and Ice at Silver Ridge: Silver Ridge Resort, Book 4**

Sign up for new release alerts and exclusives at http://www.clairecainwriter.com/newsletter

www.ingramcontent.com/pod-product-compliance
Lightning Source LLC
Chambersburg PA
CBHW051210190726
48288CB00006B/1888